Girls Fall Down

Maggie Helwig

Coach House Books | Toronto

first edition

Published with the generous assistance of the Canada Council for the Arts and the Ontario Arts Council. Coach House Books also acknowledges the support of the Government of Ontario through the Ontario Book Publishing Tax Credit Program and the Government of Canada through the Book Publishing Industry Development Program.

LIBRARY AND ARCHIVES CANADA CATALOGUING IN PUBLICATION

Helwig, Maggie, 1961-
    Girls fall down / Maggie Helwig.

ISBN 978-1-55245-196-0

    I. Title.

PS8565.E46G57 2008   C813'.54   C2008-901683-1

for David Barker Maltby,
photographer

Bodies in Space

The city is a winter city, at its heart. Though the ozone layer is thinning above it, and the summers grow long and fierce, still the city always anticipates winter. Anticipates hardship. In the winter, when it is raw and grey and dim, it is itself most truly.

People come here from summer countries and learn to be winter people. But there are worse fates. That is exactly why many of them come here, because there are far worse fates than winter.

It is a city that burrows, tunnels, turns underground. It has built strata of malls and pathways and inhabited spaces like the layers in an archaeological dig, a body below the earth, flowing with light. People turn to buried places, to successive levels of basements, lowered courtyards, gardens under glass. There are beauties to winter that are unexpected, the silence of snow, the intimacy with which we curl around places of warmth. Even the homeless and the outcasts travel downwards when they can, into the ravines that slice around and under the streets, where the rivers, the Don and the Humber and their tributaries, carve into the heart of the city; they build homes out of tents and slabs of metal siding, decorate them with bicycle wheels and dolls on strings and boxes of discarded books, with ribbons and mittens, and huddle in the cold beside the thin water.

It is hard to imagine this city being damaged by something from the sky. The dangers to this city enter the bloodstream, move through interior channels.

The girl was kneeling by the door of the subway car, a circle of friends surrounding her like birds. Her hands were over her narrow face, she was weeping, and there were angry red welts across her cheeks, white circles around them. Her friends touched her back, her arms, their voices an anxious chirp. There was a puddle of vomit at her feet, and she lowered one hand to wipe her mouth, leaning against the door.

A space had already cleared around them. Some of the passengers in the nearby seats held hands or tissues discreetly over their mouths, but as if this were incidental, as if they weren't quite aware of anything. As the train rocked through the tunnel, a bubble of light between the dark walls, a few people got to their feet and moved down the car.

The train came into Bloor station and jerked to a stop, and the girl leaned backwards, the pool of vomit spreading, her friends lifting up their feet with little cries. As the door opened, a mass of people on the platform surged forward, then stopped, moved back into the crush and towards another car, their eyes turned politely away.

A grey-haired man in a dark coat stood up and walked to where the girls were standing. 'Does she have an EpiPen?' he asked.

'A what? What's that?' A tall girl brushed blonde hair from her eyes. Another girl was hanging on to the metal pole, resting her forehead against it, her red tie hanging straight down, her plaid kilt rolled up at the waist, brushing her thighs. The train wasn't moving on.

'An EpiPen. For allergies.'

'I'm not allergic,' said the sick girl. The man bent down to look at her rash, keeping a slight distance between them. 'She smelled something,' the tall girl said. 'There's a gas in the car or something. They should tell somebody.' She kept talking, but at the same time the PA system gave a quick shriek, and a distorted voice announced that the train was out of service. Beyond the door of the subway car, the crowd began to move like a huge resigned sigh, pushing towards the stairways.

'They'll have paramedics here soon,' said the man. He was about to leave, it seemed, when the dark-haired girl who had been holding on to the pole suddenly swayed and put out one hand, falling to the muddy floor. The other one, the tall blonde, dropped to her knees beside her friend, crying her name.

The man knelt down, frowning. 'If you want, I could call – '

'Go away,' whimpered the first girl, dabbing at tears on her welt-covered face. 'Go away, it's too awful. It's not right.'

'It's poison,' cried a girl with curly rust-coloured hair. 'Somebody put a poison in the train.'

The girl who had just fallen lay with her eyes closed. She too was covered with a rash, but a different one, a red prickly flush all over her face and hands.

'Someone put a poison gas on the train,' shouted the tall girl, trying to lift up her friend. The crowd outside the train heard her, and the volume of their voices increased, heads turning, some people stopping where they were. The man held his breath for a second; then, as if seized by an uncontrollable impulse, he sniffed the air, deeply.

'What was it like, the smell?' he asked the kneeling girl.

The station was being cleared now, the crowd on the platform fragmenting, breaking into individuals, a blur of brown and beige skin tones, splashes of bright-coloured fabric, patterns and stripes. Announcements were sounding over the PA system, men in uniform appearing, moving people quickly to the exits. A slender woman with plastic bags in her hand stood still and stared at the train, her mouth partly open.

The girl who had fallen was sitting halfway up, clinging again to the pole. 'Roses,' she said. 'It smelled like roses.'

A heavy-set man sat down hard at the top of the stairs, his face suffused with blood, gasping for breath, and a stranger took hold of his arm and pulled him along as far as the fare booth, where he stumbled and fell.

The girl was creeping towards the door of the train, stopping to wipe at the smears of vomit on her legs, and her friend was sitting up, dazed, leaning her head against the tall girl's chest. On the level above, a woman took off her parka and bundled it underneath the head of the man by the fare booth.

The man in the dark coat started to put a hand out towards one of the girls, and then pulled it back. He looked up and saw the security guards arriving. 'They're coming now,' he said, 'you'll be okay,' and left the train, heading for the stairs. As he went up, the first team of paramedics pushed past him, carrying an orange stretcher, a policewoman watching from the upper level.

'They smelled a gas,' someone was saying at the top of the stairs. The paramedics lifted the first girl onto the stretcher. 'Roses,' she said.

One of the girls said, 'Poison,' again. The woman with the plastic bags was still frozen on the platform. Then she swayed, fell to her knees.

'Jesus!' crackled the voice on the PA, someone forgetting he was in front of a live mike. 'There's four of them down now. What the hell's going on here?'

The man at the fare booth told someone that he thought it was his heart, he was pretty sure it was his heart, but when he thought about it he did remember the smell. Yes. The smell of roses.

As more paramedics arrived, a policewoman placed the first call for a hazmat team.

The corridor was narrow and badly lit, the arms of the mall branching off in odd directions, and the stairs were filled now with more police and paramedics coming down, wearing face masks, as the crowd, expelled from the subway, made their way up. No one was paying attention to Alex, as he slid through the turnstile and up the stairs to the mall – and why should they, he was ordinary and forgettable, a thin man who looked much older than thirty-nine, wearing a reasonably good dark coat, his prematurely grey hair cut short. He ducked into the drugstore on his right, hoping it would carry disposable cameras – pieces of shit, they were, he'd never get a decent picture, but at least he'd have a camera-like object in his hands, at least he'd be able to think.

He was not the only person who had broken away from the crowd; in front of him, while he waited at the checkout with a disposable that doubled as a coupon for a Shrek hand puppet, were several people with their arms full of what seemed to be anxiety purchases, vitamin C and ginseng tablets, plastic gloves, antibacterial handwipes. Last year when the buildings fell in New York, in the midst of the aftershock a day or two later, he'd gone into the SuperSave on Bloor and watched people hoarding, all of them apparently unaware of what they were doing – smiling, chatting, walking calmly through the aisles, and at the same time piling their carts full of toilet paper and canned tuna and bags of pasta. Commenting cheerfully on the weather to the sales clerks while stacking up boxes of cheap candles at the cash register. Because you didn't admit to fear, not up in this country; it would be disruptive and far too personal, and not very nice for everyone around you. He used to consider this an appalling attitude, but lately he thought he was coming to see some virtue in it; the gentle restraint of people who live close together in the cold, and know that they must be patient.

He stepped out onto the seething pavement, between the concrete buttresses of the mall. People were standing at the curb waving for taxis, the line stretching down the block; in front of him at the corner they crowded together, surrounding the hot-dog vendor, covering all of the broad sidewalk and spilling into the street. A city bus arrived, running west, and was surrounded, rushed by a frantic swarm, a few of them making it inside, cramming up against the entryway until the doors groaned closed, and the bus swayed with the weight and set out slowly into the gridlock of taxis on Bloor Street. Another bus was creeping southwards towards them on Yonge – both lines were shut down, then.

He scrambled up against a buttress, bracing one leg at an angle and getting his head above the crush. It was nearly dark. He knew this camera couldn't really handle the complex light of the swiftly falling evening, but he turned west, tried to frame a shot of the buses, then eastwards, the spire of the Anglican church black against the ink-blue sky and a smoke of charcoal cloud, the line of raised arms hailing taxis down Bloor, an echo of upward movement. Dropping down again, frustrated by the shadows, he slid towards the curb and hopped delicately out into the road, firing shots off quickly in a flurry of car horns as the lights from the stores washed over the traffic, a choppy lake surface. Then, swinging one foot back onto the sidewalk, he realized that the viewfinder was framing the narrow clever face of Adrian Pereira.

'Hey,' he said, lowering the camera.

'Alex Deveney?'

'Yeah. Adrian.' He was still standing with one foot in the road, the traffic motionless now. He stepped back up onto the sidewalk. Adrian Pereira, observant and amused, older, his curly black hair thinner, but unmistakably himself. 'Man, it's been about a million years.'

'Give or take.' Adrian pushed a small pair of wire-rimmed glasses up on his nose. 'So I hear we've had an airborne toxic event.'

'That's from a book, right?'

'Also latterly from *Buffy the Vampire Slayer*. It's multivalent.'

'I was there, actually. I mean, I think I was. I was right by these girls who were fainting, anyway, if that's what started all this.'

'Oh yeah? So you're, like, laden with anthrax spores?'

'That's what I figure.' He wondered if he was handling this properly. If he should say more, or less, shake hands perhaps, or apologize for something. Or say something about those times, when they were young and anxious and the world was wide open. A quick sense memory of smoke and music flickered over him.

'Seriously, though,' Adrian looked around, 'I heard there was a gas on the train. A chemical leak, maybe?'

Alex pushed the disposable camera into his pocket. 'Honestly, I don't think so. It just, it didn't look like that to me. It was a weird set of symptoms, it didn't look like anything that made sense. And I was right there, it's not like I'm dropping on the pavement.' He looked at his wrists. 'I keep thinking I'm getting a rash, but it's just a nervous twitch.'

'You should talk to one of those guys,' said Adrian, waving his arm at the three ambulances which had now stationed themselves at the corner.

'I'm not attached to spending a whole night in the hospital so they can tell me I'm fine. I figure I'm being a good citizen by saving them the trouble.'

'If you say so.'

They wove through the seething stationary traffic, crossing from the northeast corner to the northwest. Alex supposed that he was deciding to walk home; where Adrian was going, he didn't know.

Adrian pulled his jacket around himself. 'Do you still see anyone from the paper?'

'Me? No.' Alex bent forward under a gust of wind, the sky fully dark now. 'I'm right out of touch with the world. Are you still playing?'

'Oh, you know.' Adrian shrugged. 'Now and then. Here and there. Mostly teaching guitar to little kiddies, actually. I feel they should have the opportunity to waste their lives in turn.'

'Hmm.' Alex saw a mass of people at the next corner, pouring out from the Bay station, waving at the bus as it rocked perilously through the stream of stalled cars. Behind them, the imploring wail of the ambulances.

'Perhaps you've been infected with smallpox,' suggested Adrian.

'Yes, very likely. Or maybe the plague. Plague would be good.'

'I'd take some Tylenol if I were you.'

One of the ambulances had forced itself through the traffic, its blue light splashing against the glass walls of the Gap.

'I see Suzanne now and then,' said Adrian.

'Suzanne.' No one called her that, back then. Except maybe Alex. 'Susie-Paul.'

He kept his voice casual, he thought. 'She's back in Toronto?'

'Did she leave?' Alex stopped walking and stared at Adrian, who put a hand to his forehead. 'I'm sorry, Alex. Of course she did, I forgot. But yeah, she's been back a long time. She was wondering if you were still around, actually.'

'Well, obviously I'm still around. I mean, people can look in the phone book if they're so damn curious.'

'I guess that's true. Nobody thinks of the phone book nowadays, do they? It's like, that's a land-based life form, we've moved on.'

'Well. I'm in the phone book, as it happens. Lumbering towards Armageddon.'

'Yeah, okay, 'cause she might want to know that.'

'It's not a question of knowing, is it, it's like, you open up the book and see it or not. I mean, if you want to know, it's not like it's an actual difficulty.'

'Yeah, okay.' He nodded towards the corner. 'I have to go north here.'

'Oh, well, okay.' Alex shifted from foot to foot, wondering if he should ask for a phone number, if that would seem too demanding. 'Good to see you and all.'

'You too, Alex. Who knows, maybe I'll see you the next time they poison the subway.'

Adrian turned and started to walk up the street. 'Hey,' Alex called suddenly. 'Hang on a sec?'

'Yeah?' He turned again to face Alex.

'What's she doing now?'

'Oh. I don't know exactly.' He put his hands in his pockets and shrugged. 'Something intelligent. You know.' And then he was gone, into the laneways and expensive boutiques of Yorkville, the crowd swelling on the street behind him.

At Yonge and Bloor, bloated figures in papery white suits crept down the stairs, breathing through masks, holding up instruments with lights and dials. The security guard who remained in the station held a towel across his face as he led the white figures towards the train. Behind smoky glass, another guard sat with his head down, trying to breathe, his hands damp.

Decontamination, said a white figure, its voice obscured by the air filter.

The guard nodded.

What about the girls? said a figure.

Telephone the hospital, said another.

Just precautionary. That's all. Can't be too careful.

After the Bloor/Yonge station was cleared at both levels, the trains stopped running north up as far as Eglinton, and south to Union; the eastbound line halted at St. George and the westbound at Broadview. And at every stop along the route the people of the city spilled out, onto subway platforms, into underground walkways and shopping malls, onto the sidewalks and roads, driven upwards into the air. At Queen, as the train pulled into the station, a forty-year-old bass player with thinning red hair, dressed entirely in black leather, was saying to his companion, 'Drummers. They're like a different breed, man, eh? Seriously, drummers are a whole different breed.'

'Yeah,' said the other man, staring out the window. 'They're totally.'

The metallic voice of the PA system interrupted to tell them that the train was terminating, and that they should go to Queen Street to catch a bus northbound. They joined the flow from the train and up the escalator, pausing on the next level. A group of people were gathered at the wall with the map of the PATH system, that complex underground skeleton of corridors and courtyards that could lead them into the malls or the banks, the bus terminal or City Hall, outlining the shape of the downtown core in concrete and tile.

'It's like they're not even the same breed as us, you know?' said the bass player, as they stepped onto another elevator.

'Fuckin' A,' said his friend.

'Somebody must of jumped on the tracks, eh? 'Cause it happens like every day, but they don't admit it. It's like a public policy they don't admit it.'

'Fuckers.'

'Or it could be one of those, you know, Middle East things, you know, about the war with Iran or whatever.'

'Iraq,' said the other man. 'They're gonna have a war with Iraq is where.'

'No,' said the bass player. 'No, I gotta tell you, man, I'm pretty sure it's Iran.'

They stepped out into the chilly evening, the corners of the wide streets filled, the tall glass windows of HMV reflecting the arms of people waving at the buses, pushing for space.

'You know what, man?' said the bass player. 'Screw this, is what. I'm seriously going home.'

Between Broadview and Castle Frank, one train waited, poised on the bridge over the ravine. A man with a briefcase took out a tiny silver phone and sighed impatiently. 'Yeah, the train's stuck again … I don't know … I don't know … ' Beside him, a pasty-faced boy in enormous pants stared solemnly at a piece of paper on which he had written the heading RAP SONG, and carefully printed *I get more head than King Kong / My style is grim and …* He studied the page for a few minutes, changed *grim* to *grem*, looked at it for a while longer, and changed it back again. In the seat at right angles to the boy was a couple, probably in their sixties, their faces pouchy and collapsed. The man was very drunk, a smear of alcohol fumes in the air around him, his eyes closed in half-sleep, his head on the woman's shoulder. She was staring ahead, not smiling, not frowning, blank and still.

Another woman looked out the window, down into the ravine, seeing a red tent half-hidden among the trees at the edge of the twisting river. She spread one hand against the window and watched the rain begin to fall, leaving tiny flaws in the water's surface, thrumming against the sides of the tent.

Even past Spadina, the traffic seemed locked in a permanent snarl, but when Alex got onto the Bathurst streetcar it was no more crowded than usual. There were no visible effects of the subway incident, but he thought that people did know somehow, fragments and rumours; he was not even sure why he thought this, except for a slight modulation in the atmosphere, a measure of silence, glances of quiet complicity between the Portuguese housewives and the Asian teenagers. He got off the streetcar at College and walked west in the darkness, the rain stinging his face, the fabric of his pants clinging to his knees and calves.

Just past Euclid, a shape moved out of a doorway and into the pool of a streetlight. A man, a big shambling man, with matted red hair and a heavy beard, three layers of ravelling sweaters, his hands shaking, his feet crammed into a pair of women's fur-lined boots that had split along the seams of the fake leather. 'Excuse me, sir?' he said, his voice soft and interrogative, surprisingly high-pitched. 'Excuse me? I hate to trouble you, sir, but I'm being held hostage by terrorists, would you happen to have any spare change, sir?'

Alex reached into his pocket and found a two-dollar coin, dropped it into the extended hand, a pale mass of flesh, blue veins standing out. 'Thank you so much, sir,' said the man, retreating back into the alley. 'I wouldn't ask, sir, only I'm being held hostage by terrorists.'

'Don't worry about it,' said Alex.

'But I'm on cleaning systems now. It's a lot better since I got on cleaning systems.'

'That's good, that's great. Keep it up.'

One day last month he had been walking in front of the Scott Mission, and two men were standing outside, men with bashed-up swollen faces and rheumy eyes, shouting, 'No war! No war! Peace for the Middle East!' He'd wanted to film them, send it to the news, grassroots political initiatives, but what happened at the Scott Mission was in a different dimension, he knew that, a borderline zone whose intersections with the world of agreed reality were tenuous at best.

His apartment was just short of Grace Street, on the third floor, up a narrow flight of stairs; when he moved in, it had been above a cluttered little store selling saucepans and floral-print dresses to middle-aged Italian women, but now the store had been replaced by a café with pine tables and rag-painted walls, and his rent had risen precipitously. It seemed odd to him that he could still afford to live here, but in fact he could – he had a good job, he was a proper adult, there shouldn't be anything so surprising about that.

He unlocked his door and went in, shouldering off his wet coat. Queen Jane shifted vaguely on the couch and batted her tail a few times, then went back to sleep. He sat down beside her, absently stroking her grey fur and inspecting his feet for any blisters that might be forming.

He took a small fabric case from his coat pocket, opened up his glucometer, unwrapped a sterile needle and looked at his fingers to see if any of them were developing calluses; the right index looked best today, so he pierced it with the needle and squeezed a dark bubble of blood onto the test strip. The sugar count was well within his target range. He slid out a syringe and a little glass bottle of insulin and carefully drew the clear liquid into the barrel, inspecting it for air bubbles, then pulled up his shirt and pressed the needle into the skin of his abdomen. He capped and broke the syringe and went into the kitchen, dropping it into the plastic bucket that he used as a sharps container, opened a tin of lentil soup, sliced a bagel and put it into the toaster.

You would expect yourself to be more curious, he thought, when a thing like this happened. You could speculate, now and then, on just how you'd react to a genuinely important incident, but really what you did, it seemed, was to incorporate it almost instantly into the flow of daily life – the way he had gone on with his routine the day the planes flew into the buildings in New York, the way he had gone from his errand at the bank to his office at the hospital, had spent most of the day at his computer, and forgotten for minutes at a time that anything was wrong. The way you could spend the afternoon in what might perfectly well have been a poison gas attack, check your skin casually for a rash, and not bother with the radio. As long as no one you knew was hurt or sick, you were at least as interested in hearing about a girl you thought you were in love with fifteen years ago.

He wondered if she still called herself Susie-Paul. Probably not. It sounded like she was using Suzanne now. Suzanne Paulina Rae.

He chewed on the bagel and the sharp crumbling cheddar, mopping up the insulin before his blood sugar dropped too low, the intricate dance of chemical balance that he could never ignore, never leave to run automatically as most people did.

There was a photograph he sometimes came across, loose among his files, not properly stored and catalogued like the others because it wasn't one he'd taken himself. A loose colour print of a dozen people, arranged against the wall of the newspaper office, all of them in their twenties, clear-eyed, effortlessly beautiful. Susie-Paul and Chris were well into the final disintegration of their relationship by then, the paper nearly as far along the road to its own collapse, and the people in the photograph were each in their various ways tense, unhappy, embarrassed. Adrian, who was by no stretch of the imagination a member of staff, had been installed on the sagging couch between Susie and Chris as a kind of human Green Line; he was frowning and adjusting his glasses, one sneakered foot curled up on the cushion beside him. Chris, in a heavy sweater and corduroys, faced the camera down, his face hurt and determined under a forced smile. Susie was looking away, apparently speaking to someone. She was wearing a little flowered sundress over a pair of jeans, and a torn brown leather bomber jacket; her hair, in a feathery bob, was dyed a startling pink, the camera emphasizing her large dark eyes.

Looking out of the frame, he thought. As if there were someone beyond the picture who had a claim on her attention, more than any of the people around her. It had always been that way.

And far over to the other side was Alex, the rarely photographed photographer, a slender young man in black jeans and a black cotton shirt, staring down at the floor, long sand-coloured hair falling over his face like a screen. Adrian probably assumed that Alex and Susie-Paul had been sleeping together when the photo was taken; a number of people believed this, it was one of the generally accepted reasons for Chris and Susie's rather noisy and public breakup and the subsequent failure of the paper. Alex couldn't remember now who had taken that picture – it didn't look like a professional shot – but whoever it was, they or the camera had been more perceptive, had understood that Alex's real position was then, as ever, at the margin, a half-observed watcher of the greater dramas.

I don't know, said the girl, lying on a cot in the hospital, her legs covered with a sheet. I don't know. I can't tell you. I don't know.

They had been doing nothing, her friends said, talking to the doctors in the hallway. They went to Starbucks. They walked in the park. They got on the subway and then she said she was sick, and they thought maybe there was a funny smell, and she said yes, there was this rose kind of smell, but she was too sick to tell them much, and then the other one fell down as well, and they could all smell it now, and somebody ought to do something because it totally wasn't right.

The white figures bent to the floor of the subway car, their heads lowered, their eyes intent behind the masks. They searched for traces of liquid or powder, greasy smears; they collected old newspapers and food wrappers and sealed them into plastic containers. The instruments registered no danger. The tests they could perform in the small metal space of the car told them of nothing, of absence. They would take their sealed containers to a secure lab for further testing. The girls in the hospital watched their blood flow into tubes that would be carried to another specialized facility, but the blood would say the same thing, it would say that it could tell them nothing.

The rain was turning into a light icy snowfall now – not too bad, not impossible weather to work in. For a minute Alex leaned back against the wall, letting his eyes adjust to the darkness before he walked to the streetcar stop.

He did not admit to urgency. He did not admit to himself that missing even a single night bothered him, that this was becoming compulsive. He had always worked on his own projects in his free time, legitimate creative projects that were exhibited and published here and there, and he would not grant that he was behaving differently now.

He took his Nikon with him, and a shoulder bag with lenses and rolls of film. The digital technology was getting very good, he could see why a lot of people had made the shift, but he still preferred film for his own work, still liked the darkroom process, the smell of chemicals and craftwork on his hands. The Nikon was his standard personal camera. There was also the old Leica, but that was special – it was quirky, felt somehow intimate and tactile. There was a particular kind of photography that needed the Leica; he didn't use it very often.

He had always done this. Maybe not every night. It was true that he spent more time on it now. He'd broken up a while ago with Kim, a graphic designer he'd been seeing in a rather desultory fashion anyway. Sometimes the people in the imaging and computer departments of the hospital went out together, but missing these occasions seemed like no great loss.

Instead he wandered – down to the junkies and evangelists of Regent Park, or up the silent undulating hills of Rosedale, taking pictures by the pale light laid down from the windows of the mansions. Through dangerous highway underpasses to the lake, slick shimmering water rasping on the shores by deserted factories. To the bus station, the railway station, the suburban malls where his footsteps echoed by shuttered stores in the evening.

Tonight, perhaps because he'd been thinking about Susie-Paul and the paper, he went only as far as the university, got off the streetcar at St. George and started walking north. It seemed surprisingly quiet, the broad pavements almost empty. Maybe the students left the campus in the evenings. Or maybe students these days didn't go out, maybe they stayed in their rooms and read books about management techniques – but he was showing his age, one of those old people who no longer complained that students were too wild, but that they were too good, they ate right and married young.

Susie had been his grand passion, he supposed. The phrase amused him. A grand passion. Everybody needed one. Not the most serious relationship necessarily, or the most real – that was surely Amy, who had lived with him, who he might almost have married – but the one that burned you out, broke you to pieces for a while. At some point in your life before you were thirty, you needed to be able to listen to 'Sad-Eyed Lady of the Lowlands' and cry real tears.

Outside the Robarts Library, he took a picture of a nervous girl buying french fries from a cart, then stepped back and shot a series of faint human figures, hurrying under the brutalist concrete shoulders of the massive building, blurred by the tall lights and the faint haze of snow. The wind whipped his scarf across his face as he walked up the broad curve of the stairway. He pushed open the glass door and went into the library's forced-air warmth. He was pretty sure he wasn't supposed to take pictures here, but he usually managed a few, inconspicuously. A row of students awkwardly curled up asleep in the chairs; an elderly man in rubber boots, puddles around his feet, reading one magazine after another.

He left the library and kept walking, east past the darkness in Queen's Park, statues and whispering men among the trees, then the cheap bright flare of Yonge Street, ADULT DANCERS and VIdEOS HAfL-PRiC, the neon signs reflecting in nearby windows like flame.

The white figures rose up from the station, the air judged innocent, uncontaminated, to the extent that the instruments could detect.

This is the nature of safety in the measured world – you can be certain of the presence of danger, but you can never guarantee its absence. No measurement quite trusts itself down to zero, down to absolute lack. All that the dials and lights and delicate reactions can tell you is that the instruments recognize no peril. You can be reassured by this, or not, as you choose.

It was later on that night, and Alex had come home, packed away his film and lenses. He was in the kitchen reaching for a jar of peanut butter, not thinking about anything in particular, when he caught himself blinking.

There was something in his field of vision.

He blinked again, and it didn't go away. He shook his head quickly, knowing this was useless. No change. Tiny black spots, just two or three. Up a bit and to the right. He closed his right eye, leaning against the counter. Standing in the empty kitchen, listening to the sound of his heart.

II

In the hour before dawn, the city is private and surprisingly cheerful, optimistic; hopeful, in the dark, of the coming day, the sunrise a slow dilution of shadow, a grey wash over the sky, tinged gently with pink.

On the Danforth, a handful of people sat in a coffee shop drinking espresso. A man and a woman, who met here every morning before work; he was bearded and aging, she was younger, black-haired, round-faced. Another woman in a second-hand army parka, reading a newspaper. A policeman buying muffins to take away. These were the ones who rose early and ventured out with the wind, at the coldest time on the clock.

Across the river, among the towers of St. Jamestown, a Somali girl tightened her head scarf, zipped up her red jacket and set out on her bike to deliver newspapers, and on the street an Iranian man who had once been a doctor cleaned vomit from the back seat of his taxi. A woman put a pan of milk on the burner of her stove, and stared at the creamy ripples on the surface.

The subway began to run, the first train on each line half-empty, the second and third filling up as the rush hour gathered mass and density. Underground bakeries drew fresh pastries out of metal ovens, the sweet hot smell of dough and yeast touching the platforms.

Alex left for work early. He had barely slept anyway. The floaters in his right eye were a shock, maybe more of a shock than they should have been, and he was far too anxious, too wound up to sleep, only skimming and plunging for a few hours through tangled twilight dreams. It was a relief to be outside, to drink hot tea with milk and sugar from his plastic travel mug as he rode the College streetcar, the world solidifying around him. On the northbound subway, a tall and muscular Buddhist monk, with orange robes and a shining round head, was fingering a circlet of wooden beads, a tiny secret smile playing over his lips, as he listened to three girls across the aisle from him having a nearly unintelligible giggling conversation on the general theme of chocolate cake.

Alex arrived at the hospital during the hollow quiet of the morning shift change, his footsteps audible in the lobby, and went up to his office, unlocking the door and booting up the computer. When he checked his voice mail, he found a message already waiting for him – an unexpected work call from the cardiac OR, scheduled to start within an hour. He downloaded his mail, looked it over quickly, then collected his equipment and took the elevator up to the surgical floor.

In the prep room, he reached into the rack for a green gown, tied on a mask and slid disposable gloves over his hands. Despite the gear, he would not be sterile, not fully scrubbed in; that was the normal procedure, the photographer only ambiguously part of the team, outside the sterile field. Thus the first and most unbreakable rule, that he and his camera must under no circumstances touch anyone or anything.

He could hear the music through the door, so he knew that Walter Yee was doing the surgery today; Walter, usually over the objections of the team, played REM relentlessly, and insisted on singing along with his favourites. He did not sing well. They were in the early stages of the operation when Alex arrived, the chest already opened. Walter was humming 'Losing My Religion,' his gloved hands moving delicately among the veins and arteries.

'Hi. I'm Alex Deveney, I'm the photographer,' he said for the benefit of anyone there he didn't know, and moved towards the table. Walter gestured with his head to indicate where he wanted Alex to stand.

'Can we get a picture of this before I start working?'

Alex nodded, framed a shot of the chest cavity, the heart's red throbbing muscle and glistening fat, then kept shooting as Walter placed a clamp on the largest artery and gestured for the infused medication that would paralyze the tissue.

'So who got caught in the traffic jam last night?' asked the anaesthetist.

'That was the subway thing, wasn't it?' said one of the nurses. 'I saw something about it in the paper this morning. Somebody smelled a funny smell or something, and the security guys went crazy.'

'Girls fainting, I heard,' said a resident.

'Oh yeah, I was there,' said Alex. 'It was very strange, private-school girls just crashing.'

'Probably dieting themselves to death, poor kids.'

'No, they were having rashes and stuff. Thought they'd been poisoned. It looked like some kind of hysterical thing.'

'I've never liked the word hysteria,' said Walter thoughtfully, as he cut into the heart and began to open it, exposing the cavities. 'I don't find it helpful. And it has a bit of a gender bias, don't you think?'

'Yeah, the wandering uterus.'

'Oh my God, my uterus has escaped!'

'It's taken off down Yonge Street!'

'Can I move over there, Walter?' asked Alex. 'I'd like to get some shots from the other side.'

'Hang on a second … yeah, okay. Linda, squeeze over for Alex there? Thanks.'

'Anyway,' said Alex, 'you can call it somatization if you want. I spent half an hour convincing myself I didn't have a rash. Like instant cutaneous anthrax or something.'

'And we're letting you into the OR? Standards are really slipping.'

'But if we don't, the terrorists have already won, right?'

Walter was singing again as he probed the mitral valve, professing along with Michael Stipe that he was Superman and that he knew what was happening. Alex took some longer shots of the gowned figures clustered around the table, then moved in closer and focused on the thick meat of the heart.

'Tell you what I saw on the subway this morning,' said the resident. 'I saw the kid who owns evil.'

'Oh yeah?'

'Really. I got on and there was this kid, this teenage boy, holding this big old box, like a computer box or something, and he'd written on it in pink marker: CAUTION, DO NOT OPEN. CONTAINS EVIL. The pink marker was what I liked.'

'Do you suppose it was true?'

'My thinking is, why would someone lie about a thing like that?'

Alex zoomed the lens onto Walter's careful hands, coated with the patient's blood. 'David, could you come over here?' the surgeon was saying. 'I think you'll be interested to see this.' The resident shifted around the table, and Alex moved back, wondering what it was that was interesting and hoping he'd gotten a good picture of it.

Where he was standing now he could see the man's face, slack and still, his mouth distorted by the breathing tube. He thought of this man getting up and walking away, damaged and healed. The heart cut open and motionless, this man as dead right now as anyone would ever be, short of the final death. He stepped back and photographed Walter leaning over the man, touching his heart with a knife.

The boy with the box of evil sat in the cafeteria of his high school, the box on the table beside him, eating a hamburger and feeling unusually cheerful. He hadn't heard about the problems on the subway the day before, and didn't know that a security guard had phoned in an alert while he was on the train, though it would have made him happy to know this.

He was a medium-sized boy with brown hair and thick glasses, and he had carried the box with him into every one of his classes that morning and sat it on the desk. When anyone asked him what it was, he said it was a prop for a play, which was almost sort of true.

The box had previously contained a computer game that wasn't much fun, just your basic maze game when you stripped away the effects, and the effects weren't so great themselves. There was nothing inside it, because he hadn't been able to think of what evil should look like, aside from maybe a lot of bugs, and you couldn't just fill up a box with bugs that easily. Or maybe if you lived in some really bad neighbourhood you could.

'Did you hear about the guy who found the biggest prime number in the world?' he asked the girl sitting next to him.

'Did he go insane or what?'

'No, he did not go *insane*, Sharon, why would he go insane? He just discovered the biggest prime number. It was, like, huge.'

'I just thought. Like the guy in the movie.'

'He was not like the guy in the movie, okay?'

'Yeah, okay, so he found the biggest prime number, what did he do with it?'

'Oh, like he had to *do* anything.'

'Well, you'd just think. What good is it if you don't do anything with it? And are you going to carry that box with you all afternoon?'

'I'm gonna carry it forever. You can't let evil run around unguarded.'

'You're such a freak.'

'Yeah. I try.' He moved the box so that the sign could be more easily read by people passing the table, and took another bite of hamburger.

Alex left the OR at lunchtime, and paused to check his blood sugar and inject his afternoon insulin before he went into his studio, checking the list of ambulatory patients he'd been assigned. A few hours later a girl came in, a last-minute addition to the list – a pale teenager, strawberry blonde, in tight jeans and a powder-blue T-shirt, carrying her coat and sweater and flanked by a nurse and a woman in business clothes, presumably her mother. He could see that her face and arms were splattered with bright red hives, but he didn't make the connection right away.

'Hi,' he said, smiling, reaching his hand out to the girl and then to the mother. 'My name's Alex, I'm the photographer.' He took the file from the nurse and glanced at it. 'Okay. Looks like they just want some pictures of that rash there. Could you put your coat down here, and take a seat in that chair? Thanks.' He checked the lights and adjusted his lens. 'I'll take some pictures of your arms first. Could you lift up your right arm?' He adjusted the lens, focused and clicked off a few shots. 'You're Christine, right?'

'Yeah,' muttered the girl.

'How are you feeling today, Christine? Bit under the weather?'

'Kind of.'

'Left arm now? Great, thank you. What happened? Allergies?'

'I was *poisoned*,' said the girl in a sudden rush of emotion. 'Somebody *poisoned* me.'

'It was on the subway,' said the mother, controlled anger in her voice. 'It was just like those girls on the news. Someone's got to do something about this.'

'Huh.' Alex took a step back and looked at the girl, her limp hair and red-rimmed eyes. 'Well, let's just get these photos for the record, and we'll see what the doctors have to say. I'm going to do a couple of profiles and then some pictures facing me, okay? So first I need you to turn your head to the right. Perfect.'

The sleet was coming down again. Alex wrapped his scarf around his face and bent his head, walking into the wind as the frozen rain rattled on shop windows, the tiny ice pellets not melting but clustering on the sidewalk, bright and slick. The wind rose and tugged at his coat, stinging the tips of his ears, as he crossed the broad intersection towards the subway and descended into the damp cold of the tunnels. The subway car was crowded, thick heat issuing from the radiators and from the bodies that pressed against him as he stood, grasping a metal ring, drowsing standing up.

In the faint elastic time of half-sleep, he thought of the falling girls, and though he didn't for a moment believe it, he began shaping in his mind a story, a man who stepped onto the train with a package. Let him be a tall man, and good-looking, and educated. He must be a man with some scientific training. He could be a chemist, say; but in this story he would be a doctor. The doctor steps onto the train with a package wrapped in newspaper. He carries it as tenderly as if it were a damaged child, resting it gently on his knee as he sits.

Motive was not a question that Alex in his waking dream considered in detail, but he did not think the man was acting out of anger. The man believes, at any rate, that he is acting out of something like love.

At a particular stop, the man places his package unobtrusively on the floor of the subway car, just beneath his seat. The movement is smooth and subtle. The package lies on the metal floor among shoes and dust.

At another particular stop, chosen long in advance, the man, the doctor, rises from his seat and picks up his folded umbrella. Quietly, swiftly, he stabs the package three times with the umbrella's sharpened tip. The train comes to a halt, the doors open, and the doctor moves swiftly out the door. An invisible twine of gas curls upwards.

The doctor watches the train pull out, and contemplates the end of the world.

At College station, Alex shook himself awake and joined the flow upwards to the streetcar stop. The car that arrived from the east emptied itself onto the street, and he found a seat by the window, rubbed his face with his hands and watched the lines of stores and office buildings gliding past.

When he was climbing down from the car near his apartment, he realized that the floaters were gone. It meant nothing, really, it signified no long-term hope, but he felt some of his fatigue lifting, his body not quite so heavy. He blinked, and breathed deeply in the metallic air, and crossed the street, the end of the world held off for now.

Queen Jane dropped off the couch in a slow jump, forelegs and then back legs in separate movements, as he walked in the door; he took his boots off and picked her up, shifting her heavy purring weight against his chest as he sat on the couch and sorted his mail with one hand, smoothing her thick fur with the other. She was clearly disinclined to move again, so he stayed on the couch for a while, wondering what to make for dinner and where he should go tonight, what he would do about the increasingly nasty weather. 'Fat old cat,' he muttered affectionately. 'Dumb old thing.'

He could go to Parkdale tonight maybe, ragged transitional Parkdale. Ten years ago, the place you didn't dare go after dark. Now the hookers and the junkies stood on the steps of boutique hotels, and there were articles in the newspapers about the neighbourhood's character and charm. That phase in the process could be something to document, though of course anything could be something to document. Wherever you went there was light, there were bodies in space.

Once Jane seemed soundly asleep, he heaved her onto the couch and stood up, heading for the kitchen. On the way, he lifted the phone and heard the rapid beeps that signalled a voice-mail message, punched in his code and listened. The person on the voice mail cleared her throat. 'Hi, Alex.'

Her voice was crazily, confusingly familiar, but at the same time he couldn't put an identity to it, somehow thought for a second that it was someone he'd heard on the radio. 'It's been a long time,' the voice went on, 'but it's Suzanne, Susie. Susie Rae.'

'We were unable to find any significant abnormalities in the blood tests performed on the young women,' said the public health officer.

'What does that mean, significant abnormalities?' asked the reporters at the press conference, the stand-ins for the worried city. 'What is an insignificant abnormality?'

'We found no abnormalities that would be associated with the release of a toxic substance,' said the public health officer.

'When you say you were unable to find them, does that mean they weren't there?'

'It means we were unable to find them with our most sensitive tests. In practical terms, it's as good as saying they weren't there.'

'But it's not the same thing.'

'It's effectively the same thing. We don't make absolute statements.'

'So you can't be sure they weren't there.'

'We can be sure that there is no cause for the public to be concerned.'

'How can you be sure of that?'

'Because we found no significant abnormalities.'

'So what kind of abnormalities did you find?'

We are not at home in the measured world. We would prefer our safety to be an unmeasurable absolute. Not an approximation. Not the mere knowledge that on this particular day we, unlike others, did not die, and that, if we are lucky, there is no specific reason to assume we will die tomorrow.

Finally Alex was undone by simple curiosity, as he had known he would be. But he put it off for a while, going to work on Thursday and almost forgetting her call, coming home and spending the evening in the darkroom he had rigged up in his apartment, printing a stack of contact sheets. On Friday morning he knew that he would phone her, but he didn't know what her schedule was. Calling her during the day seemed safer; if she had left only one number, it must be her home, and she probably wouldn't be there in the middle of the day.

Late in the morning he dialled up his personal voice-mail box from the phone in his office and copied down her number. Then he went out into the hallway and got a cup of coffee and drank it, came back and looked at a few more files on his computer. The number was nondescript and revealed little about her location. Probably somewhere in the east end.

At lunchtime he went down to the cafeteria in the lobby and bought a sandwich and a bottle of juice, and then, as if it had only just occurred to him, went across to one of the pay phones. Her number rang three times without an answer, and he thought that he would get her voice mail, and he could just hang up. At the beginning of the fourth ring he began to relax, and then the ring stopped and there was a live voice saying hello on the other end.

'Susie-Paul?' he said quietly.

'Alex,' she said. 'I was starting to think I'd called the wrong number.'

'No. No, that was me, I've been busy. Sorry.'

'Adrian said he'd run into you. It made me think I should ... ' her voice trailed off.

'Yes. Well.' He tried to think of something to say aside from *it's been a long time*, which was self-evident, or *it's good to hear from you*, which wasn't entirely true.

'Are you … you know, I'd like to see you. Could we meet for coffee sometime, or … '

He thought, *let's get it over with.* 'I'm free for a little while tonight.'

'Oh. Okay, let me … okay. Tonight's fine.'

'We could have dinner. But there's things I need to do later.'

'Sure. Is, is seven good for you?'

'Yeah, I'm, I live around Little Italy, so … '

'We could go to Sneaky Dee's,' said Susie.

'Aw, no,' he said, smiling despite himself. 'I'm too old to go in there. The young people would laugh at me. Really, I'm, like, I'm really old these days.'

'Well, don't say this to *me*, Alex. What about that place, the Thai place at Bloor and Bathurst?'

'That's not a useful description.'

'You know the one. The place that used to be the place that had the Caesar salad?'

'Oh yeah. The Royal Whatever.'

They had been to the place with the Caesar salad, he remembered now. Remembered riding his bicycle home in the middle of the night, his eyes stinging, shaky and confused. One night like all the others.

'They have this Buddha that lights up.'

'Well, you know. The Buddha's like that. Can you win little plastic prizes from him?'

'I'm afraid not. Sorry to disappoint you.'

'Well, I guess you can't have everything.'

'I'll see you there?'

'Yeah. I'll see you. Cool.'

He hung up the phone and turned around to face the lobby, shaking his head. 'Alex, man,' he said to the air, 'do you have a clue what you're doing here?'

Falling

I

After one girl has fallen, the rest are explicable; they have a template, a precedent. But before that, it is harder to understand. At the beginning of this problem, then, is a single girl, the first girl to fall.

She shouldn't have been a mystery, not even a question, this shining privileged girl with glossy hair, bright enough, well-meaning; this girl surrounded all her life with the expectation of clarity and goodness, who had collected tins of soup for the food bank, had given a talk in the school assembly about looking for the best in everyone, who had signed up to tutor an underprivileged child in math.

She had fears, of course she did, the normal kinds of fears. They read newspapers for their current affairs class, and she knew something about what went on in the world. She had dreamed for a while of the towers in New York. She hadn't seen, on the television coverage, the people who fell or leapt from the windows, but it was all they had talked about at school, a literal incarnation of that childhood game, sitting around a flashlight at a sleepover trying to imagine whether you would rather die from burning or jumping. She knew that one war was already happening, and there might be another coming, wars in distant countries but somehow close. She drew peace signs on her notebooks, picked up flyers from leafletters by the Eaton Centre, and worried vaguely, the details unclear.

But she would not say that she fell because of this. Her account was simple – she smelled a smell like roses, then she started to feel dizzy and sick, as if she had been poisoned, and began to vomit, and didn't feel better until she was carried into the open air on the street. She hadn't been ill before that, she didn't have a cold or an upset stomach, she was a healthy girl. She didn't know about the panics on the London Underground, the rumours of cyanide. She hadn't read the stories about what happened in Tokyo in 1995, when a group of elite sons and disaffected mathematicians decided to kick-start the apocalypse; never saw the pictures of people staggering out of the subway exits, clawing at their eyes.

So why would she imagine such a thing? Why would anyone?

The first girl who fell, on the day it began.

She had come out of school with her friends, in her kilt and tie and red wool jacket, her thigh still feeling intangibly damp where the geography teacher had put his hand on it after class.

'Sid the Squid,' snorted Lauren as they walked down the steps. 'God, he's so gross. He's just made of gross. And his wife is a hog and a half, seriously, I mean, she weighs like a thousand pounds.'

'She totally could sink the Titanic with her ass. I'm not kidding,' said Tasha.

The strangeness of adults, their clenched little needs.

'Yeah, can you imagine them in bed?' said Lauren. 'Oh, oh, darling, argh, I can't breathe!'

She hated her thighs anyway, they were rounded and fat, swelling against the hard chair.

'He's *repellent*,' said Lauren. 'Hey, you know what, you know the Starbucks at Yonge and St. Clair is giving away free mochaccinos?'

'No way,' said the girl, taking a tube of pink glitter lipstick from her backpack and opening her mouth slightly to apply it. She wouldn't stay after class anymore, not without Lauren, not without somebody. 'No way they are.'

'Yeah, because they had a sign in the window. But only till four.'

'I don't even think.'

'Come on, then. I'll prove you they are.' Lauren pushed her hair back from her shoulders, and led them onto Yonge Street, into the shine and flutter of retail, the glimmering windows, people pushing past them with briefcases and plastic bags. The girl had a black canvas bag over her shoulder, with a yellow pin on it showing a rabbit holding a PEACE placard, and a pink pin that said *It IS All About Me, Deal With It*.

'I just feel so cheated,' Tasha was saying. 'Because every year after sports day they had pizza, like every year, and then our year we just have chips and Coke. Literally like a single chip each. And you expect you're going to have pizza, you know?'

'I know, it's so cheap,' said the girl. 'It's like, hey, we're saving five cents, we're so awesome!'

'To me it's like a betrayal,' said Lauren.

Starbucks really was giving away mochaccinos, and the lineup stretched halfway down the block, some of the other girls from their own school, and kids from the local high school in jeans and T-shirts, their coats slumping off their shoulders. The girl checked her reflection in the glass door, wondering fretfully if she had gained more weight, if there was a visible roll of fat at her waist. Joining the wave of young bodies, pushing and giggling. Contact in the crowd between hips, legs, the bare skin of a stranger's arm, and she slid into the high bright relief of noise.

'I *so* need caffeine right now,' said Tasha. 'Or I'm physically *dying*.' They reached the counter, and the desperate boy pushed forward another half-dozen cups. Each of them grabbed one, pressing through the aisle towards the exit, sipping the foaming liquid, bitter and milky. Aware of the public school boys, watching them from under their messy bangs. She met the eyes of one boy, a nice-looking boy, someone she would probably never see again, and his look slid down her.

When they walked east along St. Clair they had become a group of five, Megan and Zoe joining them as well.

'I have to write an assignment about Guinevere,' moaned Zoe. 'Who I just hate so *much*. Did you read it? She's so unloyal. She's like this crazy old bipolar bitch.'

'We're not doing that one, though, we're doing that other one.'

'Well, God, you're so lucky. It's like a million pages of poetry. It's diseased, if you want to know.'

'Is your class raising money for the global, the African thing?'

'I think. But I'm not sure what we're doing yet.'

The girl adjusted the gold barrettes in her hair with one hand, rolled up her skirt so that it brushed high on her legs, her bare skin goosebumped with cold, thinking about the boy from the public school, with a vague distaste and a wish that he would follow them. He might have been a nice boy.

'What I think, we need to have a slave auction,' Zoe was saying. 'Because it's so the best kind of fundraiser.'

'We should make the teachers be the slaves,' said Megan, giggling. 'We should make Mr. Sondstrom be a slave. We so should.'

The girl frowned and wiped mochaccino from her pink lips, swallowing against the heat in her throat. 'Mr. Sondstrom's too gross to be a slave even,' she said. Megan didn't know. It wasn't her fault. 'He's just a squid. Sid the Squid.'

'Totally,' said Lauren, bumping her shoulder supportively. The girl finished her mochaccino, crushed the paper cup in her hand.

Turning off St. Clair, they walked past the frost-brown gardens of the residential streets, wet leaves in the gutters, heading towards Chorley Park, where there were boys playing soccer sometimes, or sometimes they would just sit on the benches and talk, their park, their place.

'But I'm going to the Eaton Centre later on,' said Megan. 'I need a new pair of shoes *so* bad. It's a critical situation.'

'You know the place called Rebels? They have the *best* shoes.'

'Megan buys her shoes at Sears,' said Tasha.

'I do not, you liar.' Megan, a year younger than the others, her position in the group subject to question.

'You totally do.'

'Oh God,' Zoe broke in, laughing nervously. 'I have to tell you about my brother. I have to tell you about my psycho brother, okay? I mean, he's got all these, like, warfare scenes in his bedroom, like, the little guys with their spears and shit. Which is spaz enough, right? But he's now he's like, okay, it's, like, this warfare is all over, it's modern times, and I'm going to do a terror gas attack, and kill them all. And I'm like, *God!* They're a bunch of *toys!* But he's, no, I'm gonna make a poison chemical from like Clorox and bleach and I'm gonna kill everybody, and I'm like, it's a *toy*, Jordan, you mutant.'

'God,' said the girl, rolling her eyes. 'That is *so* random.'

''Cause he's like, it happened in, in the Japan subway, and all these people died, so he's like, I can totally do this at home.'

'What happened in Japan?' asked Tasha, her eyebrows pinched.

Zoe shrugged. 'I dunno. Terrorists or whatever. Jordan's like Mutato-Boy, so, I mean, what does he know about it? I bet he dreamed the whole thing.'

'Would you believe,' said the girl, 'when I was a kid I was in that big subway crash at Dupont? Oh *God*, that was so scary.'

'Oh my *God*! You were *really*?' gasped Lauren, and the girl's face shone with gratified horror.

'I totally was,' she said. 'I nearly *died*.'

'Oh my *God*! That must have been so traumatic!'

'Seriously,' said the girl; though in truth her memories were vague, barely existing at all. There had been smoke, at some point – when she was being taken out of the car, there had been smoke. Before that she had been pressed against her mother, and there was some other woman pushing against her from the other side, and that woman was wearing too much perfume, floral, clotting in her throat. The lights had gone out.

'No, but I think monkeys are more morally superior than people,' Zoe was saying. 'Because monkeys don't use, like, landmines and stuff, do they?'

'Unless they were really horrible monkeys,' said Tasha, and then they were at the park.

'Well,' said Lauren. 'This is pretty random.'

And what happened in the green space of the park was something the girl didn't much want to talk about.

Things that Girls Do

He knew how it would go, Alex told himself as he walked up Bathurst Street. They would start out tentative and hopeful, full of kind feelings about the past. They would talk for a while about safe and neutral memories, about shared acquaintances, and then slowly the evening would shrivel into the dry, polite awareness that they had nothing in common anymore, maybe never had. It might be embarrassing and a bit sad, but they would walk away from it unharmed, freed from certain things. That was the way these things went.

He knew, in fact, not much about her. Once he had thought that he wanted to know her, wanted nothing more in the world, but it had never been true; whatever he had thought he felt, Susie had finally been not much more than a blank screen for his own longings. And he, presumably, had been the same for her, had acquired what identity he had from being simply not Chris.

BIRD FLU EPIDEMIC COULD KILL MILLIONS, said a head-line in a newspaper box. Maybe this would replace the fainting girls, then; that would be a relief. He bent down, glancing at a photograph of the mass extermination of chickens in Hong Kong. The story stressed that the world was overdue for an epidemic. The virus biding its time, waiting to make a grand appearance.

She was in the restaurant already when he arrived, but she stood up from the table as he came in, and there was a moment of awkward shuffling as they tried to decide whether they would hug. They did not. It had crossed his mind that he might not recognize her; but of course that was impossible. He sat down at the other side of the table, under a tourist-office poster of Bangkok.

'Alex,' she said. 'You look good.'

He was stung by the cliché, but this was what people said. He should have let it pass, said the same thing in return. He smiled a bit crookedly. 'I look ten years older than my age.'

She tipped her head to one side and raised her eyebrows, not insulted or taken aback. Almost amused.

'The grey hair's hereditary,' he added, feeling foolish now. 'Otherwise it's just my misspent youth.'

Her own face had lost the soft prettiness he saw in his old pictures, was angular and serious, her skin textured and finely lined, her eyes still large and very dark. Her hair, which he'd been genuinely curious about, was longer, past her shoulders, and a deep red-brown that was possibly her natural colour, though more likely not. A fine, complex face, a good face to photograph. But he couldn't say anything about how she looked; he had managed to ensure that it would not be neutral or safe.

The next few minutes were temporizing, the business of studying menus, ordering, a pause in which neither of them had to think about what to say next. The waiter came, and left, and space opened up again.

'I hope you don't mind that I phoned,' she said eventually.

'Of course not. Why would I mind?' He played with his cutlery, not meeting her eye and thinking, *How long have you been back, and never called me? Why did you look for Adrian and not for me, never for me?* He was more angry than he had realized.

'It's been a while.'

'Quite a while. I didn't know you were even back in the city.'

'Yes. Well.'

'I didn't have any way to know, did I?'

Or maybe this was just the edginess of an impending hypo. He'd taken his insulin before he left home, and his blood sugar must be getting quite low by now. He picked up his glass of juice and drank half of it quickly.

'Actually, I am in the phone book,' said Susie.

'Ah. Well, so am I. As I guess you found out this week.'

'I can see where you wouldn't have thought to look, though.'

'I didn't especially assume you'd be back.'

'Fair enough.'

He could, yes, feel his anger diminishing, independent of Susie or anything about her, as the sugars in the mango juice settled his blood. Sometimes it was no more than that, a process of the body, disengaged from other people.

'Alex,' she said suddenly. 'What are you actually thinking?'

He took another sip of juice. 'Nothing.'

'Alex.'

'Nothing. I just was wondering about the difference between emotions and chemicals.'

Again she seemed prepared to accept his bizarre conversational gambits. 'None, if you ask a psychiatrist.'

'Yeah. It's all blood sugar and serotonin reuptake.'

'Trick of the light?'

He thought of Walter's delicate cardiac work. 'Maybe.'

'Is that what you believe?'

This had become a discussion about something else, where either a yes or a no would have intentions that he didn't want. 'I don't know what I believe,' he said. 'I was just wondering.'

The waiter returned with their food, chicken fried rice for Susie and vegetarian pad Thai for Alex. 'You still don't eat meat?'

'I'm hardcore. In my way.'

'You really are the most incongruous vegetarian, though.'

'Well, the insulin comes from a lab now. Don't have to slaughter livestock for it anymore.'

'Okay.'

'On the other hand, I've taken pictures of doctors cutting open freshly killed pigs, so I'm still fairly compromised.' He wound the broad noodles around his fork; the sauce was sweet and ketchupy, entirely North American. 'It keeps me from thinking too well of myself.'

'Good Lord. That must be a fun way to spend your day.'

'I don't mean all the time. Not very often, really.'

If she had asked him what he did that involved pig autopsies, it might have gotten things back onto a normal course – professional information followed by edited personal details, a socially appropriate exchange. 'Do you have to watch them kill the pigs?' she asked, and he realized that Susie really was quite as odd as he remembered her being. Although he wasn't presenting a very convincing picture of normalcy himself.

'Well, yes. But it's not particularly graphic. The doctor gives it an injection and it just dies kind of quietly.' He poked a piece of tofu with his fork. 'I'm a medical photographer,' he added desperately, trying to steer the conversation onto solid ground. 'It's a research hospital, so they do have an animal OR. But it's a very small part of my job.'

'Huh. How did you end up doing that?'

Alex breathed a small sigh of relief. 'I don't know, because hospitals are like a second home to me? Basically, the job was advertised and I needed work. I still do other things, but I've stayed at this for quite a while now. It's a pretty good way to make a living.'

'And that's it?' She lifted a bit of chicken to her lips, watching him as he tried to keep his eyes on his plate. 'That's all it is?'

He felt another quick burn of irritation, but something else as well, the memory of her, knotty and actual, the girl with pink hair and erratic boundaries. 'No.' He cleared his throat. 'No. I guess it's not. It's also a privilege, isn't it? I mean … if you're not a doctor, you don't usually get to see, say, a person's cerebral arteries being cut and repaired. Or a heart, the actual thing, the way it moves … I'm allowed to see this, I'm allowed to see this kind of extremity. And there is something in it – something beautiful.' It was possible that he sounded crazy. He was increasingly unsure. 'I don't mean to be so dramatic. Lots of times I'm just taking pictures of electron microscopes for the brochures, or, you know, doctors pretending to discuss charts with each other on the cover of the annual report.' He ate another forkful of noodles. 'You call yourself Suzanne now?'

'Susie's okay.'

'Yeah, but mostly.'

'Mostly Suzanne.'

Have you ever seen a pig being killed? he thought of asking. *Have you ever seen anyone die? Why can't I decide if I'm angry at you or not?*

Her eyes weren't young anymore. They were deeper and shadowed, grown-up, the skin around them creased, and for just a moment he felt almost unbearably close to her.

'So what are you doing now?' he asked instead.

'I ask people peculiar questions,' said Susie.

'Well, yes, I see that. I mean for a living.'

'Like I said.'

'What, and you get paid for this? By the Question Fairy?'

'Pretty much, yeah.' She ate a forkful of rice. 'Okay. I'm actually a sociologist. Or nearly. I'm working on my doctorate.'

'You're an *academic*? Jesus.'

'Come on. It could be worse.'

'I guess. It's not organized crime.'

'It's not international finance. It's not the arms trade. Or retail sales. It's really quite harmless, I get my doctorate and then I go and teach other people till they get their doctorates and go teach other people. It's a little self-contained closed system, like a terrarium or something.'

'An academic. Man. What a thought.'

'You know, usually people just ask why I don't have a real job at my age.'

'I'm hardly one to be asking that,' said Alex, and then realized that he did have a real job, had done for quite some time, though it had somehow never managed to penetrate his self-image.

He could have asked her what she'd been doing in the meantime, but it was exactly that meantime that he didn't want to touch, how she went away and came back, the old scars. Behind his back he heard the sheer whistle of rising wind, outside the glass wall.

'So you're writing a thesis or something?'

'Dissertation. Analysis of relationship networks among the homeless and underhoused.'

'Okay, I can see that. That's really interesting.'

'Not so much. Not to anyone but me. Anyway, I had to kind of change the topic because my supervisor – well, never mind, it's just one of those dissertation things.'

'I wouldn't know.'

She bent over her plate, pushing at the remains of the rice with her fork. 'So. Well. So there you go,' she said, and then she looked up again and her face was cracked and vulnerable, a question in it he recognized, sore to the touch. *Do I know you? Do I know you anymore?* He felt something that he couldn't name slip loose inside his chest.

'I was worried about you, a bit,' he said. The window rattled behind him.

She nodded slowly. 'I was … I'm all right. It was just … '

'I thought probably. Probably you were okay. But I wasn't sure.'

'I know. I mean … What about you?'

'I … I'm fine now.' He looked down at his own hands, fidgeting with the cutlery, and couldn't think for a while what should come next.

'You know, hands are very interesting things,' he said finally.

'You're still a pothead, aren't you?' said Susie. And this at last was something he could laugh at, unforced.

'Really not. I'm just like this all by myself, as it turns out.'

'That's gotta save some money.'

'I spend it all on tofu.' But while he had been looking at his hands he'd also looked at his watch, and time was pressing in on him again, the handful of hours left in the evening. 'Listen, Susie, Suzanne, I'm sorry about this, but I should go. Let me get the check?'

'Oh. All right.' Her face tensed slightly, a small nod as if she were accepting the blame for this. Understanding that it had been her fault.

'I'm sorry, it's not … I just have this thing … '

'You're meeting someone?'

He wished he could say he was, it was the right excuse, free of hurt or judgement. 'Not exactly. It's … I need to take some photos. I mean, it's a regular thing I do, after work I go out and … it's a sort of project. I don't like to – I know this sounds compulsive, but I don't like to miss a night.'

'In this?' She gestured towards the window, and he turned and saw that winter had abruptly fallen, as shockingly as it did each year, the first sudden storm. Against the darkness, the wind was driving sheets of snow in a slanting diagonal blur, pedestrians slipping in their inappropriate shoes.

'Oh, fuck,' muttered Alex, brought up against the inevitable wall of Canadian weather.

'Are you on a deadline?' asked Susie.

'No. No, it's not an assignment, it's a personal thing.' He folded his arms and frowned. 'I could do the PATH system. I'm going to have to think about the weather long-term, but right now I could do the PATH system.'

'You really think you have to do this?'

'I really do.'

She caught the waiter's eye and gestured for the check. 'I could come with you.'

'What? You think I'm going to die underground in the blizzard?'

'I'd just like to come. See what you're doing. If it's all right.'

He took the check from the waiter and reached for his wallet. No one ever came with him. It wasn't the way he did this.

'I guess so. If you really want to.'

They stood up on the subway, their hair beaded with snow after the short walk up Bathurst, neither of them able to accept the tight physical proximity of the narrow seats, appropriate only for close friends or complete strangers. Discarded newspapers lay scattered around the car, under the feet of dripping passengers, repeatedly and monotonously predicting millions of influenza deaths. Alex thought of telling Susie about his encounter with the girls and their poison gas, but decided against it; he was tired of the story already.

There was a wet draft of wind on the subway platform, crowds wandering up and down the stairs, but they pushed through the turn-stiles and opened the glass doors into a warm corridor with ivory-white walls that was nearly deserted, one man in a dark suit crossing a corner in the distance. The stores to the left were closed, metal grilles pulled down.

'Isn't this a funny time to be coming down here? I mean, there's nothing going on here at night, is there?' Susie unbuttoned her coat and tucked her soft red hat into her pocket.

'Well, that's the trick, I guess,' said Alex, opening his camera bag. 'I make decisions and I stick with them, it's one of the rules. But this could work.'

'I can see it during the day. When things are open. It's not exactly picturesque, but retail's part of the urban experience, I get that. But retail that's closed for the night?'

'Just let me see what I can do.' They passed from one corridor into the next, walking by a man with an industrial bucket mop talk-ing in animated French to a woman with cornrowed blonde hair and hoop earrings, and came out into a shuttered food court. 'I like this.

The bones of the food court. Infrastructure,' muttered Alex, moving around the kiosks, kneeling, adjusting the lens. The light was dim, but it wasn't too dark, not so dark that he couldn't adapt.

'It's interesting, the shape of things down here,' he went on, a kind of half-conscious patter, not exactly meant to be listened to. 'I mean, up on the surface the city's so rectilinear, but down here it's like this wild kind of maze. And they put up these signs … ' he stepped back to take a picture of one of the glyphic, colour-coded signs that hung from the ceiling '… that make no damn sense at all, these weird triangles. I wonder about it.'

'They disorient people so they'll feel insecure and purchase more. Try to locate themselves through merchandise.'

'Maybe. I don't know.'

In the next hallway there was music from a PA system, a woman in the uniform of one of the food court restaurants talking on her cellphone. A man walking by with a red balloon on a string.

'Let's go up this way,' said Alex, gesturing towards a steep elevator, and as they rode up he tipped his head back in astonishment.

'Oh, look,' he said. 'Oh, this is lovely.'

They were in a long hallway, with a high ceiling of white ribs, arching in a luminous cathedral curve above the darkened space, and set into the floor were panels of light, glowing in the dim surround. Alex knelt on the floor and leaned back, holding the camera upwards, almost lying down on the tile, then moved in a quick shuffle to the side, trying to hold the glowing panels and the arch in a single shot. 'Isn't this lovely?'

Susie was standing with her arms folded, half smiling. 'It's a *bank*, Alex,' she said.

'So?'

'So? So it's a bank. So this is just money trying to look good.'

Alex walked to the glass wall at the end of the hallway, seeing that they had returned to street level, and squinting out towards the street. He could barely make out a sheer black cone, slick with wet snow, and the angular glass edges of the facing building, and he took a series of shots, working on intuition, hoping that the tangle of reflections would come out the way he wanted it to. 'I say again –

so? People made this. They thought it would be beautiful, so they made it.'

'You're very easy to impress.'

'Maybe so. But that's a choice too.'

A small child ran onto one of the light panels, screaming in delight as his father ran after him, dodging and chasing in the scattered darkness, and Alex stopped thinking in concepts as he raised the camera, his fingers moving as he shifted the pictures around, framing, needing, taking in the shapes of their play, before they went down again to the underground passageways.

Some of the corridors were suddenly full of people, walking north from Union Station and branching off to the east or west at different points along the route. They passed Yogen Früz stands, candy stores with piles of maple fudge in the windows, shops that sold bottles of vitamins, or silk scarves and mittens, shuttered and dark. Into another underground courtyard, white marble, with banks of ferns and violets and tiny willow trees, a small waterfall at one end with the twisted copper shapes of salmon leaping in front of it. His feet were starting to ache; he sat down on the small stairway between the ferns, thinking that if he were by himself he could take his shoes off.

'Where else have you done this?' asked Susie, sitting beside him.

'Oh, everywhere.' He wiggled his toes and rotated his ankles, keeping the circulation going. 'I mostly concentrate on the downtown, but everywhere I can get to, really. People think urban photography is all big-eyed kids in housing projects. Which, I mean, yeah, housing projects are part of it too. And police stations and stuff. But so is this … ' he waved his arm around, '… this whatever. Is this a hotel?'

'I can't even tell. It's all much the same down here.'

They sat on the steps in silence for a few minutes.

'How long were you in Vancouver?' asked Alex.

Susie took a breath before she answered, and looked down. 'A year? A year and a half, I think.'

'Ah.' He held his camera on his lap, fidgeting with the lens. And he knew that she was aware of the same thing, that she had been back in Toronto for over ten years, and she hadn't talked to him. She talked to Adrian. Not to him.

He reached over and rubbed the leaf of the violet beside him, thinking he would find that it was plastic, but it wasn't, it was real.

'Adrian and Evvy got married, you know,' Susie said at last.

It took him a minute to place the name – yes, Evelyn Sinclair, the very quiet and faintly mysterious theology student that Adrian had been with, in some uncertain way, all those years ago. 'Huh.' He hadn't expected that. 'Well, I'm glad things work out for some people. They have any kids?'

'One.' She looked over at Alex. 'How about you? You married or anything?'

'Nah.' He rotated his ankles again. 'Came close to it once, I guess. But it didn't happen. Basically I stick with my cat.'

'Not the same cat, surely.'

'Oh yeah. She's very old now, but she's still around. She's like my life partner. What about you? Married?'

'Was for a bit. Not anymore. It wasn't a good idea.'

'Anyone I know?'

'Nope.'

Alex stood up. 'Okay. We've been in retail long enough. Let's check out Metro Hall and call it done.'

This meant another series of corridors, and a brief emergence into the damp clatter of the St. Andrew subway station, before they reached an orange hallway where the air was indefinably different, where there were no shops on either side. In the corner two figures lay rolled up in dirty sleeping bags on the tile floor, food wrappers scattered around them.

'See, this I understand,' said Susie. 'We've moved from retail space to civic space now. It's a less censored environment. Inclusive.'

Alex lifted his camera. He shouldn't do this, shouldn't photograph homeless people who were asleep, helpless to give permission, but his cannibal eye demanded the picture, and he didn't really try to resist. They walked into another hallway, a glass wall down the left side; he knew there was a sunken pool outside, surrounded by granite boulders and pine trees, a tiny replica of the Canadian Shield down below ground level, but at night there was nothing visible, only thick black beyond the glass. Up a spiral stairway, and another man in a small foyer just a few feet from the cold, asleep sitting up, a grey blanket draped over his shoulders. Susie shrugged on her coat and pushed the door open, and then they were out in the wind.

The snow had stopped, leaving a sugared dust drifting and whirling across the pavement as they stepped outside. Alex squeezed his eyes closed and opened them again, not quite able to move forward until he had grown used to the dark, hoping that Susie wouldn't notice this.

'So you're finished?'

'I guess so. Yeah.'

'Did you get what you wanted?'

'I'll have to wait and see. I never know till the pictures are developed if they're going to come out or not.'

They stood on King Street, awkward, putting off the moment of leaving, not so much because they wanted to be together exactly, but because they didn't know how leaving was supposed to go. A few yards away, a man in a blue suit with a paper bag over his head was playing a guitar and singing 'Blowin' in the Wind,' a light frosting of snow on the top of the bag and the shoulders of his jacket.

'He's actually not too bad,' said Alex.

'What do you suppose the paper bag is about?'

'Gotta have a trademark of some kind.'

Susie started walking north, for no clear reason, into the featureless side streets, and Alex followed.

'There was that guy who used to play the accordion down by the church on Bloor. And he had that nasty dog, the one that bit people. I don't know what ever happened to him.'

'I'm kind of hoping he got arrested,' said Susie. 'The Spits, though, they were the best buskers ever.' She took her hat out of her pocket and pushed it onto her chestnut hair. 'You remember the Spits?'

'Of course. Of course I do.'

'I was just thinking about them is all.' She looked around at the dark windows, the warehouse doors of the small empty street. 'So. Do you want to get a coffee someplace?'

'Yeah,' he said. 'Let's do that.'

They came out onto Queen Street, filled with light and crowds, and ended up at the Black Bull because it was later than he had thought, and the coffee shops were closing. He took the glucometer out of his camera bag to check his blood sugar, and decided that he could order a drink and a grilled cheese sandwich. The bar was loud and dark, the air thick with smoke and the wet smell of beer.

'Whatever happened to the all-night doughnut stores? Do kids not stay up all night anymore?' asked Susie, as she looked around at the crowd.

'They must,' said Alex, lifting his glass, the beer malty and pleasantly bitter. 'I'm hoping they just go to places we don't know about.'

He leaned back in his chair, feeling the warmth of the alcohol running through his limbs, and then noticed the TV above the bar, figures in white hazmat suits moving behind police tape at the Spadina subway station. 'Christ, what now?' he muttered, and stood up and walked over to where he could hear the newsreader explaining that the station had been shut down when someone found traces of white powder on the floor. That there were rumours of irregularities in the blood tests. The chair of the transit commission was dragged onto the camera, blinking and irritable, and then they moved on to the next item, a French diplomat saying something at the UN Security Council, the news crawl under the picture rolling out fragmentary stories of weapons and spies.

'That's so not true,' said Alex, thinking he was talking to himself.

'What isn't?' said Susie beside him.

'Oh. I thought you were still at the table. I mean the blood tests. The blood tests were fine. People are just making shit up.'

'This is the poisoned girls?'

'So-called. Yeah.'

'It always starts with girls. They're like a highly reactive compound.'

Alex walked back towards the table with her. 'I'm very interested in teenage girls, actually,' she went on. 'Oh my God, that sounded bad. I hope no one was listening.'

'Don't worry. Sex panic is over. It's totally nineties.'

'You're sure they weren't really poisoned?'

'I was there. Like I keep telling everyone, I was there. I'm not poisoned, so you tell me what's going on.'

'I don't know. Maybe there was poison in the air and you just got lucky and missed it. Or maybe not. Like you said, what's the difference between emotions and chemicals? Something knocked them down. Who am I to tell them what it was?'

'But you don't believe it was some kind of actual chemical, do you?'

'I believe that belief in poisoning is moving through population groups. I believe there are actual chemical changes involved in belief.'

He took a bite of his sandwich. 'Honestly, I'm tired of the whole thing.'

'Okay by me.' Susie shrugged, sipping her beer. 'So, this project of yours.'

'Yes?'

'You go out and do this every night?'

'One or two nights I stay home developing. Weekends I go out in the day, it's not that I'm doing night shots on principle.'

'And the idea is what? A book of some kind? A show?'

'There isn't an idea as such.' He swirled what was left of the beer in his glass. He didn't have to say any more. He shouldn't. 'I just want to get as much of the city on film as I can.' He paused, glanced up at her. 'As many parts of it as I have time for.'

'Time?'

He had gotten too close to stop. 'I don't know how much longer I'll be able to work,' he said, and finished the glass quickly.

She was waiting for him to go on, but he couldn't, not on his own.

'That doesn't make sense to me,' she said at last. 'Alex, is something wrong?'

He looked down at the table, folding his hands into fists. He was at the verge of it now, the worst thing in the world, worse than anything she or anyone else had ever done to him, and he had never said this aloud to a human being before.

'It's called diabetic retinopathy,' he began slowly. 'It's … it's an eye condition that varies a lot in severity. The capillaries in the eye, well, they overgrow, and the excess ones, they're very fragile, they, ah, they can break or, or hemorrhage pretty easily. Most people have some background retinopathy when they've had diabetes as long as I have. It doesn't – if it's just minor, it doesn't do anything really. But in my case it's started progressing. Apparently fairly quickly.' She was watching him, her face still. He couldn't lift his head.

'I, ah, I don't know what else to tell you. It's not affecting my vision very much yet, but when it does, it can be fast. I mean, it's always different but, well, this is potentially the bad kind. The kind people go blind with.' He stared at his hands, knuckles pale and knotted. 'There are, ah, laser treatments that can slow it down quite a bit. You can't stop it, but you can slow it down. But, see, there's a cost, you're, well, basically buying some central vision by losing peripheral. Maybe some colour perception too, maybe some night vision – well, I've lost some of that already from the condition itself. Maybe after the treatment somebody can't see in very bright light either, or maybe sight's just generally less acute. And you, you don't do the lasers once, see. You stop the deterioration for a bit, and then it comes back and you start, ah, bleeding inside your eyes again, and you have to do the lasers again, and you lose more peripheral, more acuity … What they tell you is, they can keep you from going blind now, and it's true, they mostly can, but … I mean, they're trying to preserve enough vision that you can read a bit and basically walk around. Not enough that you can, that you can drive a car, say. Or, say, be a photographer. That's the bottom line here.' He realized that he was breathing heavily, his voice sounding choked and strange. 'I've started seeing floaters,' he said, resting his forehead on his hands. 'The little black spots, you know? They're blood spots, actually. It means there's bleeding inside the retina. Not a lot. It hasn't got in the way of anything yet. But it's … you know, there's no way out here. There's just not a way out of this.'

'Alex.'

Don't try to touch me, he thought. But she put her hand on his arm, and he flinched away.

'Sorry,' she whispered.

'I mean, I knew I wasn't going to be running around when I was ninety. I always knew that. Diabetes … it's a chronic condition with a reduced life expectancy. Prospects are getting better, but that's what it is, and you know my blood sugar control was a problem for a long time. Partly my own fault. Whether you have complications … glucose control counts for a lot, and then some of it's just luck. And I'm not very lucky. It happens to be my eyes.'

He watched her hands, on the table near his own, and noticed for the first time that she bit her nails; they were short and uneven and ragged. There was a scar across the back of her right hand, a soft puckering of the skin, and he thought he remembered it from the days at *Dissonance*, her fingers resting on the keyboard of the old type-setting machine. She wanted to take his hand right now, he knew that, wanted to hold his hand in hers or put her arms around him, because that was what people did. People who had known each other, a long time ago.

'I can't talk about it, Susie. I'm sorry, but I just can't talk about it.'

'No. It's all right.'

Tell me a story, he thought.

'So this thing about teenage girls. You know, when I was a teenage girl I wanted to be a prophet,' she said slowly, almost as if she'd heard him. 'Which is pretty funny, because I wasn't any more religious then than I am now. But I really wanted to, I wanted to be seeing lights on the road to Damascus and getting the word straight from God.'

'What was God going to say to you?'

'Well, I don't know, do I? I never did get the word. Basically I just wanted everybody to stand around and marvel at me.'

'Oh, they probably did anyway.'

'Sure. Whatever.' She shifted in her chair. 'You want another beer?'

He paused and then nodded. Susie came back into his life, and instantly he started taking chances with his blood sugar. He couldn't let this go much further. But one more beer was not a big risk.

'Evelyn's got the word from God, you know,' said Susie, when she came back to the table with the glasses.

'This we always knew.'

'Did Adrian tell you what she's doing? She's a priest now, isn't that something?'

'Can women do that?'

'With the Anglicans they can.'
'And do the people marvel at her?'
'Honestly? I don't see how they couldn't.'

These are some things that girls do.

In this city and in other cities, there are girls who cut their arms with the blades of razors. In the moment before they strike, all the anger and confusion in the world crumples up into their hands, sweat beading on their foreheads, and the blade slides into the skin with a sharp and accurate pain. The thick line of blood pours out like peace.

There are girls who starve, their hearts thin and pure, dreaming of the day when they can walk invisibly through the leaves in a trance of harmlessness. To do no damage, to touch no thing.

In Kosovo, girls fall down in their classrooms with headaches and dizziness and problems drawing breath, gasping words like *gas* and *poison*. Lines of cars stream towards the hospitals, filled with half-conscious girls with racing hearts, driven in by their terrified families, and doctors hand them sedatives and vitamins because they can think of nothing else to do. On the west coast of Jordan, Palestinian girls fall down in dozens with spasms and blindness and cyanosis of the limbs, stricken by some illness that can't be rationally diagnosed, and they are given oxygen in the hospital until they somehow get better. On assembly lines in factories in Asia, girls collapse in convulsions, one after another, moving along the lines like a chemical reaction.

Then there are girls, sometimes, who gather in groups and choose one of their own to cast out, a girl like them but faintly different. Perhaps they surround her underneath a bridge by a river and begin to hit her, and her blood falls on their clothes, and in the nicotine air there is somehow no way to stop, and perhaps when she runs away they drag her back, and when she falls in the water for the final time they do not pull her out.

In little ingrown villages around Europe, girls walk into the fields and see the Virgin Mary, who has ditched her son and gone out to travel the world, whispering secrets to them that they must tell everyone, that they must conceal forever. The Virgin Mary wears blue, and hints at revolution.

'Tell me about your dissertation.' He was drinking his second beer very slowly, knowing that ordering another one was out of the question.

She opened a bag of potato chips she'd brought from the bar. 'You'll only make comments about academics.'

'I won't. I promise.' He reached over and took a chip, then made a face when he realized it was barbecue-flavoured. 'God, how can you eat these? Sorry. I *am* listening.'

'Network analysis as such is nothing new.' She ate around the edge of a chip as she talked, then broke the centre between her teeth. 'But it hasn't been applied so much to these really marginal populations. People think, I guess people assume they don't have relationships as we understand them, that they're not ... they're somehow outside the social world. Like they don't – you know, that there's no one they know or care about? But they do, they have a world that's as complex as anyone's. Hierarchies. Networks of acquaintance. I don't know, people they love.' He looked at her torn nails again as her hand moved on the table. 'I don't know what more to tell you. I go around and interview people. Fill out questionnaires with them. I doubt that this is going to lead to anything useful at all, but at least I'm providing them with a few hours of cheap entertainment.'

'But do you like it? Is it what you want to be doing?'

'It is, I think. Yes.' She ran her finger around the inside of the bag to capture the last of the salty dust, then licked it off, delicately, with the tip of her tongue. 'To me, it seems like a good thing. I don't know why. But I'm surprisingly happy as an academic.'

'That's good. It really is.'

There was something she wasn't saying. How did he know her well enough to know that? He shouldn't be able to tell these things, but he could.

'Maybe it's not so different, what we're doing,' she said. 'Putting together pieces of the city.'

'Mmmm. I don't know if I put them together, though. I think I just … watch them.'

'Well, that's all right. That's all right too.'

An hour or more after midnight, the rhythms of the city change, the last subway trains running almost empty, the night buses beginning their schematic crossings of the major corners; the streets still crowded where there are clubs and bars, and elsewhere quiet, single figures walking alone, the streetlights detailing their clothes and hair.

Before the final train set out for its run to Kipling, a man walked by the McDonald's inside Dundas West station, his pockets filled with sweet crumbling cookies flavoured with rosewater, and stood on the platform, his face shadowed with thought. In Kensington Market, a white limousine crept silently along the narrow street like a dog tracking a scent, gliding up to a house with darkened windows, a world of illegal need.

At Spadina, the police rolled up their yellow tape, the white powder pronounced harmless though of uncertain identity, icing sugar from a spilled box of doughnuts according to one report, though this could not be confirmed. The city's sadness left untreated.

Alex couldn't remember the last time he'd had to leave a bar because it was closing. It had started snowing again while they were inside, and the clusters of young people coming out of the clubs up and down the street were obscured by the white blur.

'So where are you living, anyway?'

'Danforth and Pape,' said Susie, pulling her red hat down over her ears.

'Yikes. That's a long way to go this time of night. You should've told me, I wouldn't have kept you out so late.'

'It's okay. There's buses.'

'You don't want to get a taxi?'

'I'll walk up to College with you. I'm fine with the College streetcar.'

The snow surrounded them, sealing them in a soft enclosure, so that anyone more than an arm's length away was part of a separate world, the traffic hushed and smooth.

'It's not that I didn't think about you, Alex,' Susie said, her voice low. 'All this time. I did. I hope you believe that.'

They stopped at College and Spadina, where he had to turn west, and stood on the concrete island where the streetcar would arrive, shifting from foot to foot. There was an edge of danger in the air, as if anything, absolutely anything, could happen next. He bent down so their faces were close together, his hand hovering near her shoulder – she was a tiny woman, really, though most of the time she made you think that she was taller somehow. He felt a rush of heat in his chest, a memory of desire nearly as strong as desire itself, the girl with candy-coloured hair who stood on a stool and wrote on the walls of his darkroom with a black marker, *Watch Out, The World's Behind You.*

'Call me,' he said.

'I will.' She pushed back a bit of her hair, this new glossy mahogany, almost natural. 'I'll call tomorrow.'

'Goodnight, Susie-Sue.'

She smiled. 'I always used to know you were really wasted, when you called me that.'

'I'm fairly sober right now.'

'I know.'

There was no good way to leave, but he saw the light turn green and moved quickly, walking almost backwards and waving. 'I'll talk to you.'

'Yes. Goodnight, Alex.' Then he reached the sidewalk at the south side of College and the lights of the streetcar were arriving from the west, and he turned away, his hands in his coat pockets.

He had reached his house and was putting his key in the door when the red-haired man scuffled up the sidewalk towards him. 'Excuse me? I hate to trouble you, sir, but I'm being held hostage by terrorists, would you happen to have any spare change, sir?'

'Yeah, I must have something.' He rummaged in his pockets for change and found a two-dollar coin.

'Thank you very much, sir. I wouldn't ask, only I'm being ... '

'Yes. It's all right. How are you doing?'

'Oh, I'm doing okay, sir. I could be much worse. But I think maybe there was a breakdown in the system a while ago. Like a malfunction, if you know what I mean.'

'Really?'

'Yeah, because it was a while ago, I know that, but normally the cleaning systems should prevent that kind of thing. I think the government's working on it, though.'

'I expect they are, in their way.'

'Because you don't want that kind of malfunction if you can avoid it.'

'No.'

'But I'll tell you what confused me, sir. What really confused me was when the pretty people were falling from the sky. We need to think about that in an analytical way.'

'Yes,' said Alex, suddenly so tired he could hardly stand, supporting himself with one hand on the brick wall of the building. 'I'm sure we do.'

'Anyway, thank you very much for the help, sir. Because you've got to add it up, you know? And when you get five dollars and seventy-six cents, that's a very good one, because when you've got that you can get a breakfast. I'll let you go now, sir.' And he turned and walked away, his ankles collapsing in his ludicrous women's boots, under the veil of the snow.

II

The Susie year, he sometimes called that time in his life; and he hadn't thought of it all that often, not recently, but there were pieces of memory, now and then, so bright and clear they were almost like fiction.

He remembered this, waiting in the parking lot behind the newspaper office, Susie and Chris inside, fighting again about something. It was a warm September night, the sky clear, the noises of the street at a distance. He sat down on the hood of Chris's old car and fished a joint out of his pocket, lit it up and waited. There was a steel band practising somewhere, and pop music leaking out of one of the student pubs, and if you listened to them long enough they gradually melted together into some quite new and original style, full of offbeats and strange harmonies.

He wasn't sure how long he waited. He never paid attention to how long it took, because he knew that she'd come in the end. That she always did. He'd finished the joint and was reaching for another when he heard the soft thud of the back door, and Susie-Paul walking across the asphalt towards him. His medic-alert bracelet flashed dull copper in the small flame from his lighter.

'When's the last time you checked your blood sugar?' she asked, pulling herself up to sit beside him.

He passed her the joint, exhaling. 'This afternoon.'

'You gonna check again soon?' She took a drag and handed it back.

'I'm not sure it's necessary. It was fine in the afternoon.'

'Check it, Alex. You're working into the middle of the night. And you know you don't notice when you're going hypo.'

'That's not even true.'

'It's true enough. Jesus Christ. One ambulance ride was enough for me, thank you.'

'I have no memory of this.'

'Of course you don't. You were having a fucking hypoglycemic seizure in an alleyway off Bathurst, for God's sake.'

'Oh well. That was like months ago.' He sucked in the harsh burn of the smoke. 'Anyway, my brain's been through lots of stuff.'

She leaned back on the car hood. 'Chris is such a prick sometimes.'

'Mmm.'

'Yeah, well. Never mind.' She took the joint from him and held it up between her fingers, against the dark sky. 'So, I got these two press releases today. One was from the police union saying this year's Our Cops Are Tops parade is on the 27th. Which, imagine them sending this to us, I just don't know. The other one was from some of the communists, a talk they're having about how great everything is in Albania. On the 27th. What this says to me is that a frighteningly large part of the population is actively longing for a police state.'

'Mmmm,' said Alex. 'We could declare a day.'

'We could what?'

'Declare a day. You know, like an annual thing. We Want A Police State Day.'

Susie laughed. 'No, it has to be more obsequious. Please sir, may we have a police state? Please May We Have A Police State Day. We could have T-shirts.'

'A logo.'

'Press releases from an untraceable fax number.'

'I can quote you under an assumed name. You can be Ramona Albania.'

'Excellent.'

He exhaled slowly, watching a small blue drift of cloud move behind the trees.

'Hey,' she said. 'I have something for you.'

'Mmm?' He turned his head towards her as she reached into her shoulder bag and pulled out a tiny origami fish, made from multi-coloured paper.

'I found it someplace. I just thought you might like it.'

'Hey. Thank you.' He sat up and took the fish in one hand, its fragile brightness against his palm. 'That's beautiful. Thank you.'

'Yeah, it's nothing much.'

'No, it's lovely.' He passed her what was left of the joint and sat with the fish cupped in his hands. For a while he said nothing, breathing the scent of leaves and tar in the air, the night moving like syrup, the slow stoned feeling that everything was surrounded with a penumbra of meaning, secretly connected at some deep level he could almost, almost grasp. She reached out and brushed her hand against his, the light touch moving through his whole body as she withdrew.

And then just as suddenly she was gone, dropping the roach to the pavement, the shades of pink in her hair shifting in the small light as she walked away. Up the street to the pay phone, Alex still lying on the hood of the car, watching her in the aura of a street lamp, glowing at a distance. It was always that quick. He saw her pick up the receiver, dialling someone. Someone else.

You can be sure of the presence of danger, but you can never guarantee its absence.

She cheated on Chris, everyone knew that and presumed that Chris knew as well; there had been someone named Gord, someone else named Mike Cherniak. Not Alex. Never Alex.

Some days she would flirt with any random freelancer or bike courier who came into the building. He could see her turning it on like a power switch, the shimmer, subtle but radiant, the way she brushed back her hair, the arch of her neck. And there wasn't any purpose to it; the next time the same man showed up she was likely to be absent and distracted, as if she had proved that this was within her power and had no more need of him.

Alex didn't think that it was the same with him, he thought that there was something different between them, sharper and more actual. But he knew he was probably wrong.

Inside the production room – was he remembering the same night, some other night? Did it matter? – he squeezed a drop of blood from his thumb onto his glucometer. 'It's a bit low,' he admitted. 'Not so bad, though. Not really.'

'Lemme see.' Susie reached over and took the glucometer from his hands, studied the numbers. 'You liar,' she said, pushing a box of Smarties across the desk towards him.

Alex rolled his eyes, but took a handful of the candies and ate them.

'You need to eat a meal is what you really need.'

When Alex was fifteen, he had learned that he would be sick for the rest of his life, entirely dependent for his survival on hypodermic needles and bottles of clear liquid. Before he was twenty, he had been told that his statistical life expectancy was under fifty years – later, someone else told him this wasn't quite true; they told him a lot of things, but mostly that he would never be well. That his body had identified a part of itself as a foreign invader and destroyed it. That he could never be far from his insulin kit, that each mouthful of food should be scheduled and calculated, that he could not live like other people. That he had no choices.

It had occurred to him that he let himself edge near hypoglycemia just so that Susie would worry about him, would pay attention. But there was more to it than that, some clear wild feeling of precision and marginal risk, playing the numbers, jumping at danger and backwards, always escaping, always still alive.

It was late, past midnight, but Spadina was still busy, filled with the smells of food and car exhaust. They walked down into Chinatown, to a little restaurant with ducks roasting in the window, skin sizzling under a lurid orange sauce, and Susie-Paul ordered something identified on the menu as mixed meat, a pile of mushrooms, soy sauce and fried internal organs. Stoned and light-headed, he imagined what the deep musky tastes must be like, the feel of the tough bits of flesh between her teeth, salt and crisped fat. She speared a bit of unidentifiable animal protein and he shook his head.

'God, Susie. You're eating, like, bits of lung and thyroid there. I don't even want to watch.'

'Yeah, and you inject yourself with animal insulin three times a day.'

'Which I'm not happy about, believe me. But it's not like I'm stuffing the whole pancreas into my mouth.'

'Am I giving you a hard time about your food?'

'It's rice and vegetables, what is there to say?'

'I think it's morally wrong to be a vegetarian, if you must know. I think you should admit that you too have known sin.'

Alex looked at her sideways. 'You have no idea, Suzanne,' he said quietly.

She picked up another piece of meat on her fork and bit into it, her teeth meeting between the thick fibres, a piece of a body, a piece of a heart.

This wasn't where anything began, of course, or for that matter ended. It was a nearly random piece of that summer in 1989, an unfastened bit of memory. Alex had been the lead photographer at *Dissonance* for a year already, though in 1988 he hadn't seen much of Susie-Paul, or hadn't paid much attention. He worked part-time in the darkroom at SuperPhoto, and arrived at the office in the late afternoon during production week, developing the film and doing some of the layout. For the rest of the month he took assignments as they came from Chris, going out to clubs to photograph concerts, setting up portraits to run alongside interviews. This was maybe where he first learned to move invisibly through the room as a receptive camera eye, backstage at Ildiko's or the Horseshoe, the musicians sweat-drenched and giddy with adrenalin, their hands bleeding, torn by the strings, the blur of cigarettes and beer and hash, or the bands slightly higher up the scale who could afford lines of coke. The guitarists crashed out on smack, the skinny introverted vocalists who drank mineral water and stared at the floor, all of them pinned in the flash of his camera at this high wild vulnerable moment, the second after the applause was over. Alex crouching down in the corner, the watcher.

He wore earplugs so he could sleep at night through the non-stop party upstairs, or lay on the floor with his head between the speakers of his sound system, smoking pot and listening to his own music – cassettes that he knew to be just slightly dated, odd in a way that wasn't the cool kind of odd, Jesus and Mary Chain, the Violent Femmes, Dagmar Krause singing Brecht. He took photographs of the heating pipes and the baseboard, feeling their textures with lights and lenses; of the girls who sat on the curb outside, braiding bits of multicoloured wool into each other's hair; of his vials of insulin and the drop of blood at the tip of his finger, the thick pads of Queen Jane's paws, the dresses hanging on the racks outside Courage My Love, their folds and textures; of the dirty snow in the gutters, streaked with mud and gravel. He was careless about his blood sugar; he knew it swung wildly up and down, that he miscalculated dosages, got times mixed up. He would go late at night, in the snow, to Sneaky Dee's, a narrow little bar that never closed, that smelled of spilt beer at dawn and served tortilla chips and coffee to derelicts all night, and sit in a corner booth and drink Coke and eat nachos, and forget again to test his glucose levels.

He could have gone to his parents' house for Christmas, there was no real reason not to, but he hadn't for years now. He could go back to a place where he was the invalid son, the permanent sick child, or he could wait here in the city. Because he did believe he was waiting for something, though he had no idea what it was. He sat in the basement late at night, listening to the wind, filled with inarticulate expectation, as if he needed only to stay here long enough, to be infinitely patient, infinitely open to the vacancies of the city, and it would reveal itself to him, would hand him something, something vital. If he only made enough space in his life, if he only cleared enough away.

Early in January, he was standing outside the New Moon Café on Harbord Street, camera strung round his neck, warming his hands around a styrofoam cup of coffee while a police car glided slowly past him, banners and waving arms reflected in its windows.

'They call it Operation Mountain Rescue,' said Chris, coming out of the restaurant with a hot chocolate. 'I don't know where they think the mountain is.'

'I heard it's a guy's name,' said Adrian.

They were on the north side of Harbord, with the other journalists and the curious residents of the neighbourhood, and people going in and out of the restaurant for coffee and warmth. About halfway into the road, the police had set up a line of metal barricades, and behind them was the second circle of people, waving signs and chanting, pushing each other, breaking into sporadic scuffles. The third, innermost circle was behind a wooden fence, in the yard and on the steep stairway of a narrow Victorian house with hanging plants in the window, a crowd packed so tightly they were almost immobile, sudden earthquake shifts coming from nowhere that would send some of them tumbling down the stairs or clinging to the banister. The people pressed up against the fence were pushing for space to breathe, their faces pinched with cold and pain. Somewhere in that third circle was Susie-Paul, who that morning was not someone he noticed especially was Chris's pretty girlfriend, a colleague at the paper whose reviews reflected a frightening interest in critical theory, a nice enough person overall.

'It started out about six this morning,' said Chris. 'At first you had the people from the clinic guarding the door and the anti lot pushing in from the yard, but I think they're all mixed up together now.'

Adrian, who was wearing fluffy pink gloves and a scarf with airplanes on it, sat down on the restaurant steps. 'Sometimes I wonder if we just ignored them they'd all go away. Like kids with tantrums, you know?'

'I don't think that's how they work.'

The owner of one of the little groceries had come outside and was taping a sign to his window, a piece of cardboard with the printed message PRO-CHOICE, PRO-LIFE, ENOUGH IS ENOUGH! DEMONSTRATE AT QUEEN'S PARK AND LEAVE US ALONE! Someone behind the fence started singing 'Jesus Loves the Little Children,' and a part of the crowd on Harbord took up the song.

Alex wandered for a while around the edge of the outer ranks, taking some casual shots but seeing nothing that wasn't a predictable demo picture, so after a few minutes he swung his legs over the barricades and pushed deeper into the crowd. Everyone inside the barricades was chanting or shouting, and taking occasional swings at each other with mittened hands. Alex was shoved from behind and ended up on his knees, but he realized this might be a more interesting angle anyway, so he fired off a series of shots, a baby with a PRO-CHOICE sign pinned to its snowsuit, a man waving a Bible over the heads of the crowd.

'Brothers and sisters!' shouted a red-haired woman out the window. 'All of today's procedures have been moved to the Scott Clinic. They *will* see all patients scheduled by us today. If you are waiting for a procedure, please do *not* stay here, please go to the Scott Clinic. Supporters, I repeat, DO NOT come over the fence!'

Alex pulled himself up on one of the fence pickets, shouldering a space for himself, and stared into the tightly packed mass of people in the yard, who were swaying slightly, struggling for footholds, a flash of pink hair near his shoulder.

'Hey. Susie-Paul?'

She lifted her head and managed, with some difficulty, to turn in his direction. 'Oh. Hi there, Alex.'

'Not the church and not the state!' shouted someone into his ear.

'So how's it going?'

'Women must control their fate!'

'I think I have a broken rib,' said Susie, wrapping her arms around a railing post and biting her lip with the effort of hanging on. 'Otherwise I'm good. There are people actually underneath my feet, you know.'

'Jesus loves the little children,' sang a woman softly, sliding down the steps and vanishing under someone else's legs. Somewhere up towards the door Alex could see the two policemen who had been caught in the crush elbowing each other and giggling. 'Wait'll you tell your wife you spent the whole day pressed up against a bunch of women, eh?' one of them was saying. Then the radio at his belt crackled into life, and he lifted it, and slowly raised the other hand to his nightstick.

What happened after that was so fast, so unexpected, that Alex didn't register much of it at the time. He was twisting around by the fence, framing another shot, when he heard sirens, and then half a dozen police cars and a paddy wagon swept around the corner and uniformed men and women leapt out, formed a wedge and slammed into the crowd, pulling the barricades down and tossing them into the road, shouting, '*Go! Go! Go!*' Alex was knocked off his feet, face down into the pavement, his hands dragging against the snow and gravel as he rolled, blue legs and black boots pounding past him, and they began pulling people over the fence and throwing them onto the side-walk, forcing their way to the door. He saw a nightstick swing into a man's head. The man howled, his face ribboned with bright red blood.

'Clinic volunteer!' a woman inside the fence was screaming, holding her hands in the air. 'Clinic volunteer! Don't hit me!' Others were shouting now too, clustering into a corner, one woman sobbing. Bodies were flying over the banister, and Alex saw Susie-Paul cling-ing to the railing, her feet kicking helplessly in the air. The woman who had been singing was lying prone on the stairs, a policeman bending her arms behind her. He realized that there was a rough selection happening, that the clinic volunteers were not being smacked with the nightsticks but herded into the far part of the yard, and they themselves had understood this now too, holding up their hands before the police and shouting, 'Clinic! Clinic!' Then a police-man grabbed Susie-Paul by the collar of her coat and yanked her up, half over the banister, and she gave him a wild look and her lips pinched closed and she said nothing, nothing at all. She folded her arms around her body and he lifted his nightstick.

It couldn't have been more than a few seconds, it couldn't really have been as long as it seemed that she was hanging there in midair; almost immediately, someone else was grabbing her leg and shout-ing, 'She's with us, she's with the clinic, she's with the clinic!' But for a moment Alex didn't even think; he vaulted over the fence into the yard, half-emptied now, and ran towards her, and as the policeman let her drop he arrived below the stairs and she fell against him. He sat down under the sudden weight, leaning back against the bricks of the building and tightening his arms around her.

'Oh Christ,' she said miserably. 'There was no reason for them to hit people like that, Alex.' She clenched her fists and leaned into his chest. 'They shouldn't fucking hit people like that.'

He tried to catch his breath, thinking suddenly, impossibly, *You are mine.*

Someone was running up the stairs, unlocking the clinic door, and he heard a siren wind slowly around the corner. He could smell the sharp sweat on her face, feel the feathery edges of her hair. *You are mine.* He knew it wasn't true. But he was happy.

Adrian and Chris were coming through the gate. He touched one hand quickly to the back of her neck and let it drop, and then she stood and walked towards Chris. Alex wished that he had seen Chris hesitate for a moment, a flicker of jealousy, but he didn't. Why should he? Someone should have caught her, and Alex was nearest, it wasn't a problem. Alex wasn't a problem.

'What the hell was that all about?' said Adrian, staring around the yard at the huddles of confused and trembling volunteers. 'Did something actually cause that, or did the cops just have some kind of collective brain aneurysm?'

Alex got up, still feeling that strange shimmer of happiness that seemed not to depend on anything real. 'You're okay?'

'I hurt, but I'm okay,' said Susie-Paul, standing lopsided against Chris's shoulder. 'I think everything's just bruised, not broken.'

'Maybe it's legal to blockade a building till one p.m., and then after that it's a felony? Is that their thinking?' said Adrian. 'I mean, I'd just like to know what went on here, because that was fucking weird.'

'At least they arrested them. Eventually.'

'Alex, are you all right?' asked Chris.

'Yeah,' said Alex, leaning back against the building, smiling slightly. 'Yeah, I'm good.'

They walked up Spadina, the four of them, and ate lunch at a greasy spoon on Bloor Street. Then Chris had to meet someone at the paper, and Susie wanted to go home and lie down. Alex walked to the subway station with Susie and Adrian, and as they went inside he turned, and then turned back again.

'Susie-Paul? Hang on.'

Adrian waved and went through the turnstile, and Susie came back out the glass doors.

'Can I take your picture?'

'Sure,' she said. 'If you want.'

So he stepped back and raised the camera, light pouring into the lens, and there was this picture of Susie-Paul, still a bit shaky, quizzical, her features outlined with shadow, her dark eyes on Alex, open. He pressed his finger down and the camera snapped, the last frame on the roll.

'Okay. That's good.'

He lowered the camera, and she smiled and shrugged.

'I own your soul now,' he said softly.

'Really?'

'Mmm-hmm.'

She paused as if she were considering this, smiled at him again and went into the station.

III

On Monday morning, two girls fell down just inside the front hall of Jarvis Collegiate, their lips turning blue, and as they were taken away to the hospital the school was closed and emptied, the students sent out to cluster on the sidewalks, uncertain if they would be going back in; and this time the television cameras arrived as well, leaning in to record the faces of the girls as they were lifted into the ambulance.

The hazmat teams knelt in the hallways, their swollen white hands lifting paper and dust from the floors. The girl in the stretcher covered her face, a ring of braided wool around her wrist, a picture that would play on the news again and again.

In another school, further to the north, the first girl who had fallen stood on the basketball court, her hair tied back; she dashed forward, grabbing for the ball, and felt her own athletic body as a betrayal, the movement of her breasts an intrusion, the softness of her thighs, no longer the simple child's body she could trust without thinking. This body that bled and ached and fell. She ran down the length of the gym, the ball smacking against her hands, dodging outstretched arms, heat pulsing under her skin.

Lauren reached towards her and she twisted away, a quick stab of anger, unexpected. Early in the morning she had sat in the assembly hall and watched Lauren walk out onto the stage, tall and confident, her skin clear. Lauren started to read, and it was something about remembering what was right in the world. Women in Africa doing whatever. Making jewellery or something.

Zoe, who hadn't spoken to any of them since the day in the park, was sitting against the wall of the gym and drawing on her hand with a ballpoint pen. She must have begged off with cramps, Zoe was always doing that.

The girl jumped towards the basket, feeling the flex of her long legs, the pull of her breath. The ball touched the rim and bounced back, someone else leapt and caught it, and the mass of bodies was moving down the gym again; she wiped the back of her neck and turned with them.

Lauren, on the assembly-hall stage, saying that people could always do something to make their lives better, no matter what. And the girl had thought of what she had seen in the park.

She'd thought she couldn't stay in this room anymore. Didn't want to see Lauren ever again.

Lauren said that hope was the most powerful thing in the world, and the girl thought, *You don't even know what you're talking about*, and, *Everything you're saying is a lie.*

She had stood up and walked quietly to the supervising teacher, and said she had her period and had to go to the washroom. Outside in the hallway, she listened to Lauren's voice. In the background, the receptionist's radio whispered about the girls at Jarvis Collegiate falling down, about poison. Women in Africa, stringing tiny beads. The shudder of her own nerves.

Nicole sprang towards the basket and the ball fell heavily home, into the net and down. The girl bent over, hands on her knees, breathing heavily, her face flushed.

Everything you're saying is a lie.

You know that.

The ball was coming her way again, the other team moving down the court; she dodged, underestimated, missed. Ran alongside, loping, feinting, pulling air into her lungs as a thin pain shot up her side, her neck hot and damp.

Thought about the girls at Jarvis, what had brought them down. She supposed that these girls had secrets of their own. That all girls had secrets of some kind.

In the hallway, listening to the receptionist's radio, she had walked to a window and looked out at the small line of trees that surrounded the school grounds, the busy street beyond. *Similar to the incident several days earlier,* said the radio.

The girl thought that someone could live in the woods at the back of the school grounds. Maybe they could. She wasn't sure.

What it would be like, out there in the cold.

They were under the net again, her legs aching, she saw an opportunity and dashed forward and the ball met her hands, solid, that satisfying weight. She spun on the balls of her feet and passed it to Kirsty, and Kirsty grabbed the ball and leapt, her arms arcing high, high into the air.

Snow was mounded up in the gutters and against the walls of buildings, streaked grey and brown. In his office at the hospital, unaware of the falling girls at Jarvis, Alex stood up from his computer and looked out the window, his arms folded.

Susie hadn't called him, of course, and he almost didn't want to admit how relieved he felt. He'd woken on Saturday with a hangover not so much physical as emotional, the cloying sickness that came from an excess of closeness, from saying too much, feeling too much. He spent the day walking by himself in the snow, breathing in the bright chilly air, silent, not even taking pictures; and when he came home and there was no message on the machine, his chest felt suddenly light, something like fear lifting away. On Sunday he took a pile of clothes to the laundromat, and then went so far as to phone Kim, who told him to fuck off, a response he found oddly cheering.

He turned back to his computer, to the pictures of a rose-coloured circle of exposed brain tissue framed by green sheets, silver instruments smeared with blood, and he thought about the intricacy of the vessels, the exchange of fluid and the electric life of nerves.

The person he really had to call was his ophthalmologist. He had to tell her about the floaters, he'd put it off too long already.

He thought of Susie at the bar in the Cameron House, wearing black tights and an emerald-green sweater that came down to her knees, the sleeves falling loosely over her hands, turning away from him in the swirl of noise and music to smile at someone else; and went back to the photos, clicking ahead in the sequence, a walnut-sized tumour in a metal bowl.

Later, as he walked through Davisville Station on his way home, he saw a woman in a tailored coat wearing a surgical mask over her mouth, and on the train, which was not as full as usual, another mask on the face of a man holding a newspaper. But otherwise the journey was normal, someone eating french fries from a cardboard container, someone reading *Shopaholic Takes Manhattan*, everyone pretending not to notice the man in the mask.

He played with his idea of the imaginary doctor, imaginary terrorist, leaving the cherished packet of chemicals under the seat. The man would wear an expensive coat. The umbrella, too, would be expensive. Had he already begun to talk to his patients, in some veiled strange form, about the attractions of death? Written for them prescriptions more powerful than they needed, or simply given them mad unworldly advice, to drink glasses of vinegar, to consume silver foil? But the man is not just mad, he does not act alone, he is part of something large. He loves this thing that he is a part of, and he believes that he loves people too, specific individual people, maybe his parents, a wife, a mistress. He desires for all of them the end that will come.

This was a fairy tale, of sorts, Alex thought. The bad wizard. It happened to be a fairy tale that sounded true to him – or not so much true, he didn't think it was something that was really happening in this city, but somehow credible, appropriate. The man in the mask must have a narrative of his own that he believed, other people on the subway told themselves other particular stories. The man on his street told a story about cleaning systems, and it might be a useful story, in its way.

He got off the train at College, moving in the swaying stutter of the crowd, past tables where people in Cancer Society T-shirts were selling pizza slices. And he was thinking of her again. The ridiculous ease with which she could have moved back into the centre of his life and tossed it all up into the air like paper, the quiet safe place he had so strenuously constructed for himself.

On College the pigeons wheeled in the upper air, seeking shelter for the night, as the streetcar pulled up to the curb, and the slanting red light of sunset caught their wings, a shimmer of brightness and shadow, and Alex felt suddenly stabbed through the heart.

He came home and fed his cat, put on a scarf and gloves and a black wool cap and walked east, past Yonge and into Allan Gardens, where a few men were lying curled on benches under the walls of the conservatory, broken glass and torn paper around them. In the doorway of a blank concrete building, a young girl with round cheeks and a short blue skirt, orange highlights in her teased dark hair, was standing with her legs in that angled posture that meant invitation, that meant commerce; Alex lifted his camera, and then lowered it again. The girl scratched the back of her arm and shivered. But she might be older than she looked, her youth an illusion of cosmetics and distance; it might be so.

He walked north on Parliament and came within a few minutes into Cabbagetown – the shops along Parliament a weird jumble of discount outlets and expensive cafés, a doughnut store with the window half boarded up, a shop that sold designer pet supplies. He went into another doughnut store and got a cup of tea, warming his hands around it at a little table. Angry men were playing cards and drinking coffee, and Alex faced away from them and took pictures of their reflections in the glass.

And it didn't surprise him, it didn't surprise him even a bit, that the phone rang almost as soon as he walked in the door of his apartment, while his fingers were still stiff and white with cold. It seemed like something already agreed, that it would be Susie's voice at the other end of the line, asking him to meet her the next evening.

own your soul now, Alex had said, and she had seemed to believe it. She had been so young, after all, and more uncertain than he had ever realized.

There was a day he'd been taking photographs, as the clinic escorts and the patients dashed through the gauntlet of screaming protesters, Susie-Paul holding her coat over a patient's head as she ran, flinching as some small hard object hit her cheek. On the final sprint to the steps of the clinic, Alex slipped and fell, and cut his hand open on a rock. It wasn't serious, but it was a dirty cut and it bled quite a bit, smears of blood on his sleeve, not what anyone needed to be looking at in the pastel waiting rooms with the twining plants. He went into the kitchen at the back of the house, where one of the staff members was making tea and a security guard was monitoring the closed-circuit camera feed, and washed his hand in the sink. He was scrubbing it under the running water, watching the red drizzle spiral down, when Susie came in with cotton and gauze.

'Let me do it for you,' she said. She was quick and efficient about wrapping it up and taping it, but then she didn't let go of his hand.

'You're all right?' she asked, and she was holding his hand in both of hers.

'Oh yeah. Nothing to it.' He felt perfectly calm and perfectly safe, and without much thought he leaned down and kissed her forehead, and she laid her head against his chest. At that moment, he was sure, he might have put his arms around her and kissed her on the lips, but there were still facts out there – he was in a room with other people, people who were now watching them, in a place where they had to deal every day with certain extreme consequences of human behaviour, and there was blood on his shirt. *She lives with Chris.*

He watched her through bulletproof glass as she walked down the wooden steps to the tiny yard, her boots over frozen mud while a line of protesters tossed pamphlets and plastic embryos at her head. A heavy man threw himself into an icy puddle in front of her, clutching his chest and crying, 'Don't kill your baby! Don't kill your baby!', his voice audible even through the thick window as Susie side-stepped him, refusing to run, walking carefully and deliberately into the alley and away.

Susie at the pay phone up the street, biting her lip, one hand pressed against the glass. He shouldn't have been watching her, but he was. Whoever she was talking to. He had no way of knowing.

Susie standing on a chair in his darkroom, in the red light, a marker in her hand, writing on the walls.

'You need something in here, is all. I mean, you nearly live here, you might as well decorate.'

'It's not even our wall. It belongs to the university paper. They're not going to love this.'

'They can cope,' said Susie. *Your young men shall see visions and your old men shall dream dreams*, she wrote, under a string of New Order lyrics. Alex imagined a sketch he could add. Maybe he had done it later, with paper and pencil, back in his apartment. But if he ever did draw it, he lost it later on.

Spring night, late spring, the dark air mild. Alex was high and euphoric, dazzled. He'd been smoking hash, and drinking too much beer, which wasn't a good idea, he wasn't in control of his blood sugar, but he was trying to balance it out by eating french fries and ketchup. Walking on a wire. Out on the dance floor of a club on Bloor Street, a bit unsteady on his feet, the flash on his camera going off in chains of light as the keyboard player climbed up onto his Casio, sweat dripping from his forehead and soaking his shirt, and began to play the heating pipes with a pair of drumsticks. Alex firing off another shot, knowing that by some process he himself didn't under-stand, he would come out of this with pictures that were clear and dry and precise, recognizable Alex Deveney photos, all this heat and desire purified into an image, a hieroglyph of objective thought.

The band left the stage and the taped music came on, the bass shuddering up through his feet in time with his pulse. He leaned against the wall near Adrian's table, wiping his face with the neck of his T-shirt.

Adrian had brought Evelyn with him, and she was sitting beside him, reading a book in the flickering light; this was a bit of an event, since none of Adrian's friends could remember having ever seen Evelyn before, and some of them had recently expressed the opinion that she was imaginary. They were in the middle of a conversation which was incomprehensible to Alex, but evidently intense and somehow entertaining.

'So I told my supervisor about it,' Evelyn was saying, 'and he said to me, "You used the word *apophatic*, didn't you?" and I said, "Yeah. I guess I did." "Well, serves you right, doesn't it?" he said.'

'Did you say *affective*, too?' asked Adrian.

'Oh, I don't know. Probably.'

Adrian lit a cigarette and held the pack out towards Alex, who hardly ever smoked tobacco, but that night he wanted cigarettes with the same hunger he wanted everything, dope, music, love. He pulled one from the pack and took out his lighter, squinting down at the fire. He seemed to be having trouble getting the flame to connect with the end of the cigarette.

'Alex. Man,' said Adrian. 'You're really shaking.'

'I'm okay.' He managed to light the cigarette and lift it to his mouth.

'I don't think you are, actually. I think you're going hypo.'

'I told you, I'm okay,' said Alex impatiently, and started to walk away, but he lost his footing and nearly fell, and Adrian grabbed hold of his arm.

'That's it. Come with me.' He steered Alex towards the vending machine by the bar, the lights moving dizzy against the walls.

'You have money?'

'Of course I have money. Jesus.'

'Can I trust you to buy yourself a chocolate bar?' asked Adrian, glancing back at Evelyn sitting with her book. 'Or do I have to stand here and watch you?'

'I will buy myself a chocolate bar, mother. Scout's Honour, okay?'

Adrian went back to the table, and Alex put a hand on the vending machine to steady himself, blinking a few times until his vision cleared. The machine had several kinds of candy, but he realized now that he was both very stoned and very shaky, and somehow it seemed impossibly hard to operate. He pulled a handful of change out of his pocket, but when he tried to work out what he needed the numbers kept blurring in his mind, breaking up along the shiny glittering edges of the coins under the flickering bar lights, too damn complicated, and then it was quite difficult to get them into the narrow change slot, he didn't know why they made those slots so narrow anyway. So he didn't notice the voices behind him until he was fishing out his chocolate bar and heard a glass smashing to the ground; and even then, working the complicated foil wrapping off the candy, he didn't pay attention until he heard Susie-Paul, on the verge of tears, shouting, 'Fuck you, then! Just fuck you!'

His mouth full of chocolate, he turned and saw Susie-Paul and Chris, their faces pale and angry. He couldn't tell which one of them had thrown the glass. They were close together, facing each other across the glittering shards.

'You're behaving like a child,' said Chris, the words hissing between his teeth. 'Grow up, will you?'

'Do not, do *not*, patronize me like that, I will *not* put up with that,' wept Susie, and raised one hand, her arm flexed, palm open. Chris grabbed her wrist and pushed her arm down. 'I told you,' he said, 'calm *down*, nobody wants to see a scene in a bar here.'

'Fuck what they want!' She pulled her hand away from him. 'You can't just blame this on *people*, you have to *talk* to me!'

Alex pressed his own fists against his mouth and swallowed, trying to fight back an explosion of anxious laughter. They hadn't seen him. This was something arcane and private, and he shouldn't be watching it.

'I *do* talk to you, I talk to you all the fucking *time*, what the fuck do you want me to *say*?'

'Don't ask me what I *want*, this is not about what I *want*. Don't fucking make this be about me, because this is not *my* problem.'

'Well, I don't know whose problem it is, then, because frankly you're the one acting like you're crazy.'

'How DARE YOU!' screamed Susie. She was suddenly moving, she slammed her hands against his chest and he stumbled backwards. 'How *dare* you say that! Get the fuck away from me, you fucking shithead!'

'Jesus Christ!' Chris swept a pile of napkins off the bar with his arm as he tried to regain his balance. 'I might as well, 'cause there's no fucking point to *this*.'

'Fuck off, fuck off, fuck off!' Susie shouted, and shoved him again, hard. He grabbed at the bar to steady himself, then turned and stalked towards the door and out, and he didn't look back at her as he left.

The rest of the chocolate bar was melting in Alex's hand. He took a short step forward, then back, his ears ringing with the music surrounding them. He could feel the shakiness of the hypo subsiding, but he was still dizzy. His head filled with space. She was sitting on a bar stool sobbing, and her hair was the colour of cotton candy, her dress was peppermint, green crushed velvet, ragged and soft. She would never cry like that because of Alex. He knew this, and the knowledge hurt him. She dried her eyes with a napkin, and he could see the dark smear of her mascara on the paper.

She got down from the stool and walked slowly back towards the dance floor, and as she passed she saw him. She gave him a small vague nod of recognition but nothing happened in her eyes at all. He didn't matter in this, not even a bit. There was no reason that he should.

Alex stood by the wall and closed his eyes, hearing the shift in sound as the tapes ended and another band came out onstage. Looked across the room and saw her kneeling down by Evelyn's chair, Evelyn shaking her head and putting one hand softly on Susie's back. Susie wiped her eyes, said something to Evelyn, stood up and shrugged and moved onto the dance floor.

He wrestled a second chocolate bar from the machine, broke off a piece and ate it, and went to the bar and ordered another beer. He understood precisely how dangerous this was, but he needed to drink, he needed to be more drunk, as far outside himself as he could get.

He slumped into a chair beside Adrian and watched Susie-Paul out on the floor, tossing her head furiously, light and shadow moving across her body, the sway of her hips, the sinuous arch of her pale bare arms. Nothing made sense. The singer edged anxiously around his microphone, thin and awkward, belonging here as little as anyone else, in a swirl of rising music.

The bar was emptying out, gradually, the lights turned on to reveal puddles of beer and smashed bottles across the dance floor. It was more than an hour after last call, and Evelyn was nearly at the end of her book. Alex was rolling an empty beer bottle around on the table, watching the yellow smears of light in the amber glass and, at the edge of his vision, Susie-Paul, standing near the stage talking to a little group of *Dissonance* people. Most likely he could have stood up and joined them. The bottle slid off the table to the floor. Then the soft green folds of her dress as she moved away from the group, and he lifted his head and wondered how he could ever have doubted. She would come after all. She always would.

'Alex,' she said softly, sitting down across from him. 'I'm sorry I didn't say hi before.'

'No. 'Sokay,' he said. He had a vague awareness that he was smiling at her like an idiot. 'You were busy.'

'Not so much. It was just too noisy, you know?'

'I just said. It's okay.' He reached across the table and squeezed her hand, and she squeezed back and didn't let go. Adrian picked up his guitar and started to fiddle with the tuning.

'I should've talked to you sooner.'

'You can talk to me whenever you want.' Alex no longer had a clue what was going on, but he wasn't sure he cared. Her hand small and hot and soft in his.

'I guess you saw ... ' she waved her free hand in the air.

'Mmmm.'

'I'm sorry.'

'I don't care, Suze,' he said, slurring a bit on her name. 'It doesn't matter at all.'

'I'm not really like that.'

He drew slow circles on the back of her hand with his thumb. 'It's okay, Susie-Sue. It's okay.'

The bartender had put on a tape, some kind of quiet folk music that was meant to get people out of the building; it was playing behind them now. And then, without calling any attention to herself, Evelyn put her book down on the table, walked out onto the floor, and began to dance, alone among the broken glass. Dark and slender, a strange formality in her movements, her toes pointed, as if she might have studied ballet years ago. For a moment Alex felt like there were two different screens in front of him, foreground and background fluctuating, Susie's eyes, her fingers touching his palm, and Evelyn dipping and bending at a distance on the empty dance floor, Adrian watching her intently and making no move to join her. The room filled with mystery. A slick sheen of light on Susie's gold-painted fingernails, the barely audible singer on the tape invoking lies and dreams and windmills.

'I'm glad you stayed.'

'Of course I did.'

'It would've been awful if you hadn't stayed.'

Heat gathering between their two hands, a film of sweat.

'I don't want you to think …' she went on.

'Shhh. You don't need to talk about it.'

The song ended, and Evelyn walked off the floor, self-contained, silent, and Adrian put his guitar back in its case and got up. She stood in front of him and they looked at each other, nothing else, and left the room together.

The bartender turned the tape off and began to collect empty bottles from the tables, the clatter of glass sending back a hollow echo. Alex sat very still, hardly breathing, his ears still humming in the absence of music.

'They're going to kick us out of here soon,' said Susie.

'We could go somewhere,' he said softly. 'If you want.'

She hesitated, putting her other hand over his and stroking his thumb with her own.

'I think I should go home,' she said at last.

'Are you sure?'

'No.' She drew her hands back, their fingertips still touching. 'But … I think I should go home. I need to go home.'

At the bus stop he put his arms around her and kissed the top of her head. 'Susie-Sue,' he whispered, as the Bathurst bus arrived, filled with the lost and desperate flotsam of the night city. She climbed on board and rode away. Alex found the pole where he'd chained his bike, fumbled with the lock until it came apart, and kicked off, weaving along the road. In a final grand gesture of self-destructiveness, he reached his house and passed it, kept riding into the blurred and shining night, further and further south until he reached the lake, passing empty buses and street-sweeping machines spraying water on the road, grinding their huge black brushes, spinning in darkness.

It was nearly dawn, and he was halfway sober again, when he rode back along King Street and saw that he was, without any conscious intention, riding by the house where Chris and Susie lived. The light was still on in their apartment. He stopped for only a minute, one foot on the sidewalk, looking up at the window and thinking of their lives, of a deep and complex privacy that was going on without him, that he would never be able to enter.

V

When the bright young men released sarin on the Tokyo subway, the gas soaked into the clothes of the passengers. Many of them pulled themselves out of the subway and went to work, their pupils contracted, their breathing restricted, sarin leaking from their jackets into the office air. Others were lifted into cars and ambulances and sent to the hospital, and the nurses and doctors who treated them found their own eyesight growing dark, their own muscles weakening. This is mentioned as a risk in the literature on chemical incidents.

The girl with the braided wool bracelet who had fallen on the steps at Jarvis Collegiate sat up in her hospital cot and watched a resident walking away from her stumble suddenly, grab for the wall to support herself, and slide to the ground.

The young resident's pupils didn't contract. Her blood tests didn't show the low cholinesterase that would signal sarin, or the blood acidosis of cyanide. Her white cell count was perhaps slightly elevated. Some of the others who worked on the girl said later that they felt sort of ill, not exactly sick, but not quite well.

The resident had dyed blonde hair and long thin fingers and no known allergies or medical conditions. When she tried to describe the smell she spoke at first about exhaust fumes, and then about water and metal, but finally she could only say that it was not quite like that, that it was a smell like the absence of smell. The precise smell of nothing.

Susie was doing interviews at the drop-in at a church on College – not far from his house, she told him. He knew the place, of course, a little red-brick building with a low slanted roof, but he'd never been inside. All things considered, he shouldn't really have been surprised to arrive and find Evelyn, who seemed scarcely to have aged at all and was looking not especially priestly in jeans and an old duffel coat, coming out the side door.

'Alex? Suzanne told me she was meeting you here. How are you?'

'Okay,' he said nervously. 'Yeah. Not bad. You?'

'I have to go to a meeting right now, I'm sorry, but everybody's inside.' She swung a backpack over her shoulders and climbed onto a bicycle. 'Call Adrian sometime,' she said, kicking off the curb. 'He needs a peer group, nobody knows how to talk to him.' But she disappeared into the traffic before he could think of a response.

He opened the door that he'd seen her coming out of, and walked into a small hall filled with dishevelled men and a few women, lying or sitting on mattresses, a pile of folding tables stacked against one wall. There was a TV set in the corner playing *Titanic*, and some of the men were watching this and drinking from styrofoam cups, others reading crumpled copies of the *Sun* or *Employment News*. One man was sketching tiny painstaking patterns into an old notebook. Pinned on the wall was a bad drawing of Archbishop Romero, and pieces of cardboard with phrases written on them in capital letters. PLEASE SPEAK SLOWLY. I AM LEARNING ENGLISH. CAN YOU HELP ME FIND THIS ADDRESS? There was a strong smell of unwashed bodies in the air, cut through with overbrewed coffee.

Adrian was sitting cross-legged on one of the mattresses, talking gently to a man with a twisted, tearful face and unpredictably moving hands; in the kitchen, a woman who looked roughly a hundred years old was slowly cleaning a pile of roasting pans, and a frizzy-haired girl, probably the Pereira-Sinclair child, was sitting on a stool frowning over a copy of *Harriet the Spy*. There was something bizarrely domestic about the whole scene, Alex thought. Dinner with friends in Bedlam.

Susie was in a corner of the room, sitting on a folding chair with a clipboard and talking to an old man in a baseball cap. 'So you'd say he's a close friend?' he heard her asking. The man shook his head.

'Not close so much. But I'd say reliable, when he isn't drinking.'

Susie nodded and wrote something on her clipboard. 'And does he know that other guy you were telling me about, that Steve guy?' Then she noticed Alex, and gestured him over with her pencil.

'It's okay,' said Alex. 'I'll wait.'

'I'm nearly finished.'

The man in the baseball cap was holding on to a clear plastic cane filled with dried roses, petals of faded red and yellow and cream, packed tightly together. Nearby, a grey-haired woman was pacing in tiny wired circles, strung out, shaking, oblivious to the world – crack or crystal meth, he thought. On the TV screen, the steerage passengers on the Titanic were singing and dancing and demonstrating their working-class virtues.

'Filtered water,' said the man in the baseball cap. 'That's what I told him. You drink filtered water, the skin problems clear right up. This lady gave me one of them filters for the tap in the rooming house, but the schizophrenic guy took it off because he thought somebody was watching him through it. Mr. Sandman, he tells me. Watching him through the water filter.' He shook his head. 'You could write a book, darling, I'm telling you.'

Susie made a note on her clipboard. 'So, is the lady someone we've talked about before?' she asked.

'No – no, I guess not. So she'd be another one on the chart, eh?'

'Yeah ... you know what, are you going to be up at Bloor tomorrow? Somebody's waiting for me right now.'

'Okay, well, thank the people here very much for the delicious meal, and I'll see you then.' The man tipped his baseball cap, then stood up and left the hall, leaning on his flowering cane.

'Joseph's quite interested in the project,' said Susie, coming over to Alex. 'And he's got a social network like you wouldn't believe. I could spend a year just mapping his contacts.'

'Ah,' said Alex.

'We can go if you want. I think Adrian's busy talking to Luis.' She pulled the door open and waved at Adrian, who glanced briefly away from the tearful man and nodded quickly.

'Luis gets very angry at Thomas Aquinas,' Susie explained as they went down the steps. 'He's an ex-seminarian or something. He'd really rather talk to Evvy, but Adrian can handle him. Me, I just wave my hands around.'

'What did Thomas Aquinas do to make him angry, then?'

'I told you, it's all beyond me. He's just like, fucking Aquinas, I hate the stupid fuck, and I'm like, sure. You bet.'

'Maybe they had a fight about a girl.'

They stopped at the traffic light at Augusta, just north of Kensington Market. 'Do you want to get something to eat?' asked Susie.

'No, I ate at home. Just a coffee shop's fine.'

'We could go someplace in the Market, if you wanted. I think the Last Temptation's still there.'

'Oh God. Please, let's not.'

'Your old house is a vintage clothing boutique now,' said Susie, pressing the button for the light. 'But you know what? They've still got that crazy painting you did in the basement.'

'They must be ill,' said Alex, though what he wanted to ask was why she had gone to his old house, how she had ended up in the basement there anyway.

'How come you never did more paintings?' They crossed College Street and went into the Second Cup.

'Because I suck. Taking photos is the only thing I'm good at.'

He ordered a camomile tea, wanting something as pale and bland and harmless as possible, determined not to be put off balance.

'So, how are you?' she asked, stirring cream into her coffee.

'I saw my ophthalmologist,' he said, and then clenched his nails into his hand, immediately regretting the words.

'Yeah?'

'I don't know. Nothing much to say. She's making an appointment for this,' he cleared his throat, 'this laser thing, but I'd actually rather … I'd rather not think about it too much.'

'Okay.'

'The only … there's a small risk of a hemorrhage in the meantime. But that's treatable. More or less. And it really is a small risk.'

'If there's anything I can do … '

'There's nothing anyone can do. It's a bit like death that way.' He stared down at the hot golden liquid. 'I'm sorry. God, I'm sorry. I shouldn't be going on like this.' He was starting to feel as if his identity was coming apart. The cool, dry, solitary person he had become was a real Alex, was perhaps always the part of him that had taken the photographs, but the hungry chaotic Alex that she had known had been real too, and seemed closer now than for quite a long time.

'No, please. I mean, I'm glad you're telling me things now. You used to worry me so much, you know. You remember when you had that seizure on Bathurst? Seriously, I thought you were dying.'

'Oh. That time.' He bent a stir stick in his fingers, searching the blank spot in his memory between the Bathurst streetcar and a hospital bed, the late spring night when his high-wire act with his blood sugar finally crashed. 'Well, honestly, I don't. Remember it, I mean. You know, insult to the brain and all. But I guess I could have been dying – I mean, I could have died – if you hadn't been there. So I probably owe you some kind of apology.'

Susie picked up her coffee and sipped it carefully. 'Less than twenty years late, eh?' she said with a faint smile. 'No, really, thanks, Alex. I mean that.'

He did remember waking up, not knowing why he was in that bed but knowing he had gone somehow way too far. That whatever he had done, it had been partly because she was there, because she was all sugar and danger to him, and he pushed every limit when he was near her. 'What happened, even?' he asked. 'I mean, I know in general what happened, but I don't think we ever talked about it. Did we?'

'I did tell you after,' she said. 'I told you in the hospital. You don't remember?'

'The whole night's kind of spotty. I'm sorry.'

'I don't know. I probably should've noticed something earlier, but there were a bunch of us in this club – I was at the other side of the room, I think – and it seemed like all of a sudden you kicked over a table. There was just this crash. You were shouting, I'm not sure what, pretty loud, and kind of staggering – I figured you were on something, maybe. Or just really drunk. And it was weird because, you know, you were stoned all the time anyway, and I'd seen you drunk before, and you never got mean, so I was confused. Anyway, I thought the bouncer was going for you, so I took you outside. And I was trying to talk to you, but you weren't making much sense, or actually any sense at all, and then you just slid down the wall and started seizing.'

'Fuck. I *am* sorry.'

'I was still thinking drugs at that point. I didn't even notice your medic-alert bracelet till the ambulance got there. So I guess I could've done better. Given you some glucose or something, if I'd known what it was. Heck of a way to find out, by the way.'

'Wow. I mean, I sort of knew about this, but – hell.' He picked up his cup of tea. 'So, I never really asked you, why did you even do that? I mean, why you specifically? You didn't have to.'

'I did have to, I think. That's what … okay, this is going to sound like I'm changing the subject, but I'm not.' She raised her thumb to her mouth and began to chew the edge of the nail. 'See, I didn't tell you the whole truth about why I'm doing what I do. My research, why I do it. I've been thinking about that. It bothered me.'

'Okay.'

'I mean, not that I have to tell everybody about everything, but it seemed like … it's been bothering me is all.' She bent down to her shoulder bag, where it lay against the chair, took something out and slid it across the table towards him.

'This is my brother,' she said.

It was a cheap snapshot, overexposed. Susie with a version of her hair that he'd never seen, longer and brilliant red, sitting at a table with a man in a denim shirt and glasses. He looked rather like her, though without the brightly dyed hair, of course; his features differently proportioned but the dark eyes much the same, his expression somehow familiar. But something about him was wrong, the strained effort in his smile, the way his eyes evaded the camera. There was a birthday cake in front of them, and a single half-deflated balloon pinned to the wall.

'Actually he's not just my brother. He's my twin. Which you would think would be weird enough for one lifetime, but no. Because the other thing is, he has a major mental illness. He's schizophrenic, I mean, very seriously, for a long time. It's been relatively unresponsive to treatment.' She picked up the photo again, turning it in her hands. 'This is our thirtieth birthday. It was taken on a closed ward at Queen Street. Good times.'

Alex set his spoon down on the table. 'How long?' he asked softly.

She nodded, hearing the unspoken part of the question. 'Yeah. He had his first psychotic break a while before I met you. When we were twenty, I think. Maybe twenty-one? It's hard to remember exactly.'

'You should have told me.'

'Oh sure. Because I was really comfortable sharing it with people. Because nobody ever reacts badly when you tell them you have a schizophrenic twin.'

'I wouldn't … ' he started to say, but stopped himself; of course he had no idea what he would have done, and it would be stupid to pretend he did. He felt the whole shape of the past trembling in his mind, like a picture turning animated, in jerky stop-motion. Susie at the pay phone, up the street from the office, biting her lip. 'Still,' he said. 'Still. You should have told me.'

'Okay. Maybe I should have. Anyway, I'm telling you now. So you see what I mean? I couldn't just say, oh, Alex is flipping out, someone else should deal with that. It was just – something I was kind of used to. It's what I did. It was already what I always did.'

'Where – ' he started, and then thought that was probably the wrong way to ask the question. He didn't know how you asked this kind of question. 'How is he doing now?'

She tore a strip of thumbnail off with her teeth, then seemed to notice suddenly what she was doing and put her hand down on the table. 'I shouldn't have brought this up,' she said.

'Is it … I'm sorry. I don't know what you want me to ask.'

'I just don't want you to – I'm not looking for sympathy, okay?' She picked up her coffee cup. 'Okay, short version. He's disappeared. But I'm working on it. I'll find him. It'll be okay.'

Alex frowned, running the bent stir stick in automatic circles through his tea. 'I don't think I'm quite getting this. Have you talked to the police?'

'You know what? They really don't want to know. You'd be amazed how much they don't want to know about, about crazy people. Like you're supposed to just, like it's a usual thing to just lose track of them.'

'How long has he … '

'Three months, give or take. After our mother – she had cancer, she died last spring. A little after that, Derek went off his meds, and he, he just got worse and worse, and then he was gone. He's been on and off the street before, and he hadn't spoken to either of our parents for years before they died, but he never cuts me off. Never.'

She put the cup down again. 'He's my twin, Alex. He doesn't cut off from me.'

'You mean he hasn't before.'

'Let me tell you. When I went to Vancouver? He phoned me every day. Sometimes three, four times. In the middle of the night, whenever. He's always – he phones me, he comes to my house, God, I used to wish he *would* leave me alone. I mean, Derek didn't break up my marriage, I did that all by myself, but it can't be much fun having your brother-in-law going through the fridge throwing out all the food that's been injected with mind-control chemicals. But the point is, Derek does not cut me off. If he has – well, he has, this time he has, and that's got to mean it's really bad. I have to find him.'

Alex stared at the table and took a breath. He thought of not saying what came next, what was obvious. 'You realize,' he looked up at her, 'that he could be dead.'

She looked back, not angry, just very concentrated, very precise. 'Yes. Of course I do. I know that he hasn't picked up his disability cheques. And it's not like I have these twin-magic superstitions, like I would automatically know if he died. But if he were dead there would be a body. There'd be an unidentified body of the right age, with the right dental work, and I do have a missing-persons report in. If he were dead, I think I would have found him. I think he has to be alive to hide this well.' One hand moved back towards her mouth, but she stopped it, and gripped the coffee cup instead. 'I will find him. That's not even the part that bothers me. I'm just – honestly, Alex, I'm scared. This is different than it's been before. I don't know what sort of shape he'll be in, I don't know what to expect.'

Their hands were very close on the tabletop. She wouldn't ask him for what she wanted. He would have to say it himself. And of course he would say it.

'I could help you.'

She pinched her lips together, as if this were something she wanted so much she could hardly agree to it.

'Really?' she said softly.

'Sure. I could come with you. I don't mind.'

'God, Alex. Thank you.'

'I mean, if you want me to.'

'Yes. I really do.'

'Well. Then obviously.'

He knew he was a bad choice, a foolish complicating choice. He thought of Evvy and Adrian, the people who understood these things, who would have useful ideas. But he knew well enough why she hadn't gone to them. Evelyn would have been perfect, she would have dealt with it calmly and efficiently and kindly, and she would have done it exactly the same way for anyone, anyone at all who walked through the door. Alex would do this, if he did it, not because it was the right thing to do, but because it was for Susie. Because still, even now, he would do anything she needed.

'Are you taking pictures tonight?'

They were standing just outside the door of the coffee shop in a raw wind, wondering again what should come next.

'The weather's a problem,' said Alex. 'It's harder inside, I mean you have to get permission more inside.' He folded his hands into his armpits. 'Look. If there's some other way I can help – trying to find him ... '

'You don't have to worry about that part. Really. I talk to so many people on the street. Somebody's bound to have a lead on him eventually.'

'Yeah, just, if I can help, you know?' He felt the sting of freezing rain on his face.

'You could do one thing.' Susie reached into her pocket. 'The last address I had for him was a rooming house around here, kind of your neighbourhood. You could just knock on the doors there and ask if anyone knows where he went. I mean, I already tried, but not everyone was home, so it's worth trying again.' She fished out an old receipt from a bank machine, and pressed it against the wall of the building to scribble an address on the back. 'Anyway, I was thinking about your photos,' she went on. 'Harbourfront's a semi-public space that's indoors. We could go down there together if you wanted to.'

'I don't know.'

'Okay, sorry. I shouldn't interfere.'

'It's not that.' He thought again about what could happen if he touched her, and it was like a wave of vertigo, the abandonment of the rational world. 'It's really not that. I'm tired is all.'

'Yeah. Sorry. I didn't mean … ' She pressed the button to cross over to the streetcar stop, the car weaving towards them along its worn tracks.

'Another time maybe?' said Alex, as she flashed her Metropass at the driver. She was already halfway up the step, the doors sighing closed.

'I'll let you know when I find Derek,' she said.

Alex turned on College and started walking to the west, his hands in his pockets. He only meant to go home. But his route took him past the little church again, and Adrian was standing outside leaning against a tree, smoking a cigarette.

'Hey,' he said. 'I thought you might come back this way.' He exhaled smoke, rubbing one slender arm with his free hand. 'I'm taking a break from my duties as hired muscle.'

'I find it hard to imagine you as muscle.'

'I'm about as close to muscle as we get around here. We're the church of the tiny weak saints.' He reached into his jacket pocket and held out a pack of cigarettes, but Alex shook his head.

'You know I live just over at Grace? It's funny I've never seen you in the neighbourhood.'

'We've only been at this church a couple years,' said Adrian. 'And it's not like anyone's standing on the street with a megaphone.' He dropped the cigarette butt and ground it out with his boot, and he and Alex stood for a minute in the wind.

'I noticed a phenomenon at Mass on Sunday,' said Adrian eventually. 'Even before these latest girls at Jarvis. I noticed three or four people wouldn't drink from the cup. There's this little old lady who usually sits behind me, she's the angriest little old lady in the world, and the whole time she was muttering, "There's *no* excuse for this! It's a *terrible* shame! Why don't they use a *disinfectant*!" Because it would be very healthful to be ingesting disinfectant. But everything makes her angry. She gets angry because there's singing at Evensong. "I can't tell you how *mad* it makes me! All that *singing*!"'

'I suppose it'll only get worse.'

'They're going to be looking for someone to blame soon. That's the aspect that causes concern.'

'So tell me. What do you think is actually happening?'

Adrian pulled up the collar of his jacket as a gust of frozen rain shrilled down on them. 'My sense is that there's a curse on the city,' he said.

'Okay, that's original at least.'

'Actually, it's more early-classical. Like yellow fever as a consequence of civic wrongdoing. Somewhat Hellenic.'

'And we're cursed on account of what?'

'Don't ask me. Maybe somebody on city council killed his father and married his mother.'

'I guess that's as plausible as anything else.'

'I have to go back inside soon,' said Adrian. He folded his arms and scuffed the dirt with one foot. 'You should stay in touch, Alex. I was sorry you kind of disappeared.'

'I never did.'

'Did so. Nobody knew where you were, even.'

'I keep telling you I'm in the phone book.'

'Yeah, that's really not quite what I meant.' He shrugged. 'Anyway. They probably need me for some manual labour. I'll talk to you?'

'Are you guys some kind of conspiracy?'

'I hardly know Suzanne, actually. She and Evvy have got quite close, but I've never really known her. I did know you, though. And I was sorry not to see you. So I'm just taking advantage of a chain of circumstance.' He pulled open the door of the church and ducked inside, glancing backwards. 'Do try to stay in touch.'

The girl who first fell was left behind by events now. She still felt less than well, still had tremors in her hands at times, attacks of fatigue, which her doctor said were due to stress, and which a medical person, who preferred not to be named by the media, suggested could be the after-effects of nerve gas poisoning. But she was no longer a focus of attention.

She sat in her room and stared at the cover of her exercise book, where she had written *Bible Themes in Literature*, and filled in the circles of the B with her pen. Then she opened it to the first page and wrote *Book of Genesis*. Paused and checked her cellphone for text messages, picked up her pen again. *Located in garden*, she wrote. *V. signif*, then closed the notebook and picked up the phone.

'Oh my God,' said Nicole. 'Did you see the show last night?'

'I cried. Seriously I did.'

'If Luke and Lorelai don't get together I'm honestly going to die. I'm not even kidding. Did you see where he … '

'Oh my God. I so did. I was like dead.'

She doodled a heart on her notebook and wrote *Luke* inside, then scribbled over it.

'So are you doing this Bible themes thing? Do you even get what this garden thing is all about?'

'Well, sort of innocence and stuff, right? So when there's, like, vegetation in literature it's like this innocence thing? You know what I mean?'

'Yeah, but I just think that's kind of fucked up.'

On the small TV across from her bed, which was playing quietly in the background, she saw, yet again, the footage of the girl with the braided wool bracelet, covering her eyes. She reached for the remote and changed the channel.

She remembered how it felt to fall, the sickness and the narrowing vision; but as well, though she had no words to express this, the slow pleasure of her surrender to the body's weight, a strange sweet chemical rush as her muscles released.

Those who did not believe in the man with the poison gas had settled on iron-deficiency anemia as the meaning of her fall, and it is true that the girl's hematocrit and serum iron were not in balance, that she ate french fries and drank Coke and avoided red meat and baked beans and multivitamins. But the girl herself knew something different. She knew she had been singled out at that moment in the subway. That she would always be, at least in some small way, the girl who fell down and started it all, and she knew there was a reason for that.

But there was no one she could talk to about it, no one who would understand why, and though she herself had only said that she smelled roses and fell, the story about poison gas and evil motives gathered around her with no effort on her part. She allowed it to happen.

Sometimes, in her room by herself, she considered other meanings. She thought that there would be a change in her life, not now, but someday, and this would be part of it. She took her iron supplements and saw, on TV, the others falling.

The rain picked up strength and began to fling itself against the windows, washing the snow down into the gutters, eating away at the low, piled drifts. A little later in the winter, a few degrees colder, it would have coated the snow with a hard layer of shining ice, and in the morning the streets would have sparkled white and silver, tree branches like black engravings on the sky, but it was not yet that time, not fully within the season.

The roof of Alex's building wasn't supposed to be accessible to tenants, but the landlord often forgot to lock the access door. And it hurt no one for him to be here, huddled against the icy rain in his coat and hat, looking out over the street lights and the trees, the peaked and gabled Victorian houses, the downward slant of College towards the Portuguese Centre and the little strip mall and the basement where the Apocalypse Club used to be. The lens of his camera dripping with water, the water becoming a part of the picture, streaking and smearing the yellow glow of windows across the darkness. The slick hiss of the cars below as they slid through puddles, someone running under a dark umbrella. He sat on the roof, sodden, focused, a single point, and the fugitive light fell through him.

The next morning a man, a forty-five-year-old insurance broker, fell to his knees as he was getting off a train at the King station. He didn't faint, but lay in a crouch in the doorway of the train, gasping for breath, his face turning purple. A man in one of the seats nearby grabbed at his own throat, and moaned, and slid down to the floor. Alarms began to sound.

Bodies in Trouble

'Sedentary middle-aged men,' said Walter Yee, standing by the operating table and watching one of his residents crack open a patient's chest. 'Both moderately overweight. You can't tell me there wasn't cardiac involvement. Were they put through complete stress tests?'

'Two simultaneous cardiac episodes? Does that seem likely?'

'Okay, I'll grant you one psychosomatic reaction. But I'd like to see the test results on that first man.'

'Dr. Ryvat in pulmonary thinks it was asthma,' said one of the nurses. 'Dr. Lissman in neurology thinks –'

'Okay, okay. When you're a hammer everything looks like a nail. I'd still like to see the tests.'

Thursday morning, and Alex was standing in a corner of the OR, waiting for the preliminaries to be finished before he moved in towards the table.

'Wow,' said Walter, peering into the chest cavity. 'Talk about accidents waiting to happen. Alex, come on over here and get some horrible-example photos.'

'People in general still think it's poisoning,' said the anaesthetist.

'There is no such thing as people in general,' said Walter. 'It's okay, Adina, you go ahead, I'll just keep an eye.'

'Of course there's such a thing.'

'No, that's sloppy thinking. There are only many people in particular.'

'Fine. Many people in particular think it's poisoning.'

'I've heard disease as well. There's a bird flu theory floating around.'

'Oh, give me a break.'

Alex was standing near the resident, watching her hands, when she faltered and paused.

'Really,' said Walter. 'You're fine for this, Adina. You are.' The resident looked up at him, looked back at the patient's heart and started to cut, then her hands stopped moving and Walter jumped forward, pushing her aside, reaching into the chest.

'Okay, okay. We can fix this,' he said, and grabbed something from the instrument tray, his eyes on the opened chest. 'Excuse me, why am I not getting suction here?' he shouted. 'Jesus Christ, people! David, why aren't you clamping?'

Alex saw the chest cavity filling with blood. He focused the lens and took a series of fast pictures.

'We can do this,' said Walter. And the photographs changed too, subtly, in their purpose, being part of the documentation now that Walter and Adina had done everything right as far as they could, that there were no gross errors but only the limits of the body; or else that there had been preventable error, that something human had intervened and broken down in disaster. Alex himself didn't know clearly what was happening, but he knew just enough to take the right pictures, pictures that would help to lay out the story when it would have to be told.

Alex had not often seen people die. But it had happened – he was part of that strange elite in Western society, one of the witnesses. This man did not die, he was not exactly dead when he left the OR, but Walter was silent and grim, and whatever would happen over the next few hours, it was clear he expected nothing good.

There was nothing different to do, nothing that had to be done but to send the photos to the hard drive by wireless transfer. Alex would hear, sooner or later, what was needed from them. He would sort and select the shots, isolate the particular details that were requested. He would know this man's heart. He might not ever find out what happened to him.

But the afternoon was lucky. Things could change like that; he could walk out of the OR shaky and sick, and then be sent on one of those assignments that was pure enjoyment, upbeat and playful. This time a girl with new prosthetic legs, a bright, opinionated kid with spiky black hair and little gold earrings who found the devices – her fourth set so far – to be totally excellent. She had never had such good legs before, she told him, doing little steps to demonstrate. The previous legs had sucked like a suckhole but these were much better, her old doctor didn't know what he was doing, not like this new lady doctor who was absolutely cool. Completely aware of the camera, and flirting with it in a little-girl way, a necklace of rainbow butterflies around her neck.

So he didn't feel so bad by the time he got home, a light snow drifting around him. It wasn't, in the end, what he would have called a bad day. It was just that he was tired, that it was too complex to absorb all at once.

He picked Queen Jane up from the bed where she was sleeping and carried her against his chest to the couch, lay down with the heavy grey cat curled under his chin, her claws hooked into his shirt at the shoulder. It was not very comfortable, and he got tufts of cat hair in his mouth when he breathed, but it was easier than trying to move her. He would get up soon and make dinner; he would spend the night at home, working in the darkroom.

He remembered, then, Susie's piece of paper. Queen Jane stretched on his chest and pushed one paw against his throat, making him cough and sit up; he rearranged her into his lap despite her cries of complaint. He could run over to the rooming house easily; it was only a few blocks away, and maybe a good time to catch people at home.

There was something to be said for getting it over with. Being able to tell her that he'd tried. Of course there was also something to be said for not trying at all, for keeping his distance from the whole situation, that dangerous maze of emotion and memory.

But he put on his coat and walked up Bathurst Street to a squat, cramped building, decaying white plaster on the front. There were a dozen doorbells of various types and ages fastened to either side of the door, some with names or numbers written in chalk underneath, some with scraps of paper pasted onto them, the letters faded into illegibility. One had a red painted arrow pointing to it, with the words DOSE'NT WORK alongside. The door itself was locked. He chose one button randomly, pushed it and waited for a few minutes, but there was no response.

Under the bells, also in chalk, someone had written BSMT APTS, and added another arrow that seemed to point south down the street. Presumably it was intended to direct people – assuming anyone ever came here – to the narrow laneway that ran by the side of the house. Alex went down the front stairs and followed the laneway to the back, where he found another door, heavy steel and painted green. This one wasn't locked, and he pushed it open and walked down a flight of stairs into a narrow corridor that smelled of cooked cabbage and damp rot. There was a row of apartments on either side, the chain-locked entrances just a few feet apart, and a sheet of drywall and a hammer lying in the corner as if the rooms were in the process of being subdivided into even smaller units.

He knocked at the door marked #15. A bare-legged girl in a T-shirt peered around the chain, shouted, 'Foreign student visa!' and slammed the door again. At #13 there was no answer, though he could hear a television playing inside, canned applause, probably a game show. He was standing in the corridor considering his next move when he heard a chain lock rattle open, and a young man with dreadlocks wrestled a bicycle out into the hallway.

'Hey, man,' he said, nodding to Alex in a vaguely friendly way.

'Hey,' said Alex. 'Do you think you could help me?'

'You here about the election or something?'

'Is there an election?'

'Beats me. But I sometimes think I should take more of an interest, you know? Getting to that age where I should take responsibility?'

'No, the thing is, I'm looking for someone who used to live here.'

'Oh, well, I couldn't do much there, I just moved in a few months ago. But you should talk to Mrs. Nakamura in #8. She's been here, like, forever.'

'Okay. Thanks.'

'No problem. Let me know if there's an election, eh?' He dragged his bicycle up the stairs, dislodging the chunk of wood so that the door swung closed, and Alex wondered if he was locked in now, but decided to try Mrs. Nakamura before looking for an escape route.

There was a mat outside #8, a pair of red slippers placed carefully side by side. Alex knocked, and heard movement, and then the door was opened by a diminutive woman in a faded floral smock, her hair tied tightly back.

'Come in!' she said, with a wide smile. 'Please come in!' She pulled the door open wider.

'It's all right,' said Alex. 'I just need to … '

'No, no. Please come in.' She tugged gently on his arm, and he found himself inside the room, which was windowless, dimly lit by a single desk lamp. 'Sit down. Sit here.' The woman moved him towards a folding chair.

As his eyes adjusted, he saw that he was in a bare and very neat space, a little writing table at his elbow. There was a larger melamine table against the wall, an old but spotless toaster oven and a radio sitting on it; a cot nearby, with a red blanket tucked tightly around the corners. There was a can of tuna and part of a loaf of bread on the toaster oven, and half the wall was covered with large colour posters of tennis players. In the centre of the room, and taking up much of the space, was an ironing board, and once he was safely seated the woman returned to it, and resumed her task of meticulously, slowly, ironing a piece of junk mail.

'You have to be careful with the mail,' she said brightly. 'In these days. I always make sure to iron. Then it's safe. You agree? I hope you take precautions. Is that right?'

'Ah,' said Alex. 'I don't get much mail.'

'I always make sure. Now, can I help you? You're from the city hall?'

The basement was overheated; he was already uncomfortable in his winter coat. He took his cap off and held it in his lap. 'No, I just wanted to ask about someone who lived here a few years ago.'

'You're from immigration? Nobody here has any problems with immigration. All the papers are in order.'

'No, no. It's just for a friend.'

The woman finished ironing the envelope, picked it up and set it neatly on the corner of the desk, then pulled over another chair and sat down near Alex. 'Let me ask you, did you hear the weather report on the radio?'

'I'm afraid not.'

'They said there could be a blizzard. I'm very worried about that. I was thinking that the power might go off.'

'I don't think so.'

'If there's a blizzard, and then ice on the power lines. The power could go off. I've been very worried. I tried to call my son, but he said he didn't have time to buy me a flashlight. But, you know, he goes to this church? All the way up at Finch? I would think if he could get all the way up there he could buy me a flashlight. Don't you think?'

'I just wanted to ask you about someone,' said Alex.

'I know. It's so good of you to come to talk to me. I called my son, you know, and I said, if you could buy me some Ritz Crackers, if the power goes off, I could put the tuna on them, and it would still be a meal, right? But he isn't very kind.'

'I'm sorry.'

'Look, look at this.' She reached into a shoebox on the small table. 'I wrote him up this list.' She found a piece of lined paper and held it out, under the lamp. Alex looked at the large shaky letters, spelling out CRACKERS RITZ. ON SHELF WITH COOKIES. Underneath, she had done a rough drawing of a Ritz Cracker and coloured it orange. 'I just thought if the power goes off I could put the tuna on them,' she said, her voice beginning to shake.

'I really don't think the power's going to go off.'

'But it did one time before. If there was ice on the lines.'

'I'm pretty sure that was different.'

'Or if the terrorists, you know. In these days, you can never be sure. If I had a flashlight it would be better, but he isn't kind to me.'

'I'm very sorry. Could you maybe just look at a picture and tell me if you recognize someone?'

'Of course, of course.' She reached out and clutched Alex's hand, and he started in alarm. 'My husband died three years ago this day,' she said. 'We were married for forty years. We were so happy.' He saw tears forming in the corners of her eyes; with her free hand she took a tissue from her pocket and wiped at them. 'He fell down with a heart attack and died instantly. My son wanted to say something at the funeral, but, you know, I wasn't sure. But you know I talked to the Metropolitan, you know, the police, and they said after a couple of years it's okay to let him into the house again, and it was ten years by now, and the police said after a couple of years I could let him be in the house, you know, not to stay here but to come in. But I didn't know about a speech at the church.'

'I'm sorry,' repeated Alex helplessly.

'I have such problems in this life,' she said, gripping the little ball of tissue. 'He is not a good son.'

'Please,' said Alex. 'Could you just take a quick look at a photo? Please?'

'You can help me,' said the woman, her face lighting up. 'Maybe, I think you can help me.' She ducked her head down, opening a drawer in the little table; her black hair parted knife-sharp in the middle, fragile and dry. 'If you wrote a letter to the city hall,' she said, bringing out another piece of pencil and a paper and pushing them towards Alex. He tried to move them back towards her, but she picked up his hand and wrapped it around the pencil. 'About the problem of the power.'

'I don't know ... '

'I can see you have an education, of course. My son, he never took advantage of an education. But you are a good boy to an old lady, aren't you?'

He angled the paper under the desk lamp and wrote *Dear Councillor*, then couldn't remember where the ward boundary lay or who her city councillor would be, so he left the salutation as it was. *Mrs. Nakamura is afraid the power will go off.* He put down the pencil.

'You tell them what I need,' she said; and this opened up such an expanse of possible longings that language was helpless. Dear Councillor, he thought. Mrs. Nakamura needs your love. Mrs. Nakamura needs her life redeemed. Mrs. Nakamura and I are waiting for rescue.

She wants a flashlight and some Ritz Crackers, he wrote.

'Draw for them.'

The pencil was not very sharp, but he outlined a rough sketch of a flashlight, and then added a box of crackers beside it, concentrating on the detailing, adding a little cross-hatched shadow, so he wouldn't have to look up and meet her eyes.

Your assistance would be greatly appreciated. He added the date and address at the top of the page, and signed it *Alexander Nicholl Deveney*, the full name he never used.

The woman picked up the piece of paper and studied it, folded it carefully twice and put it in her pocket.

'You are kind,' she said. 'I'll take it to them tomorrow. It's better than the mail. In these days.'

'Yes. I'm sure it is.' He reached for the snapshot and put it on the table between them. 'Do you know this man?'

'Oh yes,' she said. She opened the shoebox again and took out a sheet of graph paper, then took a small pair of black-rimmed glasses from her pocket and put them on.

'Yes. He is here on the chart.' She stared at the graph paper, then put her finger on one line and turned it to Alex. He saw numbers, Japanese characters, and English words here and there that he recognized. SAD MAN, said the words she was pointing to. PROBLEM IN SINK.

'He lived in #5 upstairs. But he left a long time ago.'

'Do you know where he went?'

'No, I'm sorry. He was a man who had a lot of difficulties. Was he your friend?'

'Not exactly.'

'My son is also a man with difficulties, but I don't understand them. I don't understand why he behaves that way. And he goes to that church up at Finch. Your friend, is he getting treatment for his problems? Are they taking good care of him?'

'I don't know where he is.'

'Oh. That's very bad. You will have to hope and pray.' She took his hand again. 'I will say a prayer for you.'

'That's okay. I don't really … '

'I will say a prayer for your friend as well.'

'Yes. Well. Thank you. I think I should go.'

'Did you hear anything about the weather report? They were saying a storm tonight. I just worry about the ice on the lines.'

'I'm sure it will be all right. Honestly.'

'The Metropolitan said I could let him into the house again after a few years.'

Alex stood up. 'I do have to go. I'm terribly sorry.' He took a step backwards towards the door. 'I'm sure the power won't go off.'

'Thank you,' said the woman, her eyes filling again with tears. 'It's very kind of you to come to talk to me. It's truly very kind. I'll pray for you and your friend tonight.'

'Yes,' said Alex, and backed out the doorway, turning to move quickly down the corridor, and up the stairs in two long steps. The door opened from the inside, and he pushed the piece of wood back into place, not sure if he should do this or not but thinking somehow that it was better to leave everything as he had found it. The cold air was sharp against his skin, and he pulled on his cap and stood on Bathurst Street, taking deep breaths.

It would be a pathetic report to take back to Susie, but she hadn't expected much from him anyway.

He turned onto College and walked back towards his apartment. A streetcar drove past, a small child pressing her face against the window in a comic grimace; the door of a café opened briefly, and he heard laughter, and the sound of an espresso machine. When he got to his block, he saw the man who was being held hostage by terrorists sitting in a doorway, and reached into his pocket for change.

'Excuse me, sir,' said the man, who had his arms wrapped around his legs, against the cold. 'Would you happen to have … '

'Sure,' said Alex, and gave him a handful of coins.

'Thank you very much, sir. I wouldn't ask, but … '

'It's okay. I know.'

'It's a bad situation, sir. They're upset that I have the knowledge. They don't want me to have the knowledge, about the people falling out of the air.'

Alex sighed and leaned against the bricks. For a minute he saw the whole city as one great cry for attention, and he thought that maybe people died on the street not from cold or heat or hunger but only because no one got enough attention. 'Okay,' he said. 'Why were the people falling?'

'Well,' said the man, his eyes growing brighter. 'That's the part that we need to think about in an analytical way. Because sometimes things fall down, sir, and the force of your will can't keep them standing. Because you remember how it was, sir. When the buildings were coming down.'

'Oh,' said Alex. 'Do you mean in New York?'

The man shrugged. 'The force of your will was helpless, sir,' he said. 'But this is what somebody told me who had a name tag that she wasn't CIA. You can have something come into your head, but it's up to you how you understand it to be. And this is where the analytical thinking comes in. For instance you might decide that it's a problem of the force of your will, and if you tell yourself that people can't fall out of the sky then they will stop doing it, but I haven't found this to be very successful. Or you could decide that your job is catching people, but there's the potential for harm if they're falling very fast. It was all on the television, sir. I'm sure you remember.'

'Yes, well, I think I know what you mean.'

'Or you can decide that it's an issue of enemies and take yourself in hand to eliminate them, which is very efficient in a way unless they get mad at you too, or someone comes and makes you sit in the white chair which could be very unfortunate. But that's not the part that's making the terrorists angry, sir. They've been trying to cause me harm because they're upset that I have knowledge of the components. The components of the bodies, sir.'

How much of this, Alex wondered, can a street contain? How much, before it all breaks down?

'The reassembly of the components isn't a hopeful prospect,' said the man. 'And when blood comes out of the ears, there's no possibility to survive. I've seen this in person. The components have been damaged on a wide basis.'

Alex looked at the man and frowned. 'But you weren't there, right?' he asked. 'I mean, in New York? This is something else you're talking about?'

'That's all right, sir,' said the man. 'I know what you need to ask me, you want me to tell you that I was really there or else somebody just told me about it, and I'm not offended that you want to ask me that. That's the way it is when people are talking, you need to ask certain questions, and when I answer them I always try to be honest.' He scratched the skin on one hand. 'But even when you see something with your own eyes, you don't always know what it means until somebody tells you what happened, do you? You just don't always know. So there was this noise, and this darkness. I can't remember it all fairly well. But the government's involved in my situation now. Things are looking up.'

'Okay,' said Alex. There was no more sense he could make from this, not now, there was nothing to do but accept what the man could give him. 'I'm glad to hear that. I hope it goes well.'

'We all do our best, sir. Things are looking up every day.'

'Listen.' On impulse, Alex reached into his pocket. 'Could you do me one favour? I'm trying to find someone, could you look at his picture and tell me if you know him?'

'Well, that would depend on your intentions, sir,' said the man, his heavy face furrowing with concern. 'For instance if you wanted to push him in front of a car, sir, I wouldn't want to be involved with that.'

'No, it's nothing like that. It's just his sister wants to talk to him.'

'Is she going to be respectful of the systems, do you think?'

'Yes. I think so.' He held out the photo. 'Have you seen him anywhere?'

The man studied the picture for a long time. 'I couldn't tell you at this moment, sir. There's a possibility of some help. But I think I'll need to make some enquiries with the government.'

'Sure. You do that then.'

'I'll try to look into the matter for you, sir. That's his sister? She's a very pretty lady.'

'Well. Yes. She is.'

'Okay, sir, and thank you for the change. I'll let you know if the situation is updated in any way.'

Sitting at a melamine table with Nicole and Kirsty after track practice, the girl picked at a plate of fries, the gravy salty and thick and hot. 'But honest to God,' Kirsty was saying, 'you really, like, collapsed from a poison gas? 'Cause this is getting totally serious.'

'I don't know,' said the girl, carefully licking a ribbon of gravy from her finger. 'I guess. Yeah.'

'I mean, because they keep saying it's nothing, but you know there's all kinds of people collapsing now, and if they're all getting poisoned it could be like, you don't know what's going to happen in a week or two weeks or … '

'It's stupid,' said the girl. 'Forget it. It's probably just like, they have a problem with the pipes in the subway or something, they just don't want to admit it so they blame the, you know, terrorists or somebody. That's probably, that's probably it.' She knew that whatever she said would carry a particular authority, because she was the one who had fallen first; even Tasha would never have quite the same position, though Tasha had collapsed as well. Anyway, nobody really listened to Tasha to begin with. 'Let's talk about something else.'

'I just kind of think this is serious,' said Nicole.

'No,' said the girl. 'It's stupid. It's just stupid, okay?' She pushed her hair back impatiently, the good tired ache in her muscles.

'Sure.' Nicole reached over and took a french fry from the girl's plate. 'We can definitely change the subject. It's fine.'

It occurred to the girl that she could phone Zoe, but she knew that she wouldn't, that she could never explain to Zoe what had happened, or what it had felt like, in that moment, to fall. She thought again about the woods at the back of the school grounds, the thicker woods deep in the ravines, about living out in the cold there, how dark it got.

'That new science teacher? He's a total babe,' said Kirsty.

II

'And that's supposed to mean fucking *what* now?'

Alex bent over his contact sheets, biting his lip and trying hard not to listen to Chris and Susie, who were shouting at each other a foot away from him.

'Look, don't ask me, ask your boy toy Mike out there if you want to know. As if you really don't know.'

That summer in 1989 the air was heavy with humidity, and the production room had somehow ceased to be public space, had turned into a heat-charged theatre for this escalating drama, everyone's lives invaded by it. Alex could never be sure who he would find there or what would be happening, how long it would take to get an issue out and what would be torn or broken in the interim, Chris and Susie refined into their worst possible selves, insulting each other in front of the staff, staging petty battles, destroying small prized possessions. They had never seemed so close as they tore each other slowly to pieces, passionate and obsessive, no one else around them more than a stage prop. And even then they would go home together at sunrise, come back to the office for the next evening's work. Return to their apartment, to whatever happened between them there.

Alex walked through it, quiet, an outsider, except that she would be there in his darkroom, she would touch him and lean on his shoulder and then suddenly leave; she would call him at midnight, meet him in a bar in the Market and tell him everything, and the next day he would be no one again.

He came to the office late at night, and he was in the parking lot, chaining up his bicycle, when he heard Susie-Paul crying in the darkness. He ran towards the sound, and saw the small outline of her, huddled by the wall, at the edge of the spill of a street light, barely visible.

'Susie. Susie.'

She looked up, a streak of something dark and wet on her face, and a splayed mass at her feet. Lifted her hands. He saw the shine of the edge of a knife, a heavy liquid on her fingers.

He was on his knees beside her instantly, his feet tangling into the mess of Chris's bicycle beside her, the tires slashed, the chain ripped off. She was covered with the oil from the chain. And he knew that he would have forgiven her anything, anything at all, there was nothing she could do that he had not in advance forgiven.

'Susie.'

He pulled her into his arms, and she came, smearing oil in his hair, on his neck, the exacto knife falling to the ground.

'I killed his bike,' she said.

He kissed her then, really kissed her for the first time, their tongues pressing hard into each other's mouths. They fell together in the shadow of the wall, the hot asphalt scraping his knees, her body moving against his, their legs entangled. But she slid away from him. She pulled herself up and staggered backwards, tugging down her dress, her lips swollen.

'I can't. Alex, no. I can't do this right now.'

He sat on the asphalt breathing hard, smelling of WD-40. He wanted to say something ugly and childish – *you could do it with Mike Cherniak* – and it wasn't love or kindness or even common sense that prevented him, just inarticulacy. But this too he had forgiven her, had forgiven her long ago. There was nothing else he could do. He was helpless.

There was no particular reason that Alex painted a giant bird across one wall of his room. He had been very bored one evening, and he had paint and brushes still lying around from his short-lived experiment with art school a few years before.

'Is it a phoenix, then?' asked Adrian.

'No. It's just a bird.'

'Bird of prey? Migratory bird? Pelican? The pelican is Jesus, you know. Though if I were Jesus I might be offended by that. Well, obviously it's not a pelican.'

'I don't know. It's a bird. It looks like a fierce bird.'

'I think it's an osprey.'

'If you say so. I was just thinking Jane would like to have a permanent bird to chase, but this one's awfully big. I don't think her visual field is up to it.'

'There's not a wide symbolic network around the osprey. I wonder why that is.'

'I'm thinking now I could make Jane a little bird mobile, but it wouldn't last long.'

It was a white bird with black and brown edging on its feathers, and a jagged turquoise line marking it off from the grey concrete wall, and it was somewhat larger than Alex himself. He didn't much like it; there was nothing in it that was original or real. He'd never had the right kind of eye to be a painter.

'What would you do for me?' Susie said. She was lying on his bed, wearing a white lace dress and black tights with runs in them, smoking hash, and Alex was stretched on the floor, leaning his head against the mattress. He could hear Queen Jane growling in the far corner of the room, doing battle with a sock. 'If I asked you. What would you do for me?'

'Anything,' he said. He didn't know why she was there, she had turned up at his door, it happened sometimes. He didn't ask.

'But that's not true,' she said, exhaling and handing him the joint. 'You wouldn't kill somebody, for instance. And that's good, I mean, I wouldn't want that. But really. What would you do?'

I would sit here for hours and never touch you, he thought, sucking the smoke into his lungs. *I would let you pull me towards you and then push me away again. What more do you want?*

He held the smoke in for as long he could before exhaling, leaned his elbow on the mattress and looked at her, a distant and slightly mad expression on her face that was not just the hash. He could see the dark lashes surrounding her bottomless eyes; he was close enough to count every one of them.

'I would stop taking photographs,' he said.

'No, you wouldn't.'

'I think I would.' He passed the joint to her. 'Do you want me to?'

'No.' She took a long drag, and a slow trail of smoke spun out from her lips in a complex spiral. 'If I was very sick, if I needed someone to look after me, would you do it?'

He lay his head on the mattress, pushing his hair from his face. Patterns of light from the cars that passed outside shimmered across the wall. 'Sure. I guess. I'm not a doctor.'

'Not like that.' She stared at the ceiling. 'What if – what if I was sick in a way that changed me? If I wasn't the person you knew. Would you still look after me then?'

'But that won't happen.'

She closed her eyes. He sucked the last of the smoke from the roach and dropped it into an ashtray. Her hair in the light of his desk lamp was a hundred shades of pink and gold.

'You'll always be Susie-Paul,' he said. She shook her head slowly. 'I know who you are. I will always know who you are.'

'You don't know, Alex,' she whispered. 'You don't understand.'

He felt a faint creep of apprehension. 'Is there – Susie, is something wrong?'

'No. Nothing's wrong. Not with me.'

She lay with her eyes closed for what was probably a long time.

'You still want to go hear the Spits?' she asked at last.

'If you do,' he said.

'Sure. Let's.'

They walked up Bathurst Street in a cutting November wind, icy puddles soaking in through his boots. She was very quiet, and he knew that he had let her down in some way, but he didn't know what he could say to make it better.

And then they were in the heat and crush of the basement, the music hugging them in, pools of brown water on the floor and the room filled with bodies, sweating, moving, someone climbing onto a table to dance, and the band almost invisible because there was no stage, only a strip of masking tape marking them off from the dance floor. They had a drummer and a bass player now, and the guitars were loud, high metal in his ears. He stood against the wall with Susie, sharing a bottle of beer and feeling the music shake through his body, wondering what it meant that they were there together, clearly together, and yet not really. The singer's voice rising on a long line, sweeping him upwards.

The next song he recognized – it wasn't a slow song exactly, but less fast – a song about UFOs and longing, about lights on the asphalt and aliens and escape, and Susie-Paul reached for his hand and led him onto the floor, and he wrapped his arms around her as she rested her head on his chest, swaying not quite in time with the music. And he knew this was something in her that was sad and nearly self-destructive; it wasn't what he wanted.

> *Take me away*
> *Take me away*

The first set was over, and they walked outside again, to the sheltered yard of St. Peter's Church where the sound of the traffic on Bloor Street was faint, like falling water.

'I have to tell you something,' said Susie.

'I figured you did.'

'I've decided to go away. I'm going to Vancouver for a while.'

He turned from her, leaning into a corner of the limestone wall. 'How long?'

'I don't know.'

He ran his finger across the rough edges of the stone. It was almost glowing, in a diffused beam of light from somewhere. 'Will you come back?'

'I don't know.'

He walked a few nervous steps in the frosted grass. 'You don't believe me,' he said, 'but I will always know who you are.'

She shook her head. 'You think that, Alex. But you don't understand.'

And when they went back inside, the bass player was leaning down, relentless, and the music crashing against the walls, fast and angry, the singer stretching out her arms and dancing, that ragged extraordinary voice.

> *Follow the light to where the little ones lie*
> *Watch their faces disappear in the sky*

The singer grabbed her mike from the stand and sang a long wordless cry and crossed the line of tape, dancing out into the audience and vanishing among their bodies.

Build ourselves a town
And then we'll watch it all come down

Susie-Paul spun into his arms like a collision, and pulled his head down and kissed him hard in the middle of the dance floor. And it wasn't what he wanted but it was the best he was going to get. He squeezed her against him and kept kissing her, the other people on the dance floor tripping over them, knocking them sideways, the night going on everywhere.

And suddenly nothing was urgent or desperate as he had thought it would be; as if the frantic pulse that had been beating at the back of his skull for the last year had abruptly calmed. He knew so completely that this was all he could ever hope for.

For a while they were kissing at the bus stop, muffled in their winter clothes, sucking warmth from each other, and when he drew away from her to breathe, the moisture on his lips began to freeze and sting.

He locked Queen Jane in the kitchen upstairs and unzipped Susie's dress. The skin of her shoulders was smooth and slightly freckled and tasted like sweat and yeast. He went down on his knees and ran his tongue up her thigh. Their bodies slick and wet in the hot basement, the taste of her on his lips, her mouth sliding over him, and the borders of everything turned fluid, time and space and movement. Far away from himself and falling, broken open inside her.

And then sometime during the night he started up from the bed in quick panic, his heart pounding and sweat pouring down his back. Hypo. Grabbed at the can of Coke on his desk and drank it fast, spilling part of it on the floor, and waited for the shaking to stop, and nearly wept because his blood could never leave him alone, because he could never, not for one minute, be free of this.

Susie-Paul tossed and muttered, and he went back to her, his fingers reaching between her legs, and woke her slowly, and they slid into each other again, the heat of her skin.

She left in the morning while he was still sleeping.

He wasn't sure what he had expected after that. But not complete silence. She had stayed in town for three more days, he learned later, but he never heard from her. When he called her house – he hadn't ever done this before – there was no one there at first. In the end he reached Chris, and by then she was already gone.

He knew exactly when she had left because he found out from Chris, the two of them managing to establish a very brief and unsatisfactory friendship based entirely on having been dumped by the same woman. Chris believed that Alex and Susie had been lovers for several months at least, and Alex never bothered to tell him otherwise.

He did think that she would phone him sometime, or write to him or at least send a postcard. Not so much because they'd slept together. He could accept that this was an anomaly and meant very little; but they had been friends. And he wanted to know, he was worried about her, she had seemed so damaged, and talked strangely; maybe she really was sick somehow – and then he thought of AIDS, and was ashamed of the thought, but it was true that he had been wholly careless. And he was by no means sure who else she had slept with.

She wouldn't do that, though. She was not the sort of person who would do that. He tried to keep this in the back of his mind where he kept all his other irrational fears about her – cancer, suicide. He didn't know why she didn't write. At the end of that strange awful year a man in Montreal picked up a rifle and went out hunting feminists, and fourteen women were dead, and he knew she had said she was going to Vancouver and anyway all the dead women were named, but he thought of that too, blood on her white lace dress. It couldn't be true, of course. But he wished she would write and tell him so.

Dissonance came out less and less often through the winter, and finally stopped altogether. For a while he managed to increase his hours at SuperPhoto so that he could pay his rent, and borrowed money from his parents to cover his insulin, but he knew he would have to find a better job somehow.

Finally, in the spring, he heard at several removes – from Adrian, who had heard it from Evelyn's cousin – that she was indeed in Vancouver, working as a canvasser for Greenpeace, and seemed to be more or less okay. He forced himself to go to the clinic and get tested, and he was clean, and he tried to believe that he had never expected anything else.

A few weeks later he was at the hospital to see his endocrinologist, and there was a notice on a bulletin board inviting people with photographic expertise to apply for a job, and he tied back his hair and went for an interview.

There no was precise point at which he understood that he would not hear from her again.

III

In the indigo evening, a woman knelt on her front steps with a rag and a tin of cleanser, her hands red and raw, scrubbing the stairs again and again. Every time that she started to think she was finished she would see a spot she couldn't remember cleaning, and again her mind would fill with the possibility of contagion, of the people collapsing on the subway, and what they carried with them when they left and walked into the city. She would think of vials of Asian flu inadvertently opened, of sarin and tabun deliberately released, of some tiny particle borne towards her, tracked into the house, onto the floor where her children walked, some flake of poison, of illness, of malign intent. She poured more cleanser onto the rag, dipped it in a bucket of water, and scraped it again across the stone, weeping, exhausted, shaking with cold.

She was an intelligent woman, she knew that this behaviour was somewhere within the range of an obsessive-compulsive disorder. She knew that there was no possible contaminant that would cling to her front steps or kill them all with a single molecule. She knew, as well, that the burning pain in her shoulder was the result of tension and cold, not a heart attack, not the effect of a neurotoxin. But this knowledge was useless. Her knuckles frozen white, the skin of her fingertips chafed away till they almost bled.

Inside the house, the sound system was playing, the music meant to convince her that this was less than torture, a bearable household chore. Leonard Cohen's vampire voice singing 'Ain't No Cure for Love,' over and over. She dipped the rag in the bucket again, shook the tin of cleanser over the steps, wondered what breathing it in was doing to her lungs, as the night gathered around her.

'You don't mind me coming along with you?'

It was Friday afternoon, and Alex was kneeling by a butcher's stall in St. Lawrence Market, under the high ceiling of the old hall, when Susie arrived. He had been photographing a man packing up trays of meat as the market closed for the day, working on the contrast between the slick deep redness of the steaks and the thin and papery skin on the man's gnarled hands.

'It's okay, it's good you called,' said Alex, putting the camera back into his bag. 'Besides, I bet this is something you don't even know about.'

'What, raw meat?' asked Susie, looking towards the butcher's stand. 'I know more about raw meat than you do.'

'No, this was just me killing time. We'll be going north from here.'

'And this doesn't bother you at all?' asked Susie, with a gesture towards the heaps of ground pork, the glistening coils of sausage.

'Bodies in space, Suzanne,' said Alex, standing up. 'It's all bodies in space.'

They walked out of the hall and crossed the street. She was wearing a rather elegant black and white batik dress and a red quilted jacket, not quite warm enough for the weather. 'I have to go to a party for some American hotshot later,' she said, shrugging, aware that he'd noticed. 'House of a major donor to the university, up in Rosedale. Filipina maids handing around wine and smoked salmon. And academic backbiting.'

'The maids hand around the backbiting?'

'They might as well. The upper classes can't do a thing for themselves.'

'Sounds fantastic. Don't let me keep you from it.'

'I wish you could. But I have some time before it starts.'

Outside St. James' Cathedral, a Mennonite family was handing out pamphlets in the dusk – a man in a broad hat, three small girls in calico dresses and aprons, and a pregnant, tired woman wearing a bonnet. Alex took a pamphlet from one of the girls, and after a short negotiation with the father was permitted to take a picture of them, posed stiffly in a group, their papers clutched to their chests.

Alex studied the pamphlet as he picked up his camera bag. WHAT WOULD JESUS DO? it read on the front.

'See, this is a question I ask,' he said. They walked by the cathedral garden, brown now and shrivelled, the dried seedheads covered with the powdery snow that had fallen during the night. 'What *would*

Jesus do? Would he be a fireman? A circus acrobat? I mean, you hang out in churches, you tell me.'

'Something weird, I think,' said Susie. 'This is what I'm starting to pick up, that he was a very odd guy. He'd be sitting on the church steps telling a story about mustard. He was always on about the mustard.'

'You're making that up.'

'No, really. I definitely have heard about mustard.'

'I'm going to check with Evelyn before I accept that.'

'Feel free.' Susie looked up and around at the office towers. 'Damn, we're in the business district again.'

'We should turn this way,' said Alex, pointing to a pillared corridor between two glass walls.

'I got a letter from my ex-husband today.'

'Oh?'

'He says I was a bad wife. I mean, I *know* I was a bad wife, it's his fault he married me in the first place. I just don't see the point of bringing it up now.'

'Well. Sorry.' He had no idea what his response to this was supposed to be. He and Amy exchanged polite and impersonal Christmas cards every year, and he could hardly imagine her mentioning their relationship, much less critiquing it.

'Forget it,' said Susie. 'It's a crappy day all over.'

They went on through the back streets, under grey walls, and then across Yonge and into a gravelled lot, entering an empty glass walkway and crossing out the other side, onto the little stub of Temperance Street. 'There,' said Alex, pointing across the road. 'That's the Cloud Gardens.'

Behind a five-storey building, the cold waves of a waterfall poured down the wall, reflecting coloured lights from a theatre marquee across the street. The brilliant water dove into a stone channel, framed as it fell by stepped and ragged limestone terraces and a network of metal bridges. To the side of the cascading waves, a long red oxide steel grid held squares of etched glass and beaten copper and pale concrete, rippled aluminum, green and gold metals. In the square below, curving stone walkways ran between bare oak and ash, banks of snow-covered shrubs.

'Who even knows this is here?' said Alex, waving his arm as they walked onto the largest path. 'No one even knows it's here at all.' Though this was clearly not quite true, as the bridges and terraces were dotted with clusters of teenagers, sheltered in pockets of darkness. The sharp smell of pot smoke was drifting down over the water.

'I'm thinking that's why they call it the Cloud Gardens,' said Susie, nodding her head towards them.

'Kind of takes you back, doesn't it?' said Alex, and then put down his camera bag and began moving through the paths, turning in a circle with his camera and causing some consternation among the pot-smoking teens. He had been taking pictures for a few minutes, and had climbed up onto one of the terraces, focusing down on the lights that flickered on the swift run of the water, when he saw that Susie was sitting on a rock, staring down and picking at her fingernails. 'Hey,' he called to her. 'You could come up here.' She shrugged and walked slowly towards him.

'There's something else I wanted to show you,' he said. He led her up another terrace and over one of the metal bridges to a glass door. 'It's closed right now, but look.'

Inside the glass, barely visible, was a dense foam of broad, deep-green leaves, tree trunks hanging with vines, cut through by more bridges. 'It's the top of a rainforest,' said Alex. 'They built a rainforest under glass here, over a parking garage. Just because. Just so it would be there. And no one even knows.' She had folded her arms and pursed her lips. 'This is a human thing, Susie, and I love it. You can tell me it's pointless if you want. You can tell me it's built on exploitation and I partly believe that. But you can't tell me it isn't beautiful.'

'Alex,' said Susie sharply. 'Would you quit with the lectures already?'

He stepped away from the glass. 'Excuse me?'

'I'm sorry, but you don't know what I'm thinking, do you? You have no idea what I was was going to say about this rainforest. For some reason you're trying to make it out like I'm all theory and no humanity, but you don't know who the hell I am. And you're hardly one to talk about what's more human.'

He lowered his camera and stared at her, as she kicked fretfully at the bridge with her leather boots. 'That's not fair,' he said.

'It damn well is,' said Susie. 'You've always been … you block yourself off. You always did. At least you're not permanently stoned anymore, but there's still always something in between you and the world, this weird obsessive project of yours or whatever. And you try to tell me about what's human? I don't get you sometimes.'

'This is ridiculous.' He ran a hand over his hair. 'I'm as much in the world as anyone. I've got a job, I've got people I know. Hell, I had a girlfriend until a couple of months ago.'

'Had would be the key word there.'

'Well, so what? It wasn't working out, I broke it off. It happens.' He could have said more hurtful things, and he thought of them – *you're going to lecture me about busted relationships?* – but he didn't want this to go so bad, so fast, he didn't want that.

'Yeah, because why exactly? You needed more time to wander around taking pictures of metal structures?'

He turned away from her. 'How about because I may be going blind, Susie? How about because it's not so easy to say to somebody, by the way, I may be blind soon, is that a problem for you?'

'So you're going to deal with that by cutting yourself off even more? Alex, you live with a *cat*.'

'Jesus fucking Christ!' He slammed his fist on the railing of the fence, hard enough to hurt. 'You, *you* of all people are talking to me about being isolated? You never even told me you were back. You never told me for eleven fucking years, so fuck you!' He ran down one short flight of steps, but then he stopped, breathing hard, unable to sustain anger.

'I'm sorry,' he said. Distantly, he heard water tossing in the stone channel.

'I care about you, Alex,' said Susie quietly. 'I really do. But you're already mixing me up.'

'I need to take these pictures.' He turned to look at her, standing on the bridge. Her face was half obscured by shadows. 'I need this. I know I can't do what I want to. I want to take pictures that will change people's lives, and I know I won't be able to, I know I'm not that good. But I can't help wanting it.' He walked up the steps towards her. 'This isn't about theory. This is about me. This is about me haemorrhaging inside my eyes. This about me losing the one thing I've ever had. This is about how I'm supposed to survive.'

He reached up and put his hand on her arm.

'Susie-Paul,' he said quietly. 'You're angry at me. I'm not even sure why, but I know there are reasons. But just – try to understand this.'

She looked down and shook her head, and didn't speak for a while. 'I guess I should go,' she said at last. 'I have to go and eat hors d'oeuvres with the big shots.'

'I'm sorry, Susie. Don't go yet.'

She sat down on the step. 'I think I should.'

He was leaning on the railing, drained, waiting for her to move. She would walk away this time, he thought, and that would be the end, and he wasn't even sure how that made him feel. But she was still on the step when he became aware of a noise, and then realized, to his astonishment, that his beeper was sounding.

'Good Lord.' He reached into his pocket. 'That's got to be the first time in two years this thing has gone off.'

'You have a beeper?'

'I do shifts on call sometimes. But it never actually goes off. I mean, how often do they need an emergency photo session?' He pushed a button on the beeper, turning the noise off, and breathed out heavily. 'Well, it means they're expecting criminal charges. It's got to be. God. I hate forensic.'

'Charges?'

'Maybe it's a car accident,' he said, thinking, *Assault. Rape.* 'I need to find a pay phone.'

'You can use my cell.' She reached into her jacket and took out a small phone, and he punched in the hospital number, spoke quickly to the dispatcher at the other end.

'I have to go,' he said, handing the phone back to her. 'I'm really sorry. They want me as soon as I can get there.'

'It's okay. I need to be at this party.'

'We have to talk, Susie.'

She shook her head, noncommittal. 'Sometime. Some other time.'

'I mean it.'

'Yeah.' She stood up and walked down the stairs. 'Whenever.'

But they couldn't say goodbye then, they had to ride the subway north together, awkward, edgy, until she got off at Rosedale, making uncertain promises to call.

Two people on the train were wearing surgical masks, and someone else had a scarf wrapped over his mouth. Alex stayed on until Davisville, and walked out of the station into a cold night wind. He stopped at a little restaurant, bought a falafel and ate it on the way to the hospital, tahini sauce leaking out over his fingers. Maybe he wouldn't see her again. He thought that at least, out of all of this, he knew where to find Adrian now, and that was something. It was definitely a good thing. Arriving at the hospital, he washed his hands with antibacterial soap and then called an internal number, was told to pick up his equipment and go to the burn ward.

It was going to be even worse than he had expected.

Outside the burn ward he found Janice Carriere, in her green scrubs, mask hanging down over her chest. 'What am I going to be seeing?' he asked.

She sighed. 'It looks like assault. What we've been told, he was beaten up first, then someone took a lighter to his clothes. Maybe they didn't intend to do this much damage.'

'Oh, shit. Is he … '

'I think he'll make it, but it's not pretty.'

'Is it a gang thing? Do you know?'

'Well, a group thing anyway. Gangs or not – I haven't got a lot of details. The police are over that way,' she waved vaguely, 'I had to send them out of the ward. He can't talk right now.'

'Is it a good time for me to go in?'

'Good as any. There's no procedures underway at the moment.'

He went into the scrub area, put on the gown, the mask, the gloves. You had to be especially careful in the burn ward; these were the most vulnerable of patients, their whole flesh exposed to the infective air. He adjusted his camera lens and took a breath. *Bodies in space*, he told himself, and entered the room. He smelled meat and scorched hair. .

Fire flays the skin, stripping it back off the muscle in brittle charring. And this was not something he could do quickly, however much he wanted to. He had to move slowly around the bed, the nurse stepping aside for him, making sure that it was all on film, the exact degree of harm. The arms, the legs, the hands, the torso. Black, scorched red, the parched white of dead tissue.

You could look worse. You could look worse and live, and be basically all right, after a while. You could look much better than this and still die. The man would need intravenous fluids, antibiotics, skin grafts, he would be mapped with scars like a lunar surface, but he might well live.

There would be pain. It was too soon now, the man was in shock, and drugged unconscious, but he would wake to pain, and the knowledge that his skin had been peeled back by fire.

Alex left the room, and put his hands over his eyes in the scrub area. The grilled-meat smell clung round him. He took off the sterile gown and went back to the hallway. Janice was talking to a policewoman, down past a line of empty stretchers. He signalled to her that he was finished, and she broke off her conversation and came back towards him.

'The photos can be on the hard drive more or less instantly. You want me to print them out right now?'

'That might be best.' She shook her head. 'Poor bugger.'

'You know any more about what happened?'

'You aren't even going to believe this.' Janice stretched out her hands and cracked her knuckles. 'Apparently he was standing by the subway station talking to himself and carrying a sports bag, and a bunch of drunk teenagers decided he was the subway poisoner.'

'Oh God, no.'

'That's what the police say. One of the kids also said the guy "looked Muslim," though another one is apparently calling him "the Jewish guy." So they're pretty clear that they're into hate crime, they just can't decide who it is they hate.'

'But, is he ... what was in the bag?'

'Dirty socks. Running shorts. I mean, I think he is a bit peculiar, talking to himself out loud and all, but ... ' She rubbed the back of her neck. 'It wouldn't have been so bad except that while they were hitting him, they spilled their booze on him. So when the lighter came out it had an accelerant. It's all just a mess. Anyway, if you can get the photos for the police, that'd be great.'

He went to his office, and while the photos were printing he put his head down on his folded arms, thinking about the burned man whose name he didn't know, thinking about Susie on the bridge in the city's hidden garden.

He felt nervous on the subway on the way home, anxious, as if someone were about to hit him in the back of the head or push him on the tracks. There was no reason for this, but it didn't seem familiar any longer, the empty cars estranged from him. The platforms echoing and deserted at College as he left the train and transferred to the streetcar, though it was not yet close to midnight, and the station should have been full of people, coming home from restaurants and meetings and sports events, going out to late-night clubs and parties. A man was standing at the corner of College and Yonge holding what seemed to be some kind of protest sign, a large piece of brown cardboard on which he had scrawled GEORGE BUSH TEXAS NORTH MURDER MORON BASTARD AMPHIBIAN, WE ARE NOT A MORON AT ALL.

Alex rode the streetcar to Grace, got off and crossed the street, and the man being held hostage came down the street to meet him. 'Sir, I hate to bother you, sir, you're always so kind … '

'Sure. Okay.' He took a two-dollar coin from his pocket and handed it over.

'Thank you so much, sir. I wouldn't ask … '

'Yeah. Whatever.' He didn't want to hear any more about this, about terrorists, or people falling from the sky, or blood coming out of the ears.

'Oh, oh, and another thing, sir?'

'Mmm?' He kept walking towards his doorway.

'The lady's brother, sir. The man you were trying to find. I made some calls to the important people. I can tell you where he is now, sir.'

A woman walked down Woodbine Avenue, carrying a slice of pizza in a greasy paper bag, and singing 'Life During Wartime' under her breath, a love song about tapped phone lines and vans full of guns. A woman alone at night, hypervigilant, listening for footsteps behind her, she sang to herself about burning her notebooks. Outside a subway station, municipal workers cleaned away scraps of scorched cloth and skin, while the burned man lay in isolation, his heart stuttering and slowing as the nurses ran lines of fluid into his bloodstream, fighting off shock, pulling him upwards as his body plunged down.

Two slight figures in leather jackets and fingerless gloves stopped in an alleyway near King and Bay. While one of them watched the passing traffic for police cars, the other pulled a can of paint from a scuffed khaki backpack and sprayed FEAR on the wall in black letters. They caught the King streetcar three blocks away, rode it to Spadina, and stopped in front of a blocky old office building, once again spraying FEAR against the bricks.

Across the city, harmless bacteria passed between individuals, carried by airborne particles or traces of saliva or the touch of a hand, our lives marked always by the proximity of others. And on this night or some night quite close in time, a germ woke up and began to inhabit someone's blood, in a way that was no longer innocent.

The girl who fell sat in her room in front of her laptop, frowning over an essay.

> Lord of the Flies *contains numerous characters which are all young boys. William Golding uses the characters to present many themes and big ideas that give the reader a lot to think about. So each of these characters has a very distinct personality.*

She leaned back from the keyboard, playing idly with a bangle on her wrist. On the bulletin board above her desk, beside a picture of last year's basketball team, she had pinned a postcard from a peace group, something she'd picked up outside the Eaton Centre; you were supposed to sign it and mail it to the prime minister or someone, but she wanted to leave it where it was, the hard-edged sketch of a hand, *Say No* printed across it in red.

Simon is in the choir but helps out differently to the others.

Out of the corner of her eye, she saw movement beyond her window. Someone was out there in the dark. She leaned closer to the glass, and for a moment she saw the two people in leather jackets, a boy and a girl, she thought, slipping between the posts of a fence and into the ravine. One of them carried a can of spray paint, and her hair had come loose from underneath her cap and swung down her back, dyed a startling green. She moved with quick precision over the stones at the edge of the slope.

What were they doing, those two, down in the ravine, those hidden, knowing people? The girl tried to imagine being out there in the dark, elusive and daring. The vivid figures, alone together, definite somehow in their mysterious task. She caught a vanishing glimpse of long green hair between the black branches of the trees.

This could never be her life. She could not be that kind of girl. She turned back to the laptop.

Simon is very good and pure. He meets up with a pig's head skewered on a stick, which becomes known as the Lord of the Flies.

She didn't much like this assignment. She didn't want to think about this, poor Simon crawling from the jungle into the circle of boys. Boys did that kind of thing, tearing butterflies to pieces, stomping on each other. What girls did was different.

She wondered if there was a book about what girls did, how you could talk about it. She imagined starting to write that book, what you can do with fingernails, what you can do with secrets.

She looked out the window again to see if the people with the spray paint were still visible. Nothing moved in the darkness, but written across the bars of the fence she saw a single word, painted in thick fast strokes. FEAR.

Alex took the wooden footbridge over Rosedale Valley Road, walking level with the tops of the bare broken trees, and turned onto one of the winding streets of Rosedale. Small cedars lined the sloping walkway to the house, behind a stone wall landscaped with climbing vines; there were rosebushes by the door, and holly trees, sprinkled with tiny Christmas lights, which he feared might have been planted specifically for the season.

Susie had been right about the Filipina maids; one of them opened the door when he knocked, and took his coat before he could stop her, and another immediately tried to offer him a glass of wine, smiling with the faded intensity of someone who had been smiling for many hours.

'I'm just here to pick someone up,' he said, and she showed him through the hallway, past a Chinese stone horse, a crackle-glaze vase.

There were little groups of people scattered around the sunken living room, under a Kurelek painting that he presumed to be original. But whatever the art on the walls, the late stages of every party were fearfully similar. Glasses sat abandoned on tables and mantlepieces with the acidic dregs of red wine clinging to them, in a litter of broken crackers and olive pits. On one side table, a tray holding a scatter of cheese rinds, three half-rotten grapes and a single curl of smoked salmon. Someone smoking by an open window.

From an adjoining room he could hear an emotional, muffled discussion; in front of him, people huddled on sofas, their heads bent together to exclude the other groups from their conversation. That time at the burnt-out end of the evening, the sudden intimacies and old resentments gathering like piles of cigarette ash. Susie was sitting alone in a chair by the fireplace, gripping a glass of wine. He crossed the room and knelt down beside her.

'I'm sorry I didn't get here sooner. I had to feed my cat.'

'Your guy was really sure about this?'

'It was pretty detailed. Now, remember, this comes from a man who thinks that terrorists are trying to kill him because he has too much knowledge about the components of the body. You can decide how much faith you want to put in it.'

She laughed, a bit wildly. Her cheeks were flushed and her eyes too bright. 'This is insane. I've been interviewing people on the street for months. And you talk to one guy. *One* guy. Fuck. Just … fuck.'

He put his hand on her knee without really thinking. 'Are you all right? Don't get too fixed on this, Susie. It might not even be true.'

'We'll need a flashlight,' she said.

'What?'

'I don't know if there's going to be anyplace open to buy one, is the problem.'

'Oh, Susie, no. We can't go right now.'

'Yes. We can. We have to.' She drank the rest of the wine in her glass. 'If I don't go now, I'll never go.'

'We can't. It's not safe.'

'It's fine, I've been down there before. There's a whole community by River Street, I've done interviews there.'

'Yeah, but not at midnight.'

'So he told me he wanted to see me incorporate Aristotle's *Poetics*,' said a woman on the couch, her voice rising passionately. 'Never mind that my entire argument is anti-Aristotelian! I mean, honest to God!' She broke off as if she were about to start crying.

'I can't stand it here much longer, Alex,' said Susie. She stood up, and he followed her through a hallway and into the kitchen, where a particularly well-dressed group was clustered at a granite-topped island, debating something in low voices. 'It's supposed to be a big honour for me to be invited at all, you know.' She found an open bottle of wine and poured herself another glass. 'You want a drink?' He shook his head. 'Because I'm just a grad student. There aren't many grad students here.' She leaned against the counter, her arm touching his. 'I should be honoured, right? Instead I just think, I can't deal with this world. I don't even mean Rosedale. I mean anyone who doesn't have a brother living in a ravine.'

'That covers a lot of ground.'

'I'll make an exception for Evvy. Evvy gets to be in my world.'

'I really welcome this opportunity for collaboration,' a woman at the island was saying, but Alex saw that several of the men were looking their way. This was the thing about being with Susie in public, he thought; he had to notice other men noticing her. And of course they did, she was lovely. It made him very aware of himself, a thin, worn, grey-haired man, chewing on a carrot stick.

131

Susie was drinking fast; she'd finished most of the glass already. 'If you want to go down the ravine tonight, you should at least lay off the wine,' he said.

'You're right,' she said, draining the glass and refilling it. 'That would be the smart thing to do.'

'I'm just saying.'

'Let me tell you about Derek.' She pushed a strand of hair from her face. 'Derek was brilliant. Fucking brilliant. A lot of people with schizophrenia are very bright, but Derek was, like, stratospheric. And I … I should have known something was wrong. We were so close, Alex, I should have, I did know, I must have known … ' Her voice wavered and broke and she drank half the glass in one swallow. 'Fuck that anyway. There's so many things, there's too fucking many things I could be angry about.' She reached for the wine bottle again. She was drinking very fast; she was drinking to get drunk.

'Derek doesn't necessarily present as severely delusional,' she said, stumbling over the sibilants. 'Sometimes he knows how to play the game. But he's got this whole fucked system. It'd take me all night to explain it to you, but just as an example, there's this part of it that's all about semen. Which most of the time means he's forbidden to have sex, not that this is difficult in his circumstances, but then at certain times he has to expend the semen, you see, so he ends up spending most of his cheque on hookers. Picture that he shared all of this information with me, and you'll have some idea what my family life is like. At least that's how it used to go. It sounds like he's onto a new phase now.' She lifted one hand and quickly wiped the corner of her eye. 'And I'm supposed to stand around in this fucking mansion and care about the fucking university's fucking problems?'

'We don't have to stay, do we?'

'It's hereditary, do you know that?' she went on. 'Twins. Think about it.' She took another deep gulp of wine. 'The risk's not as bad for fraternals as it is for identicals, but it's still pretty high. But I'm probably safe now. You don't often have your first psychotic break in your late thirties. It happens, but not as much. I mean, I'm fucked in every kind of way, but I know I'm not schizophrenic.'

'Let's just go,' said Alex, touching her shoulder. 'I'll get our coats.'

'Right. You do that, then,' she said, emptying the bottle into her glass, her gestures loose and abrupt. 'I'll be waiting right here.'

The living room seemed to have experienced one of those random elevations of mood that sometimes happen after midnight; people were now animated and laughing, with the exception of the anti-Aristotelian woman, who was weeping quietly while a maid tidied away a broken glass. He could smell pot somewhere, but couldn't quite tell what direction it was coming from. He walked through to the foyer, and down another hallway, past a pink-walled room with an antique writing desk and a vase of forced hyacinths, their sugary scent filling the corridor, and finally found the tired maid who had taken his coat; she sent him on to a closet where he collected it, along with Susie's quilted jacket.

When he came back into the kitchen Susie was still leaning on the counter with yet another glass of wine, looking small and belligerent as a bearded man in a dark suit hung onto her arm, talking to her intensely. Alex paused in the doorway and she turned to him; he tipped his head towards the exit and she nodded, finished the glass and pushed herself unsteadily off the counter.

'Suzanne!' exclaimed the bearded man. 'Surely you're not leaving us so soon?'

'Yes, Douglas,' said Susie. 'I am. As a matter of fact, I've just discovered that my brother is living in the Don Valley ravine, and my friend and I are going to look for him. So, you know, have fun.' She pulled Alex into the living room.

'Douglas wants to screw me,' she said. 'That's the only reason I got invited here. He's a power broker in the department, too. If I had any ambition at all I'd do it.'

'Ah,' said Alex. They reached the foyer, and she pulled on her jacket and fumbled with the buttons, reached for the door handle and then changed her mind.

'Hey,' she said. 'I know. Hang on a minute.' She grabbed one of the carved wooden panels on the wall and pulled it open, revealing boots, a tennis racket, an assortment of coats. 'Okay, no luck here.'

She opened a second panel and found a wall of shelves filled with gardening tools, bottles of antifreeze and a big industrial flashlight. 'Yes! I knew it!' She grabbed the flashlight and tucked it under her jacket, a move that did not conceal it even slightly.

'Susie! What are you doing?'

'What do you think I'm doing? Stealing a flashlight.' She giggled suddenly and put a hand over her mouth.

'They're going to notice it's gone, for Christ's sake.'

'I don't give a fuck. This is like, this is like me losing a penny. Screw them.'

'Are you twelve years old or what?'

'Come on. Let's get out of here.' She pushed open the door and they stepped out onto the walkway, a furtive little knot of pot-smoking professors huddled by the side of the house, the branches of the trees creaking in a harsh wind.

'Susie.' He put his hands on her shoulders. 'Susie-Sue. Please. Not tonight. Please just let me take you home. We can go first thing tomorrow.'

'I told you, Alex,' she said, pulling away from him. 'I have to do this now. It has to be now.'

'People are sleeping,' he said, desperate for some rationale. 'If we even find him, he'll probably be asleep.'

'No problem,' said Susie. 'When he's off his meds, he's nocturnal.' She lost her footing on the step at the end of the walkway and caught herself on the wall. 'Jesus, I didn't mean to get this drunk. No, that's not true, I totally did.'

'Okay, Susie,' said Alex, throwing up his hands. 'You win. You always win. We will go down into the ravine and look for your brother under the guidance of the man who's making great progress on cleaning systems.'

'Good. Thank you.'

'Just give me the stolen flashlight, okay?'

She walked ahead of him along the street, but then stopped at the corner, and he caught up and found her looking confused. 'This way,' he said, touching her elbow. 'Up Glen Road.'

'It's all twisty here. The streets. I never know where I am.'

'Yeah, well, you're just lucky I spend my time wandering around taking pictures of metal structures.' But she didn't react; she didn't remember.

'I forgot to ask you, that call you got. What was it in the end?'

'You probably don't want to know,' said Alex.

'No, tell me.'

'It was an assault. It was horrible. I don't much want to talk about it.'

'I'm sorry.' She squeezed his hand.

'Somebody got burned up because they thought he was the subway poisoner.'

'God. God, this is so fucked. I don't know what's happening to this city.'

'Me neither. Adrian thinks we've been cursed.'

Susie giggled again. 'Fuck. What a concept. Who does he blame?'

'The government, I suppose. That's who he always used to blame.' He detached his hand from hers and stuck it in his coat pocket. Below the road the earth fell away, another valley opening beneath them, sheer and dizzy, into a well of darkness.

'I hate this fucking neighbourhood,' said Susie, still giggling, as they left the bridge and continued north, past wide yards filled with trees outlined in fairy lights. 'I just want to scrape the paint on their Mercedes with my house keys.'

'Oh yeah. Resort to vandalism. That's always good.'

At the end of Glen Road they turned and took another short street into a park, walked across the grass until they had passed through a fence of bushes and found themselves at the top of a steep hill. Alex turned on the flashlight and scanned the bushes until he found a narrow track leading downwards into the shadows. He started to scramble down, his boots sinking in the slippery mud, but Susie tripped and fell almost immediately. 'Goddamn,' she moaned. 'This is my only good dress. Look at this.' Her stockings were covered with mud, and there was a large smear across the front of the dress; clearly not thinking, she wiped her caked hands on the sleeves of her jacket.

'Okay, c'mere.' He stretched out his hand, and she took it and and stumbled towards him, the shock of her body against his, and he thought, *Oh shit. Oh no.* He caught his breath, his arm moving around her waist to pull her closer, *Oh no.* Then, bracing his feet, he steadied them down the long slope to a forking path at the bottom.

'I think we're on level ground from now on,' he said, though she continued to lean against him, her hand pressing into his back. He didn't take his arm away. They turned to the right, the mud sucking and clinging to their boots. The wind was muffled by the wooded hills on either side of them, but his ears and fingers were stinging with the cold. He aimed the flashlight ahead, and then swung it to either side, looking for any signs of habitation.

'Wait for me a sec.' He let go of her and walked off the edge of the path, into the snow beneath the trees, circling the flashlight around him, trying to see into the woods as far as he could, but he wasn't good with darkness, he couldn't see much. She probably didn't remember that either. He stood at the edge of a deep gully, hearing water running below; came back to Susie, and she leaned into his chest again, wrapping both her arms around him.

They walked on, and then he saw a signpost on his left, between two hills. 'Okay. That'll be the brickworks.' He led her off the main track to a smaller path that ran sharply downwards, and he could make out the shape of the old brickworks now, and a smaller building at the side lit up with orange security lamps. They crossed a concrete plaza, ponds and wetlands spreading out around them, and then they were beside the great hulk of the abandoned factory, which had been haphazardly tidied and repaired, a strangely inaccessible cultural monument. The wind was worse here, howling around them in the broad exposed flat.

Susie shook her head. 'This doesn't look right,' she said. 'I don't think he'd live near a, an attraction. And it's not far from the road, listen.'

'Well, it's maybe not a very successful attraction. But I don't know. Anyway, it sounded like he was a ways behind it.'

He turned the flashlight into the factory hall, picking out the blurry shapes of men in sleeping bags among the twisted piles of old machinery, and pointed to them wordlessly. Susie left his arm and moved skittishly towards the men, veering at an angle, but then she saw empty bottles lying by the sleeping bags and shook her head and returned.

'They were drinking,' she said. 'Derek doesn't drink.'

'He could've started.'

'No. He wouldn't. Anyway, they're just crashing. Your guy said he had a tent, right? He's settled in.'

There was another mud path, narrow and sloping upwards, leading on beside a fence. It ran by the parts of the brickworks that had never been restored, that were smashed and boarded up and covered with graffiti. There were no lights here; Alex turned the flashlight on again. Susie tripped on a tree root and fell again, and cut her knee, and he bent and took her back into his arms. Thistles bit and lodged in their clothes.

The path led them around a corner, to the back of the vast dark walls. In the beam of the flashlight Alex saw a sign with a hazard symbol and the words *Asbestos and silica contaminated area. Do not enter.* They passed the warning, around the corner of a barbed-wire fence into a clearing. Not far beyond them was the railway overpass, towering on massive concrete pilasters, reaching up far above their heads, far beyond where he could see.

He stopped, and lowered the flashlight. 'Susie. Look.'

Somewhere up the hill was another light, distant, below the railway bridge, a small wavering point.

'Oh,' whispered Susie. 'Oh dear. I think it is.'

'We're going to have to get up the hill.'

At first it was thick with dried grass and weeds, waist-high for Alex, nearly chest-high for Susie, a crackling barricade. He couldn't climb up with his arm around her, but he stretched out one hand behind him, and she held it and followed him, stumbling through the vegetation. They reached the first concrete foot of the underpass, and here the slope turned muddy, and much steeper, clogged with fallen trees and stones.

Alex released her hand and grabbed on to the branches of the dead trees to pull himself along, bent over, fighting gravity. Susie, beside him, was on her hands and knees now, unable to get up the hill any other way. He slid and fell onto his hands himself, dragged himself upwards on another branch.

He reached the next concrete foot and boosted himself onto it, then stretched down and grabbed Susie's arms, hauling her awkwardly up.

Anchoring himself against a tree stump, he turned to look up the last expanse of slope. The light had gone out. Alex aimed the flashlight that way, and it illuminated the outline of a tent. A green tent, just like the man had said.

'He must have heard us coming,' said Susie.

The tent was pitched under the last wall of the underpass, where it drew even with the top of the hill. There was a small level area around it, scraped clean, and two milk crates holding something, he couldn't see what. The slope where they were was steep, precipitous; they struggled further up, mud-covered, scraped, and then, some yards from the tent, Susie put her hand on his arm.

'Stay here,' she said. 'You'll have to stay here.' She squeezed her eyes tight shut and opened them again. 'I have to do this.'

He stayed on the hill, in the wind, leaning against the broken trunk of an old tree. And he watched her, Susie, on her hands and knees in the mud, crawling unsteadily up the hill, over the rocks, towards the doorway of the green tent.

She stopped outside the front flap, still on her knees. The person in the tent must know she was there.

'Derek?' he heard her whisper shakily.

There was no answer from the tent right away.

'Derek?'

'Is that Susie-Paul?'

'Of course it is.' She sat down in the mud and wrapped her arms around her legs.

'That doesn't make sense.'

'Oh, for fuck's sake, Derek. Who else would climb all the way up here just to look for you?'

The light came on inside the tent, and then a man opened the flap and crept out, holding a lantern in one hand and a book in the other. 'Well, hello then,' he said.

He didn't look much like the man in the photo. He was horribly thin, emaciated really, and he had mouse-coloured hair down to his shoulders and a straggly beard, a scabbed-over cut on his forehead. He bobbed one leg nervously as he sat, tapping the book against his knee. The glasses were gone, and his eyes, Susie's deep brown eyes, looked freakishly large in his sunken face.

'You're not well,' she said.

'I'm fine,' said Derek. 'I'm doing quite well, in fact.'

'You look like you're starving.'

'I've been reducing my caloric needs. But I don't starve. I'm exploring the possibilities of agriculture.' He waved his hand around the small level zone. 'As you can see, I'm engaged in subsistence farming.'

'Jesus.'

'In the interim I still have some needs I can't meet from the surrounding land, but I hope to achieve complete self-sufficiency by 2005.'

'Oh, yeah. You and North Korea,' said Susie. And unexpectedly, Derek's face lit up in a luminous sweet smile. Susie's smile.

'Oh, Susie-Paul. It *is* you.' He put his hand out and stroked her arm, and she raised her face to him. 'It's always so good to see you,' he said.

'Then why have you been hiding from me?'

Derek tilted his head to one side. 'But I don't, baby girl. I never would.'

'I haven't seen you for three months. I didn't know if you were dead.'

He ran his hand down her arm again, leaning towards her. 'You're my baby sister soul. You can't be far away from me, can you? You're with me here every day. We're together eternally. You remember.'

They looked so much alike now, their eyes on each other. 'No,' said Susie softly. 'This is what you're imagining, Derek. I've never been here before.'

'I'm sorry, baby. I'm sorry you can't remember. I want to look after you. I wish you'd let me.'

He came close to her, a small submissive movement of his head. She took his hands and held them in her lap. 'Oh God,' she whispered. 'I've been so worried.'

'It's all right, baby. It's really all right. You know I'll look after you.'

She reached out and stroked his wild hair. 'Derek, Derek, it's going to be winter soon, you can't go on living here.'

'This is a good place,' said Derek. 'This is a safe place. They can't get the brainwashing chemicals at us here.'

'Oh no. Not the brainwashing chemicals again.' Alex saw a dark trail of mascara run down her face and knew she was crying.

'Susie-Paul, of all the people in the world, you are the one I need to save. I need to help you. Don't you understand that?'

'I love you, Derek, but you're out of your mind,' said Susie, her voice full of tears. 'You have a mental illness. Your theories about sodium pentothal and computer rays, they are not real. I do not talk to you when I am not here, and I have never been here before.'

'But of course you have,' he said. He touched her face, running a finger gently over her smeared mascara. 'We're the same person, baby. We were born together. We're the same body forever, and I can't be safe without you.'

'No, Derek. We're not. We're really, really not.'

'We could be. If we were together.'

'No. Not ever, Derek. That's not who I am.'

Derek moved his hand down her neck, his shoulders bending. Then he lowered himself to the wet ground and lay his head in her lap, and she curled over him, still stroking his hair.

'I know it's not easy for you,' she said. 'I know it was really, it was confusing for you when Mom died. But this is not a solution.'

Derek lifted his head and looked up at her, his legs twitching, his tongue flicking nervously over his lips. 'Don't lie to me, Susie-Paul.'

'I'm not lying. What do you mean, I'm lying?'

'Susie-Paul.' There was a dangerous edge to his voice. 'You know they're not dead. You know this is just a trick. You need to stop telling lies.'

'For Christ's sake.' Susie sat up sharply. 'Stop it, Derek. Of course they're dead. Mom had cancer. Dad had a heart attack. They died.'

'Stupid,' said Derek, the word a brittle snap. 'You know it's not true. You're letting them trick you.'

Susie choked down a hiccupy whimper and pushed back, moving away from him. 'Cut it out. I buried them, Derek, I saw the coffins going into the dirt. People die. They're dead.'

Derek shook his head again, quickly. 'They're still watching you, baby. They're still after you. I know because you tell me. You tell me all the time.'

'Derek! Stop!' She clenched her fists in front of her mouth and began to sob.

Derek was squatting by the tent, staring at her seriously, and he was twitching a bit but there was no question that Susie, muddy and drunk and weeping, looked far more crazy than he did. 'Just shut up,' she said, her face glistening in the light of the lantern, streaked and wet. 'I fucking buried them, Derek. They're under the fucking ground.'

'I didn't mean to make you feel bad,' he said softly.

Alex could hardly tell what the noise was that Susie made, but he thought it was meant to be a laugh. 'Well, that's great. That's just lovely. Everything's fine, then.'

He moved towards her again, suppliant, almost crawling, and put his hands on her knees. 'Susie-Paul. Baby sister. You know I never mean to hurt you. I'm sorry. I'm a bad person. I'm sorry.'

'You're not bad, Derek.' She wiped her smeared eyes and lowered her head again to his. 'You don't have to apologize.'

'I love you, baby.'

'I know. I know.'

Alex didn't think that he'd moved; he hardly thought that he'd breathed. But he must have done something, because Derek's head lifted suddenly and he glanced down the hill.

'You brought a person with you.'

'He's my friend.'

'I don't like that.'

'Well, tough luck,' said Susie.

Derek sat up and frowned towards Alex. 'I don't know why you have to involve other people.'

'Because other people matter to me. You just have to live with that.'

'It's really not safe,' said Derek, shaking his head in disapproval. 'I've told you that before. These are not safe people.'

Alex tried to catch Susie's eye, not knowing if he should go back down the hill.

'Anyway,' said Susie. 'None of this is why I'm here. We need to find you a proper place to live.'

'This is better than where I was before.'

Susie looked around the underpass. 'You know, honest to God, it's probably not much worse. But the rooming house did at least have some heating.'

'People tried to hurt me there.'

'What I want, what I hope is that we can find you a better place. There's some money from Mom's will, it's not a lot but ... '

The change was like an electric shock, so fast Alex was dumbfounded. Derek leapt up, his fingers reaching and convulsing like snakes, his voice a high screech.

'You *bitch*! You fucking *bitch*!' He grabbed at her sleeve, shaking her arm hard, but Susie didn't seem frightened; she dropped her head in resignation and wept but didn't move away. 'You think you can trick me that way?' he shouted, still shaking her arm, his other hand moving clawlike near her face. 'You think I'm an idiot? You *fucking bitch*!'

'Shut up, Derek,' said Susie quietly.

'Get out of here! Get out!' He pulled away from her and hurled himself back into the tent, zipping the flap closed. 'Go away *now*, bitch!' Susie buried her head in her knees, sobbing, Derek screaming from the tent, 'Go *away*! Go *away*!'

And Alex moved, scrambling up the slope towards her and taking her wrist. 'Susie. Come.' She shook her head, waving him away with her other hand. 'Come on, come on, honey,' whispered Alex.

'Go *away*, go *away*, go *away*!' screamed Derek.

'He isn't going to hurt me.'

'I'm not afraid of him hurting you. Honey, come with me.' Alex pulled her up and away from the tent, out from beneath the underpass, crawling with her, up the last steep slope to a level field, Derek howling, 'Go *away*, go *away*!' below them. They came out at the edge of the railway track, and she staggered and fell against him on the narrow outcrop before the rail. They stood in the snow, staring at each other, out of breath, Susie hanging on to his arms, Derek still shouting below them.

'I have to go back,' she said.

'What the hell do you think you're going to do? Drag him out?'

'Not like this. I can't leave like this.' She had barely taken half a step onto the plunging slope before she slipped, skidding down on her side and grabbing at a thorny branch, landing on her knees, Alex thought. But he couldn't really tell, she was in darkness now, hardly visible.

'Derek,' she called, and Derek screamed, wordless, a long keening wail. 'I'm going now,' Susie yelled above the noise. 'Derek, I will come back. We will work this out.' Alex was standing uncertainly on the tiny strip of snow between the track and the downslope, listening for trains. 'Goodbye, Derek,' shouted Susie, and he tried to make out the shape of her as she fought her way up the hill one more time. As soon as he could see her clearly, he grabbed her arm and hurried her across the tracks into the field beyond, then stopped, uncertain what to do next.

'Where are we?' she panted.

'Oh God, I don't know.' Car lights were moving below them, an arc of highway surrounding the dark wedge of the hill, a few bright windows in the apartment towers across the valley. 'Bayview. That must be Bayview.' He moved towards the lights, reaching the verge of another steep hill where brush and thistles as tall as Susie's head rose out of the snow, and he held her tight to his chest and slid downwards, a controlled fall through dry branches towards the gravel shoulder. The world mostly visible again, he stared at the passing cars, trying to orient himself, to understand where he was.

'Okay,' he said at last. 'I think I know how to get out of here.'

There was a traffic light about twenty feet up the shoulder, and it took them across Bayview onto Pottery Road. And on the bend of Pottery Road, at three in the morning, there was a man selling roses from plastic buckets, a thick luminescent green necklace wound around his forehead, glowing pink and yellow bracelets lining his arms, his piles of roses interspersed with flashing red artificial flowers. He looked at Alex and Susie hopefully as they came in his direction. ROSES $5 written on the buckets in black marker.

The thin sidewalk was intermittent; they had to walk on the shoulder most of the way, past the glowing man and up the road, across the Don River and beneath another underpass, to the foot of a hill. On their left side Alex saw a dreamlike array of wooden ponies, floodlit beneath a yellow billboard declaring the place to be Fantasy Farm. Smaller signs admonished *Fantasy Farm Is Private Property*, and *Please Do Not Climb On The Antique Carriage*. The ponies reared and pranced between pools of darkness.

On the right side was a proper sidewalk, protected from the road by a concrete divider, on which someone had sprayed the word FEAR in black paint. He stepped onto the pavement, weak with relief. 'We can follow this street up to Broadview,' he said. 'When we get to Broadview we'll be back in the real world.'

'I'm so tired, Alex,' said Susie, who hadn't spoken since the traffic light.

'I know.' He put his arm around her again. 'It isn't far. You'll be okay.'

But it was up another hill, and he was tired as well, too tired. He couldn't stop and get out his glucometer here, but climbing hills in the middle of the night would be driving his sugar down badly; he needed carbohydrates before a hypo set in.

They made it to the top of the hill, and it was Broadview and Mortimer. There were perfectly normal small houses, and a dental clinic, and rows of little strip malls on either side of the street, the stores locked for the night. There had to be someplace that was open, he thought, seriously worried now about his blood sugar. Anyplace. And yes, there was a lit building about a block away.

'Let's go that way,' he said, and got close enough to see that it was something called the Donut Wheel Diner – perfect, he would be all right.

It was a small place, doughnuts in racks behind the counter, plastic-wrapped sandwiches, and a big handwritten sign over the cash that said WE NOW SELL BEER!! It was long after last call, but the one other patron had clearly taken full advantage of this opportunity before going to sleep at his table.

He asked for an orange juice and a cream-cheese bagel, which would very possibly send his sugar too high. But he was beyond calculation, had been unprepared for any of this, had let Susie lead him to the brink of disaster yet again.

Susie rubbed her head, squinting against the light. 'Oh God,' she muttered. 'I think I'm starting to sober up. Oh God.'

'I'm pretty sure I could get you a beer,' said Alex. 'I think it's like a doughnut speakeasy.'

'When I want you to be funny I'll tell you,' said Susie.

'Black coffee?'

'Please.'

They sat down at a little round table, and Susie sipped her coffee and rubbed her head again. She was covered with mud, and her stockings were torn, a rip down one sleeve of her jacket, a thin scratch on her cheek. There was mascara all over her face and she was not nearly sober yet. Alex reached across the table and took her hand; the palm was scraped and bloody.

'Are you all right?' he asked.

'That's a strange question.'

'I'm sorry. I didn't know.'

She lifted her free hand and began to chew on a dirty thumbnail, and this seemed to Alex like a gesture from a distant past. 'He's my brother, Alex. In our own sick way, we've always looked after each other. I can't just leave him there and let him freeze to death.'

'He seems pretty determined.'

'Well, he's insane, isn't he? That helps.'

He ate his bagel with one hand. 'Let me take you home,' he said again. 'I can get you a taxi.'

Susie shook her head. 'We're near my house. It's a ten-minute walk.'

'I'll come with you, then.'

'I think I can get home safely.'

'I know. But I'll come with you.'

And it was a plain, human place again as they walked. Small brick houses with snowy lawns and strings of red Christmas lights over the eaves, the windows dark, residential streets as quiet as sleep. She stopped at a house on Carlaw, just north of the Danforth.

'I rent the second floor here,' she said.

They sat down on the top step of the porch. 'I just need to catch my breath a minute,' said Alex, looking at her dark hair lying against the pale line of her cheek.

'Sure.' She rested her chin on her knees. 'He never got to have an adult life, you know,' she said quietly. 'Not really. He was ... he was just so young. When he ... There were so many things he never got to have.' She ran her thumbnail back and forth across her lips. 'Sometimes I think I'll forget how it was. It'd be easier if I did.'

'Tell me.'

'I don't know. What can you say? He was never ordinary. He had this – there was this magic thing about him. Something ... so bright and ... strange – he had these giant diagrams he'd drawn, hung up on his walls – and I never understood hard science, but they were really beautiful. The structure of things. He understood that. And – I wasn't alone. That was the thing. Derek was there. I was never – there was someone who cared about me. Always. That's all, that's ... He was going to be a chemist. That's pretty fucked, isn't it, if you think about it?'

'The difference between chemicals and emotions?'

Susie lifted her hand, palm up.

'Neurotransmitters,' she said. 'The dopamine hypothesis. Serotonin. I know all about these things, Alex. The neuroendocrine system, I get that. But what does that mean? This is my brother. This is who he is. There is no real Derek somewhere else. That brain is real. And it suffers.'

'I know.' He could hear traffic in the distance, but the street was still and empty.

'We're all the same as Derek, you know. In the end, we are. We're all just trying to hammer together some kind of self around the chemical reactions.' She ran a hand across her eyes. 'Look at us. You get angry for no reason when you're going hypo. I stole a flashlight tonight because I got drunk. Is that real? Is that chemical? What's the difference? You fell in love with me back at *Dissonance* because you were smoking too much pot.'

'No,' said Alex. 'No. That wasn't why.'

But the truth was that he had, back then, never known why, and never wondered; his emotions had been instant and opaque and he had expected nothing else. He had known so little about her.

'Why didn't you ever call me?' he asked, his voice very low.

'It was too hard,' murmured Susie, staring out at the street. 'It was just too hard.'

He raised his arm, and the motion had the weird dreamy slowness of an inevitable act. With the mingled hunger and sickness of someone going back to a familiar drug, he stroked her hair away from her face. He kissed her neck and tasted salt. She turned towards him and reached up, her mouth soft against his.

'Oh no,' he whispered, after a while. 'No, this is a very bad idea.'

'Yes,' said Susie, running her hands down his chest.

He bent and touched his lips to her hair. 'This is a train wreck,' he said. And then he was kissing her again, she was sucking his tongue, pulling him further into her mouth, and it went on forever, and he thought that he could dissolve in this, in this sweetness, the joints of his body coming undone. Wrecked, addicted, gone.

In her bedroom they stood apart from each other for a moment, still fully clothed, hesitant, and he was much more afraid now than he had been in his twenties, older than he should be and far too aware of all the things that could go wrong. Then she moved towards him, and he lifted her small burning hand and licked the drying blood from her palm.

Plague Days

erek Rae's life in the ravine is, after its manner, a life well-organized. His time is measured by the regular catastrophe of the trains passing over his head, thunderous and dirty, an assault of noise. The days and weeks are shaped by weather, the poison sun and debilitating humidity of late summer shading slowly into the long cold nights and the sheltering snow.

He doesn't know that the girls are falling down. It is a shame, perhaps, that no one has told him, because Derek is closer to the heart of the problem than anyone thinks. But this is how it is, he doesn't take the subway, he doesn't read the newspapers.

Though Derek is radically isolated, he is not in fact quite without human contact. He is known to the street nurses, for instance, who bring him the bottles of water and tins of Ensure that now constitute his entire diet; the nurses have not passed this information on to his sister because Derek does not speak to them, so they are unable to determine whether they have his consent.

Sometimes he comes out of his tent and sits in Chorley Park, but he does not think he will do that again after what happened the last time.

When it becomes most urgently necessary – no longer very often – he will cross over to Broadview and ask for change until he can afford to visit one of the city's more desperate and undiscriminating sex workers. His library is made up mostly of books and magazines he has found lying in bus shelters or coffee shops, though in a few cases he has stolen them from the public library, because books are a singularly pressing requirement, the one thing left that resembles his vanished life. Sometimes he finds mittens and hats discarded on the hiking path, and these sustain him in the coldest weather.

None of this represents the truth of Derek's existence, his passions and his miseries, the battles he wages all alone against pains and fears and the forces of universal gravitation. The raw courage that is required of him every day. His hard-won choice to continue living, when so many possibilities to stop are offered at every hand, the cars on the highway, the trains on the tracks, an end to the daily loss. None of this represents Derek's soul, scraped bloody, howling, fighting always to hang on, a solitary superhuman ordeal, unacknowledged by the world, unrewarded.

These things are known. Somewhere, they are known. But they are not to be spoken of.

And up and down the city, people pursued their lives, their own small braveries and defeats; they walked dogs and drilled holes in the street, wiped the noses of other people's children. At the corner of Bloor and Spadina, just before dawn, a shirtless man pulled out a knife and began to cut his arms and chest, spilling gouts of raspberry blood on the sidewalk, and as the police took him away he spoke of crimes against order, of the subway cars falling apart in rot and atomic disintegration, entropy calling them home.

Later, at this same corner, a woman would stagger and fall, and hives would break out on her face. The panhandlers who sat on the newspaper boxes, blind drunk at ten in the morning, laughed at first, and then watched her twisting on the street, biting her own lip until she drew blood, and one of them ran and pounded his fist on the window of the bagel shop until he saw the waitress pick up the phone to call 911. Then he ran, staggering and falling with his friends, to the park down the block. They lay on the dead grass of the park and laughed again and wept.

In the hospital, the burned man dreamed of paper snowflakes, clean-edged and white and cool, falling to cover his bed. His body a field, extending through space. He lay beneath the blue light of the dream, the taste of dirt and honey in his mouth, and the paper snow filled the concave vault of space, this man his own world in his opiate sleep, the fire on the far horizon.

The first thing Alex thought when he woke up was that he had to make sure Susie was still there; and she was, though she had pulled the covers over her head and was nearly invisible. Of course, it was her apartment, so the chances of her leaving in the night were minimal. He moved closer to her, in the warm envelope of the duvet, running one hand along the curve of her spine and pressing his face into the soft skin of her neck, but she didn't seem close to waking, and his second and much more rational thought was that he didn't know what time it was, and he needed to find his insulin kit immediately.

He pushed himself out of the bed with an abrupt silent movement. The bedroom was chilly and dark, a heavy curtain over the window; he found his underpants and jeans near the bed, then crept into the middle of the room, going more by touch than anything else, and located his coat, and the fabric purse in the pocket. There was more light in the hallway. He left the bedroom, easing the door closed behind him, and sat on the hall floor to check his sugar. It was too high for a morning level, and it must have been much higher in the night. That was no good. Not as instantly life-threatening as a hypo, but it was the high levels that did the lasting harm, that set the capillaries overgrowing behind his retinas, that threatened neuropathy, kidney problems, heart failure.

Acting automatically, he calculated his dosage, drew up the clear fluid into a syringe and injected, tucked the used needle back into the kit. But this was a whole new problem; now he needed to eat within the next half-hour, preferably sooner, or his sugar would plummet.

The kitchen at the end of the hallway was small and cramped and rather untidy, but there was a large window looking out onto the backyard and the alleyway beyond. A dirty dish and cup in the sink, a kettle on the counter, a coffee maker; some bits of paper stuck to the refrigerator door, reminders about dental appointments and books due at the university library. Tentatively, he opened the fridge. A bottle of cranberry juice and a carton of milk, takeout containers with noodles and leftover chicken wings inside, part of a loaf of rye bread, a cinnamon bun in a paper bag, plastic-wrapped chunks of havarti and feta cheese, some organic rhubarb jam from a health-food store. On a shelf nearby, a jar of peanut butter and a tin of cocoa. He took the peanut butter down and made himself a sandwich, poured a glass of juice. He would have liked some hot chocolate, but he thought he should cause a minimum of disturbance, he shouldn't seem to be laying claim to her kitchen.

About ten-thirty, according to the clock on the stove. He sat down at the table and looked out the window into the backyard, chewing the bread and peanut butter. It was a very clear, still morning, the sky a low field of white cottony snow falling slowly. Someone ran along the alleyway with a dog. Looked like a Labrador. Some kind of big dog, anyway.

Floaters. He'd noticed them already, of course, though he couldn't say exactly when. Sometime after he came out into the light. Floaters, impossible to count how many, dancing like burnt-out novas at the margins of his field of vision. Tiny hemorrhages, the possible forerunners of something much worse; stress-induced explosions of the proliferating blood vessels. He couldn't let this go on, couldn't go on doing this to himself. He had to tell her that this was impossible, he wasn't able to climb into ravines in the middle of the night or crash his normal routines without warning, he had to stop following her everywhere. Even if every minute that he wasn't touching her was a kind of disaster. Suzanne Rae, his personal crack cocaine.

He was still eating the sandwich when the bedroom door opened, and adrenalin shot through his body so he could barely swallow. She walked uncertainly into the room in a bathrobe, and he couldn't make out her face when she saw him – she was grimacing against the light, one hand shielding her eyes. She went to the sink, took down a glass from the shelf and ran the tap.

'I don't normally drink like that,' she said with her back to him, and swallowed the water quickly, leaning on the sink.

'Yeah. I can tell.'

She turned around, biting her lip and frowning. 'Oh. I didn't mean to imply … ' She pushed a matted bit of hair from her face. 'Alex, I'm really glad you stayed,' she said shakily.

'I'm sorry about … ' he waved vaguely at the sandwich. 'I had to eat. I know it's not very good manners.'

'Sure. Much better you should just drop dead.' She walked to the fridge and took a can of coffee from the freezer compartment. He could see her breasts moving under the bathrobe, pale skin half-shadowed and secretive. She fumbled with the can and started to spoon coffee into the machine, and then halfway into the process she dropped the spoon on the counter and put her face in her hands.

'I'm so fucked up right now,' she said.

He stood and put his hands on her shoulders, touched the back of her neck. She smelled of sex and stale alcohol, and she had bits of twig in her hair. There was no limit to this.

'I guess it's just as well you met Derek. It helps if you know.'

'I don't understand everything.'

'No. Nobody could.'

His skin was goosebumped, without a shirt in this cold room. He closed his eyes so he wouldn't see the floaters, and crossed his arms under her breasts, holding the warmth of her against him, the curve of her back pressed into his stomach.

'Tell me something pretty,' she said. 'Tell me about one of your places.'

'I'm not good at describing things. That's why I take photographs.'

'But try?'

'I don't know. Have you seen the terraced garden in High Park?' She shook her head, and he felt the movement against his lips. 'There's these waterfalls,' he said, keeping his eyes closed. 'They built this series of waterfalls and pools down one side of the valley. It feeds into Grenadier Pond. There's stone bridges over the pools, and this stone pagoda where the ducks live, little brown mallard ducks. And flowers growing in the rocks all down the hill. There's, well, I don't know the names of all the flowers. Lilies I know. Some of them are kind of pumpkin-coloured, and others are more yellowy, like, like the inside of a nectarine. And there's, um, these pale flowers, white with a kind of wash of purple or pink, on long stalks, and the ones like bottlebrushes, bright red and yellow. And green, all this green falling down the rocks, little tiny green leaves and blue flowers, and I think some pine trees? I don't know if I'm remembering the pine trees or making them up. I guess it's actually kind of fakey and pretentious. But it's still nice.'

She took hold of his hands and moved them further down, the robe parting slightly so he was holding the soft drift of hair and wet flesh. 'Oh,' he said, as she pressed back harder against him, and he felt his knees loosen as he dipped his head and sucked on the small lobe of her ear, his tongue against a nub of scar tissue where a piercing had healed badly. She turned around in an awkward tangle of legs and fingers, and he lifted her onto the counter as she reached for the zipper of his jeans.

Her body had no overlay of memory for him; that one sad stoned trembling night had been too brief, too long ago. His head bending down to her, mouthing her dark pink nipple, this was now, this existed for itself. The salt slickness of her cunt. Not the body of a girl, but a woman at the end of her thirties – a woman who had never had children, who was strong and fit, but adult, aging, skin and muscle loosening. Immediate and real.

They lay down on her bed, exhausted. Her eyes were bloodshot, and he was nursing a cramp in his calf. Skin on skin, clammy with sweat in chill air, and he felt the heat from her flushed shoulders like a coil of wire.

'I'm sorry I shouted at you,' said Susie. 'Back at the rainforest place.'

'The Cloud Gardens. It's okay. You had a point.' Though he could not even clearly remember, right now, what they had said to each other. 'It's a very tiny rainforest,' he said, spreading his hand over her ribs. 'Like, in an elevator shaft. It's the oddest thing.'

She kissed him again, and even the sour taste of her mouth was too much for him, he wanted to draw every bit of her inside him, into his blood. Over and over, she could break him down.

The light was fading already in mid-afternoon, and snow was still falling, soft and slow, the kind of snowfall that never seemed heavy at any one time but accumulated into thick billows and drifts, pressed down on the sidewalk by pedestrians and melted into shades of tan and deep brown by the cars on the road.

Alex sat on the floor of Susie's living room, drinking coffee and staring at a newspaper, where a picture of the burned man dominated the lower part of the front page. The man was, as it turned out, neither Muslim nor Jewish but a Portuguese Catholic, and was described by his family as 'odd.' He thought of phoning Janice Carriere to see what was happening, if the man was still stable, if he was awake at all.

Susie came into the room, dressed now in a sweater and skirt, and sat down in an office chair at a worn wooden desk with a rather expensive laptop resting on it. Ikea bookshelves around the walls, and a large map of the city taped up near the desk, with annotations in green and red ink, a scatter of shelters and homeless communities – the Scott Mission, Seaton House, the cardboard neighbourhood under the arc of Bathurst where it rose, just past the Gardiner. *Bastard Bridge*, she had written here. A yellow post-it note read *prelim interviews only, revisit*. On the desk, a thick sheaf of papers, several different pens including some stolen from hotels, a glass paper-weight with a sea urchin inside it. She looked up at the map.

'That's where he is, right?' she asked. Alex stood up and looked where she was pointing.

'Yeah. That's it.'

'There'd be much easier access from Bayview, wouldn't there? I'll try that next time.'

Alex frowned. 'You're going back?'

She looked up at him, surprised. 'Not this minute. But yes. Of course I am.'

'Do you think that really makes sense?'

She opened her mouth, then looked away quickly. 'Well, it's not like you have to come with me,' she said.

'That's not what I meant. I'm just not sure it's a good idea.'

She picked up her coffee cup with both hands and bent her head to drink. Her hair was wet and shining, the desk lamp picking out erratic highlights, a dark syrup stream. 'That's not your problem, is it?'

Alex tried not to feel as if he had just been punched in the stomach.

'I don't want you getting hurt is all,' he said.

'Schizophrenics are rarely violent. That's a TV myth.'

'I didn't mean physically.'

155

'I told you. It's not your problem.'

He rubbed the back of his neck, feeling tension gathering in the air. This was bound to happen, he'd known that; the history and the hurt would come rushing back. They couldn't talk about anything without the static in the way.

'I'm sorry I involved you at all, okay?' she said. 'It wasn't fair. I can deal with this myself, I always have.'

'Susie-Sue. That's really not what I meant.'

'I know what you meant. You meant that I should just leave him there.'

'Not exactly. No. I just don't see why you have to go up there yourself. It's too hard on you.'

'And who the hell else do you think is going to? The prime minister? God? No one cares about him but me, Alex. No one else even tries.'

'Okay, okay.' He walked a few steps around the room, not sure where he was going, and stopped in front of a picture pinned to the back of the door, a child's drawing, a stick person with strangely angled arms under a huge sun.

'Miriam did that,' said Susie. 'Evvy's little girl. Years ago, of course. It's supposed to be me.'

'I should think that's an honour.'

'Not really. Kids'll draw anyone who passes by at the right moment.'

'Anyway,' he said, 'I should go with you. You shouldn't be alone.'

She shrugged. 'That's up to you. I'm all right on my own.'

'You didn't think so before.'

'Yeah, well, that was stupid. I shouldn't have asked you.'

'Yes, you should. Of course you should.'

She sat under the desk lamp, broken reflections of light moving on the surface of her coffee, bright threads in her hair trailing down past her angular cheekbones. Her head turned away from him.

'Maybe I should go home now,' he said.

'Maybe.'

'I have to feed my cat.'

She nodded.

'Will you tell me when you go to see Derek again?'

'I suppose.'

'I want to come. Really.'

'Yeah, okay.' She got up from the chair and hugged him. Her hair left a damp patch on his shirt.

'I'll talk to you soon,' he said, his fingers digging into the fabric of her sweater.

'Well, it's all right. I should work for the rest of the weekend. I'm writing this paper for a journal.'

'But soon.'

'Sure. I'll call you. Or you can call me. Whichever.'

Saturday evening on College Street, the sidewalks busy despite the snow, despite even the falling girls, people still determined to prove that they were the kind of people who went to College Street on Saturday night. The lights of the clubs and restaurants glowing against the cold as Alex sat on the streetcar, looking at the burned man's face in a discarded newspaper. He thought again about phoning Janice, just to ask. Otherwise he might never know.

This seemed to be his place in the life of the city, and in Susie's life too, somehow, a devoted observer at the margins of the crack-ups, the big stories. Susie and Chris, Susie and Derek. At least he had managed to miss the episode of her marriage, whatever that had been about. Someone else had presumably held her hand for that one.

… which could indicate the presence of a viral infection, said a side-bar to the story. *The possibility of a large number of casualties*, it said, *in the hypothetical case of the deliberate release of* H5N1 *influenza, or bird flu. But the chances of such a release being successful are far from clear.*

He imagined his murderous doctor striding through the snow with an oily package, thinking of love and killing, elegant, serious, sometimes uncertain. How many people in the street were carrying their own terrorists in their heads, and what shape did they take? Foreigners and police, dark men and angry children.

On College, a block from his house, the window of the little grocery was broken, chunks of safety glass swept into a pile on the sidewalk. It could have been a child playing ball, but everything now seemed to assimilate to the city's larger narrative, and he assumed it was a crime of fear. The owners of the grocery Lebanese maybe, or Iranian, or mistaken for whatever.

Maybe it was just an accident.

For a little while he studied some contact sheets that he had left out on his desk, but the floaters were bothering him. And he was very tired, that alone was putting his eye off. He took a cassette out of the cupboard and slid it into the machine. One of Adrian's old tapes – how long had it been since he'd listened to Adrian sing? It was another regression to the past, maybe, but one that at least wasn't confusing or dangerous, just Adrian's odd propulsive wandering songs, his inscrutable lyrics.

Queen Jane crawled up onto his chest, the weight of her pulling him down towards sleep. He shouldn't really sleep on the couch, he'd just end up with a stiff neck, but he was disinclined to move. The tape clicked and began to replay. He should go by the church and see Adrian sometime, he thought, as he slid into a disordered space of dreaming.

The snow stopped that night, but the temperature kept dropping for days, the wind howling in white swirls up and down the streets. The floaters were persisting. Alex told no one at work, but it was a constant low-key struggle not to raise his hand to brush them away, not to blink and shake his head every few minutes; they were in the way of his focus, distracting him. And reminding him, reminding him as long as his eyes were open, of that bleak space breathing in from the future.

But they would recede, maybe they were already receding a bit, it was hard to tell. This time, next time, they would still go away. Probably damage to the retina would be minimal, for now.

On Monday night he was walking west on College, towards his apartment, with his hat pulled down to his eyebrows and his scarf over his nose, and then sirens were coming from all directions at once, and the street became a sea of red light, fire engines and ambulances and police cars all meeting at a point on the north side, a restaurant with a broken window. He didn't want to know what it was about. In between the emergency vehicles were little groups of people, hugging each other and crying, and broken glass on the road. A man was holding up his hand, thin streams of blood running down his arm.

Alex didn't want to know what it was about but he was reaching into his camera bag nevertheless, he'd need a long exposure for this, the light would be tricky to handle. He took a picture of the bleeding man, of the police entering the restaurant.

And he was packing his camera away when something came towards him out of the dark, shining and unpredictable, a fluttering thing, and before he knew what he was doing he had put out his hand and caught the string of a gold foil balloon in the shape of a star.

Then the whole cluster of balloons tied to the restaurant's patio fence broke free and were swept up in the wind, into the bare branches of the overhanging trees, into the awnings along the street, a flock of golden stars reaching out of the damage. Alex stood in the street and held on to a string.

Sometime before the day that Susie had fallen from the stairs of the clinic, that Alex had caught her – though his memory was inevitably coloured now by what had come after – he had been sitting outside his house in the market, trying to fix the advancing mechanism on one of his old cameras, when she came down the street with a bag of potatoes in her arms.

'Hi,' she said as she passed the steps. 'It's Alex, right?' He nodded, glancing up at her and then looking back at the camera. 'Aren't you cold out here?'

He shrugged. 'One of the kids in my house dropped some acid last night. He's been playing the same chord on his guitar over and over for, like, the last twelve hours. I needed a break.' He lifted the camera up to the light so he could get a better look at the insides. 'My definition of responsible drug use is if you're going to play the same chord for twelve hours, you don't inflict it on anyone else.'

'Okay.' She shifted the bag of potatoes on her hip. 'I wanted to tell you I liked your photos in the last issue.'

He didn't know what to say, so he shrugged again.

'Sorry, you're busy. I should get home anyway.'

'No, it's all right.' He didn't want her to leave for some reason. 'You can sit down if you like.'

She put the potatoes on the steps beside her. 'You fixing that?'

'Trying. Not actually doing it.'

'You could always go over to the Last Temptation, it's warm in there.'

'I don't mind. This is cheaper.'

He spent a few more minutes prodding the gears of the camera, Susie sitting beside him without speaking, her breath a white cloud in the air. He was slightly stoned himself, and not really able to focus on the task that well.

'The thing is,' he said, and was surprised to find himself speaking, 'the thing is, maybe if I just sit here long enough, then ... ' The sentence ran out on him and he stopped.

'Then what?'

'I don't know.' He put the camera in his lap and tucked his hands into his sleeves, thinking about wanting things that could never be named.

'Well, if you sit here long enough, your toes could turn black and fall off. That'd be something.'

'Yeah, I guess it would.'

They sat in silence for another minute. 'Where does your family live?' asked Susie.

Alex snorted. 'What? You're gonna call my mother and tell her I'm sitting outside without a hat?'

'Oh, come on,' said Susie, but she smiled. 'I'm just asking.'

'Kitchener. If you must know.'

'Do you see them much?'

'Not so much, but we get along okay. They're all right.'

'My family's in Scarborough.'

'Oh. Hey. I'm very sorry.'

Susie laughed. 'Yeah, no kidding.' Taking off her mittens, she pushed back her hair with one hand. 'I was wondering,' she said quietly.

'Yeah?'

She studied her nail polish, the same pink as her hair. 'If people – if anyone ever escapes from things. Gets away. I mean, do you think it's possible?'

The size of this question confused him entirely. 'I, ah, I don't know. I mean, um, is this a person and their family?'

'I suppose so. Yeah.'

'So what … what's the family doing, you know? I mean, is there a problem?'

'Never mind. That was a stupid thing to say.' She put her mittens back on and stood up, lifting her bag of potatoes. 'I better get home.'

'I'm sorry,' said Alex, and he meant it though he wasn't sure what it was attached to.

'Thank you, Alex. Maybe I'll see you around.'

On Tuesday morning a woman collapsed at Kennedy station, and later she would say that it was the smell of flowers without air, of flowers that took the air away. Another woman would say that she saw a man with a beard, and something on his head, it might have been a turban, and he was standing by a pillar and watching them, like he already knew what would happen.

The hazmat teams descended with swabs, collecting fragments of matter far below the threshold of vision, which would be taken to protected labs and cultured. Trace elements would grow in the petri dishes, but there would be nothing that could be blamed, nothing that could act as an explanation.

Loose pages of newspapers, crumpled words, blew along the platform in the wind of the trains, *respiratory symptoms, H5N1, variants of anthrax.*

Alex rode home through a depleted rush hour, barely recognizable as such, the traffic in the stations thinned out and moving nervously. It had been last Tuesday night he'd met Susie at the church, and he was fairly sure that churches coordinated their meal and shelter programs with each other, that they each took particular days of the week. For all he knew, Evelyn had people sleeping in the hall every night, but it was more likely that her church was responsible for Tuesdays.

He walked east on College to the little brick church. It was dark when he got there, but still early evening, and the first thing he saw was a line of men and women stretching out the doorway; inside, he made his way past rows of tables where people sat over plates of lasagna and mashed potatoes, to where Evelyn was standing in the kitchen, staring at something on the counter and raking her fingers through her hair.

'Okay,' she was saying as he came in. 'So someone has given us a casserole made from permafrost. This is just something I have to come to terms with. It's all just part of the rich incarnational parade.'

'Hey, Alex.' Adrian came in through a side door, and glanced down at the frozen casserole, which was leaking trails of water onto a cutting board. 'You didn't get bombed out of your house last night, did you?'

Alex blinked. 'What's this now?'

'That restaurant where the bomb went off. Don't you live over that way?'

'It was a *bomb*?'

'A very minuscule bomb, though,' said Evelyn, poking at the casserole with a knife. 'And of poor quality. Nobody was really hurt. They don't have access to the good explosives down at the low end of organized crime.'

A large man in a ragged jacket got up from his table, coming to lean in the doorway of the kitchen. 'There's something I can do to help, maybe?'

'I don't think so, Vojcek, not right now. You can collect the plates in a few minutes, I guess.'

'Aye-aye, captain,' said Vojcek with a brisk salute.

'You're kidding me,' said Alex. 'A bomb? Was this connected to, I mean, was it some kind of hate crime or ... '

'Nah.' Adrian bent down to turn on the dishwasher. 'These two guys have competing establishments. They despise each other. It's, I don't know, who does the better calamari in mango sauce with chipotle reduction or whatever. So one of them hired somebody. This is what I'm told, at any rate. But I suppose it's part of the overall municipal malaise.'

'Is the terminal stage of capitalism,' said Vojcek. 'Soon we are a communist dictatorship, and I will flee to New Zealand.'

'Attaboy, Vojcek,' said Adrian. 'Keep looking on the bright side.'

Alex left the kitchen and went back to the hall, where servers, at a table against the far wall, were scraping food out of the bottoms of the pots. A young woman with shining dark hair and the tense brightness of insanity in her face took his arm with a terrified smile. She was wearing a long orange scarf over her head, a blue sweatshirt that was slightly too small, grey pants that were slightly too large.

'Is this a safe place?' she whispered, and then laughed. 'Is this a safe place? I have to face my fears, you see – there are people trying to drive me crazy, there are people out there trying to drive me crazy, and you have to ask why? Don't you? Don't you have to ask why?' She held on tighter to Alex's arm. 'Are they benefitting financially, are they benefitting spiritually? Is it a question of the war? Everyone here knows my obsession, you see, everyone knows my weakness ... and it's hard when there are people all over the streets trying to drive me crazy, do you know what I mean? Is it clear? Do you think this is a safe place?'

'I think so,' said Alex. 'Sure. I think it is.'

'I have to face my fears,' she said, and then turned her head as if she had heard something, and pulled her scarf tighter around her hair and crept into a corner, nodding and moving her lips.

The frizzy-haired girl he had seen last week slammed suddenly into the hall, apparently in some temper, and stomped past the tables into the kitchen, kicking off her boots and whining in a high unintelligible voice, Evvy's own voice soft at first and then sharpening, and the child stormed away into some other part of the building. Evvy leaned back against the counter and ran a hand over her face, and Alex wanted to do something but he knew that he couldn't. Adrian moved closer to her and touched her arm.

'Domestic crisis,' announced Vojcek cheerfully, picking up plates from the table beside Alex. 'Is difficult child. Has poor sense of responsibility.'

'Mmm,' said Alex vaguely.

He didn't know how much he really expected Susie to be there. Not much, he thought, though he knew he was unnaturally aware of every person who opened the door.

Evelyn had come out of the kitchen now and was sitting cross-legged on the floor of the hall, sorting through a box of old mittens. A short woman in a red hat walked across the room, and for a moment things were suddenly vivid and sharp at the edges; but it wasn't Susie after all, in fact she looked almost nothing like Susie. He went into the kitchen, where Adrian was turning an unlit cigarette in his fingers and staring at it with a vague suppressed longing.

Susie probably wouldn't come. There was no real reason to suppose she would.

'I was wondering about taking some pictures,' he said. 'I mean, I know I'd have to ask people. But would it be okay to try?'

Vojcek had no problem posing for a portrait, and neither did Joseph with the flowering cane; he spent a long time with Joseph, working on the textures of his skin, the fleetingly sweet expressions in his eyes, and trying to get the cane into the shots in the right way. Luis didn't want to be photographed, and it was clearly a bad idea to ask the woman with the orange scarf. A girl named Mouse asked to be photographed with her ferret, which was living inside the sleeve of her coat.

'Isn't that a bit funny?' asked Alex, slipping into the kind of easy patter he used with teenage patients. 'A mouse with a pet ferret?'

Mouse grinned and chewed a loose bit of her hair. 'I know a girl called Kat who has a hedgehog, what about that?'

'A pet hedgehog?'

'Yeah, but it kinda sucks as a pet. It can't cuddle you or nothing. And it's not very friendly. Actually it's kinda mean. It really brings Kat down sometimes.'

'Maybe she needs a better pet.'

'Well, she don't want to give up on this hedgehog. She thinks it can, you know, rehabilitate.'

He was focused now, working, and happy, and not even too bothered by the floaters, which were definitely diminishing, and then he heard the thud of the wooden door. Susie was partway into the hall, unwinding her scarf, when she saw him, and stood still for a second before she walked towards him.

'I was just leaving,' said Alex.

'Are you sure?'

'I think so, I think I should go.'

'I need to do some interviews, but if you could wait a little while … '

He knew if he looked at her eyes he was lost. But really, he was pretty much lost anyway. He shrugged. 'I guess I could wait.'

He took some more photos while Adrian and Evvy and a few others folded the legs of the tables and stacked them up, lay down mattresses, rolled out the TV. The movie was something about a comet destroying all life on earth, and the general level of interest seemed low, though Mouse said that there was a really excellent tidal wave later on, and the woman there died, and it was very sad and she'd cried like anything.

'The fire next time,' said Evelyn.

'Nah,' said Adrian. '*Men in Black II* next time.'

Susie had set up a couple of chairs in the corner, and now and then he heard scraps of conversation. How many friends in this place, in that place. Would you say they were close friends? What kind of thing do they help you with, do you help them with? What word would you use to describe your relationship?

Adrian squatted down on the floor beside him while he was packing up his camera. 'Did you know Suzanne was coming?' he asked.

'No.'

'Is it okay?'

'It was a very long time ago,' said Alex, which was such a blatant lie he could hardly imagine anyone believing it.

'If you say so.' Adrian stood up. 'I guess I should see if I'm needed somewhere.'

He should have told Adrian about the floaters. He could have told him that at least.

Susie crossed the room towards Evelyn, and they spoke for a minute with their heads close together, and then Evelyn stepped back and laughed, and moved in a quick twirling step that made Alex think of her dancing. He tried to remember when he had seen her dance. Susie hugged Evvy lightly, and looked over at Alex, and he picked up his bag and came to her.

They went outside, into a wind that was very strong now. 'I have to remember to call you Suzanne,' said Alex.

'You don't really.' She played with the fringe of her scarf, and the wind blew her hair across her face, obscuring her expression.

'So did you, did you get that paper finished?'

'Well, it's not like – it takes longer than that. I, ah, I did some work on it, I guess.'

They stopped walking at the same time, and then he took hold of her and kissed her, pressing her against the wall of a bus shelter, half angry, half desperate, her hands gripping his arms. He didn't consciously think that her mouth no longer tasted of hangover and bad sleep, but he took in the sugar trace on her lips and the smell of her breath. Reese's peanut butter cups, a small cheap treat for herself, bought at the 7-Eleven or the newsstand in the subway. An innocent, silly thing.

She had no mittens, and she was walking along the street blowing on her hands. He wanted her to be inside, somewhere warm. They ended up at the Kos Diner, piling their layers of heavy outdoor clothes on empty chairs; it seemed obvious that she was coming back to his apartment, but somehow he couldn't say this, neither one of them wanting to take a step they couldn't reverse. Susie ordered a coffee and french fries. Her hair, loose and disarranged, seemed to be a slightly different colour, a bit more golden.

'I found a magic star last night,' he said. 'But Adrian tells me it has a mafia connection.' He told her about the restaurant and the flock of balloons, trying to make it sound entertaining rather than grim, wanting her to smile.

'Do you suppose it's a sign of some kind?' she said, shaking a blob of ketchup onto her plate.

'Gotta be.'

Susie dipped a french fry into the ketchup and sighed. 'Derek sent me a letter,' she said. She reached into her shoulder bag and took out two ragged pieces of notebook paper covered with tiny dense handwriting. 'The street nurses gave it to me.'

'Is this good or bad?'

'I'm really not sure.'

Alex moved his hand towards the letter and looked at her, and she nodded, so he pulled the papers over to his side of the table. The script was slanted, rushing forward on the page so that words ended up on top of other words, lines snaking up and down the margins. There seemed to be no salutation, nor anything resembling the beginning of a thought.

> i was talking to the doctor that time and he said have you thought about your hostelity, I could use the help. because the hired help, yes they do, the hired, the hived, the halt, the lame, they are always helping. okay that was not my point. so he said that about the hostile and i said, what the fucking shit, i can get hostile on your ass if you keep going on about it. so he fucked me up the ass that's all the doctors do every day they're back at it. i was bleeding from my anal passage because of the fucking of the doctors and that's why I got the cancer in there and my penis also.
>
> but you find a safe place and be in it. because the sodium pentothal and others you may not beawar of, hypnium oxygenatium and also wood alcohol derivatives as such. this is why the kalorie intake. you see it is kalorie, not calorie as they tell you, kallos = beautiful but it's a risk you take. but you find a safe place.
>
> baby sister we were born together in one bloody body and they say it isn't the same dna but that's a lie, on top of me and because they say we are not, no no, go away, but i look after you. they tried to do it again to you but i put my mysterious protection in place. you are very beautiful susie-paul. i will make it all right.
>
> not even to get into the subject of the suicide missions they are asking me to undertake, but i say, no, we are not going in that direction. to the undertaker ha ha. all in little pieces. with involvement of the following persons, mr kofi annan, mr vladimir putin = whore, mrs margaret thatcher + tony blair, mr president of the united stated union of holy matrimony which is to say fucking in the bleeding orifices. the oval orifice. ha ha ha.

but it's not my point okay okay. but only if you would come here and stay with me. that would be better.

once upon a time there was a little girl. and the birds ate up her eyes. but she lives happily ever after at the end, this is my mystery power.

but stopping the crying is a problem of our time, he cries too much.

There was more, but Alex couldn't keep reading. He turned the papers over in his hands and briefly thought that he might cry himself, watching Susie eating her french fries, eyes on her plate.

'He spends a lot of time writing,' she said. 'This is on the coherent side.'

Alex slid the papers across the table. 'He's in love with you,' he said quietly.

Susie shrugged. 'That's not the form of words I'd choose to describe it. I'd say I'm the focus of a lot of his obsessions. But I don't know. Maybe that's not much different from what normal people mean by love.' She pushed back her hair, and Alex bit his lower lip. 'He wants me in there with him, you know. I mean, not so much in the tent or wherever. In his world. With the plots and the brainwashing chemicals, inside that system. I even feel guilty sometimes that I'm not.'

'Oh God. Susie.' He wasn't sure it was the right thing to do, given the conversation up to that point, but he reached across the table for her hand. She moved away, in what might have been an accidental gesture, and he took a french fry from her plate instead.

'But I'm not inside it, am I? And poor Derek's not my bad angel. I have my own ordinary failures, and that's a big thing, really. People don't know.'

There was nothing he could say – there was nothing he could do, short of kneeling and putting his head in her lap – so he said nothing. A flicker crossed the path of his sight, and he moved his head, and caught himself making a brushing motion at one of the floaters. She noticed the gesture, but she didn't know what it meant, it had no implications for her. *My eyes are bleeding.*

'Anyway. What's the news in your life, aside from magic stars?'

'Nothing much. Day-to-day stuff at the hospital.'

My eyes are bleeding because of you.

'I don't want to keep you if you're busy.'

'No. I'm not.' He watched the shifting highlights in her hair and wondered how long he would be able to see them. That was the kind of detail he might lose. 'I got a good run of photos at the church.'

They sat without speaking for a while, Susie eating her fries with her fingers.

'I'd like to photograph you sometime,' he said.

'You already have. A bunch of times.'

'Yeah, but ages ago.'

Slowly, Alex was becoming aware of noises behind them. Voices at another table growing louder and more agitated.

'Come on. I know you were taking pictures of me last week.'

He shrugged; it was true, though he'd been only half aware of it at the time. Susie in the darkness of the Cloud Gardens, looking at the ground. 'But I mean properly.'

'Yeah, okay. Sometime.'

He saw movement, real movement, not black spots, from the corner of his eye, and heard a woman's voice, high and scared, saying something about roses. 'Oh man,' he said, and turned his head in time to see her – in her thirties probably, in a furry green coat – crash heavily to the ground beside the door. Alex stood up from the table.

'Shit,' said Susie, and they both started to move towards the woman, but half a dozen other people had already reached her. As someone tried to lift her up, she vomited onto the floor, splashing her coat and a man's shoes. Alex heard her saying the word poison, the word terrorist.

'Let's just go,' he said. Another man was clinging to a table, his heavy shoulders hunched over as if he were barely supporting himself, red blotches appearing on his face. But Susie's expression was lit up with professional fascination. 'Oh no,' she said, excited. 'I have to stay, I have to watch this.'

An ambulance had already arrived, then a fire truck. Two more people were sitting on the floor holding their heads. The paramedics were wearing masks that covered their faces, blue gowns over their uniforms and green plastic gloves, and they lifted the woman carefully to her feet. She staggered and fell against one of them, and he turned his head to the side as he held her up. Strips of bacon, neglected on the grill, began to shrivel and blacken, harsh smoke curling into the air around the counter.

'This is really, really interesting,' said Susie, moving closer to the centre of activity.

The paramedics led the woman and the blotched man out of the restaurant, the firemen passing oxygen masks out among the crowd. The scorched bacon was spitting fat, and Alex felt a heave of nausea. A dark-haired waitress ran back behind the counter and scraped the strips of bacon off, tossing them into the sink. The deep fryer and the coffee maker were smoking as well, she turned them off, unplugged the coffee maker and threw it hastily into the sink. Susie moved back a step, took Alex's arm and pulled him forward. He put one hand over his mouth, thinking he was about to be sick, a horribly familiar smell of burned meat in his nostrils.

'Here's what I want to know,' she whispered. 'Do the ERTs think this is a poison gas? What procedures are they employing for these incidents?'

'I just don't want to be taken in for decontamination or whatever.'

'See, look at this, the medics have the masks but the firefighters don't, and that doesn't make rational sense. But it's like … they have a kind of ambiguous response to this. Like it's, hmm, liminal between real and imaginary, you know?'

A fireman stretched an oxygen mask towards them, but Alex waved it away. He was afraid that Susie was going to put on a choking fit in order to get into one of the ambulances – there were two outside now – but she was busy with her clipboard and pen. Police cars pulled up at the curb, and then everyone inside the restaurant was being led out, standing for one shocking moment outside without coats, pressing against the wall for shelter.

'They're not sure what they're doing,' said Susie. 'A lot of this is improvised.' Policemen began coming out with armloads of winter clothes, purses and bags, dumping them on the sidewalk. He pulled his coat on, and his scarf, but he couldn't find his hat. Susie had brought her bag outside with her, but she still had no coat, was hunched over and windblown, scribbling notes. A heavy man lean-ing against the wall seemed to have a nosebleed; he was clutching a wad of bloody tissue to his face, his mouth wide open. A cyclist with dreadlocked hair rounded the corner, staring at the crowd as he passed, and shouted, 'Valium! Take Valium!' as he sped into the dark-ness along College.

'Susie. Aren't you freezing?'

'Just a second.' She wrote another sentence, then bent down to a pile of clothes on the sidewalk and tugged her coat out. The woman who had fallen was being lifted into the ambulance.

' … set up a decontamination tent?' he heard one of the firemen saying, and then another fire truck arrived, and a white-suited hazmat team climbed down. A woman stood with her mouth partly open, pinned down by the sight of these swollen figures moving clumsily towards the door of the restaurant. Alex grabbed the sleeve of Susie's coat and pulled her along the street, out of the light from the windows.

'Can we go now? Please?' He stood behind a newspaper box, sepa-rated from the crowd, his hands in his pockets. Susie looked back almost regretfully, but Alex started walking quickly west on College, and she came with him, trotting to keep up.

'I'm glad I saw that,' she was saying. 'It really is a thing that's worth studying.'

'I just don't want it happening around me all the time, is what I want.' He took a breath, and the exhaust-filled air seemed clean in comparison, his nausea subsiding.

'You notice it's always just one or two people? It's like a mass phenomenon that's at the same time highly atomized, I think that's almost unique. I wonder what they were talking about just before she fell.'

'It seemed to come out of nowhere, more or less.'

'Nothing comes out of nowhere, believe me.' She blew on her hands again, rubbing her knuckles.

'And why does that sound like a pop lyric?'

He was walking more slowly now, safely away. As she drew level with him he reached out almost absently, and his fingers touched her shoulder and then moved back.

'I'd like to talk to that first girl. She's the real key to all this.'

'She looked pretty ordinary, I have to tell you,' said Alex, shrugging. 'I don't know, I think one of her friends had a pierced navel, if that's any use.'

'Gotta be useful to someone.'

'I wouldn't count on that.'

They had gone by Palmerston now. As they passed the streetcar stop Susie paused and made a small uncertain gesture.

'Well,' said Alex, 'I live over by Grace. It's just a few blocks.'

She nodded, and as they crossed the street his arm moved around her waist, his hand running up and down the soft curve of her hip as she leaned into him for warmth. He could have told her that it wasn't a good time, that he needed to be at work in the morning. He wasn't entirely sure how he felt about going to bed with Susie knowing that her twin brother's chronicles of anal rape were folded away inside her shoulder bag. But it was like this, it would be like this, he had never been truly alone with her.

Inside the apartment she stretched up on her toes, trying to touch the gold balloon above her head, car alarms going off on College Street.

The fear had been always visible, the men with instruments appearing on television almost as soon as the first girl fell. But when real disease awoke in the city, it happened so quietly that hardly anyone noticed.

It woke, like the fear, in the body of a girl, though a very different girl, a strung-out child with a push-up bra and a chronic cough and track marks, two miniskirts and some fishnet stockings and undiagnosed fetal alcohol syndrome. This girl began to feel sick, as if she had the flu. For a while she kept working, and it wasn't so bad as long as she could get a line of coke from the guy who ran her, back in the parking lot behind the Salvation Army building, or even just some booze, but then he didn't like his girls to be that far out of it, he'd smack you around if you got too wasted, but it was hard to work otherwise when she felt this sick. And then it got worse, and then a lot worse than that.

She was lying in her bed and she couldn't even tell if she was cold or hot except that it hurt, whatever it was, it was hurting. And bad dreams. Choking in her sleep, down her throat, jamming it, couldn't breathe, and she couldn't get away from it, and she wanted to scream, but she was pinned down, too heavy, but it just hurt so much. Dirty girl. And some of the johns were freaks. The things they wanted her to do. The light scooping into her eyes like a jackknife, it was in her head now, it was all pain blowing up her head, and it was too heavy, she couldn't move her, her, it hurt too much. And what they wanted her to do. Perverts. But when you spread your legs. Dirty girl. And it hurt, in her, in, in, and in her body, and it was shredding into black, dark dark, and her neck snapped back, and her body turned to stone.

The guy who ran her came in, and then left. By the time her friend found her, hours later, and called an ambulance, she could no longer be woken. The ambulance came and took her away; and in the hospital she died.

As she was still dying, the procedures for a meningitis outbreak were set into motion.

The staff at Public Health acted quickly when the hospital phoned them. They placed a story in the local paper, they put up flyers in the neighbourhood where the girl had been working. But the desires of the street move so strangely, so covertly, and they follow no reliable pattern. The public health officers knew they would not reach everyone they needed to, and perhaps not anyone they needed to, but there was not much else they could do.

The other girl, the first girl who fell, walked quietly into the kitchen of her house and opened the cupboards, searching through the canned goods, turning the tins around in her hands as if she were considering something. Tomato soup, stuffed vine leaves. A jar of peanut butter. She wasn't sure how much she could take without an explanation, and she didn't think that she could explain why she needed to do this. A tin of coconut milk. Finally she took two cans of tuna, hesitated, and put one of them back on the shelf.

She picked up her coat, a rather expensive leather coat, and slid the can into her pocket.

Just going for a walk, she said, poking her head around the door to the sitting room. She'd be back by ten to finish her homework. Anyway, there was a TV show she wanted to watch. Her father nodded, and she checked for her keys, her cellphone, and went out into the wind.

She walked around to the back of the house and looked down into the ravine, but there was no one there. It would have been strange if those people had been there anyway, that green-haired girl and her friend. They had come, and performed their task, and vanished.

The fence had been painted over, but she could see the shadow of the word FEAR, a grey shape underneath the white paint.

A few streets over it was there again, FEAR, on the side of a little florist's shop. All the things she could never do, the places she couldn't go. The kind of person she could never be.

The girl stood in a park at the north end of Rosedale, her hands in the pockets of her coat, fingering the can of tuna, watching figures pass under the wide blurred halo of the lights. A woman with a fawn-coloured pug on a leash, the collar of her own coat pulled up around her face. A jogger with a scarf tied over his mouth, finger-less gloves on his bunched hands, his running shoes kicking up snow. The girl looked at an empty bench near the bushes, the damp mahogany-stained wood showing some decay at the edges. She turned her head to either side, as if checking for watchers, then moved reluctantly, uneasily, towards the bench. She took a five-dollar bill from her pocket and put it on the wooden seat, then pinned it down with the can, a strange coded offering. Walking away from the bench, she waited at the verge of the park for a while longer, look-ing as if she expected a great bird, perhaps, to arrive and carry her gifts away. But she couldn't stay out forever, she had homework to do, parents who kept her mostly to a curfew. The tuna and the money were still sitting on the bench when she left. She would never be able to know who would take them, or what meaning someone might see in the gesture.

On Dufferin near Lake Shore Boulevard, two police officers arrested a man in a turban who had left his bicycle leaning unattended against a wall, with plastic bags hanging from the handlebars.

If you were frightened enough, they could look like something else, those bags. Bulky packages, brown paper with grease stains. It could be groceries. It could be terror.

The policemen pushed the man onto his knees on the sidewalk as he came back to his bicycle, and bent his hands behind him, binding them with cuffs.

They drove along Lake Shore for a while, and then they stopped at a Tim Horton's, and one officer stayed in the car with the man while the other went inside to buy coffee and a box of maple-glazed Timbits. The officer in the car asked the man if he thought he was a smart guy. The man said no, he did not think that he was a smart guy at all.

As they went east, the sidewalk was lit up with a small flame, and on the steps of a small office building a circle of women were passing a burning coil of sweetgrass between them, wafting the smoke with their hands. The police car slowed to watch the ceremony, but didn't stop.

They drove further east, and then turned south, driving through blocks of boarded-up lots and a small sad diner with a neon canary above the door, down to the ports. The man realized now that they were taking him to Cherry Beach, and he knew what this meant, he had heard about what the police did at Cherry Beach. They drove on, past the green ice-edged water of the canals, the metal heft of container ships, bars that advertised themselves with drawings of martinis and dancing girls, and stopped by a stand of bare trees near the edge of the water. The officers pulled the man out of the car and he stumbled, his hands still cuffed behind his back, and they watched him as he struggled up and walked, at their orders, towards the lake. There was a small hut leaning over the water, its white paint cracking, and a half-submerged picnic table. At the shoreline the water was frozen, a lace of hard ice, shards and peaks, and it caught the distant light and cast it back in a faint shimmer. The man went down on his knees by the pebbled shore, and lowered his head, and waited for the clubs to descend.

Towards morning, a girl fell down at Yonge and Eglinton, and the sun rose on the hazmat squad.

II

There were mornings when Alex turned on his radio with the thought, almost the assumption, that he would hear about a major terrorist attack in one of the central cities, London or Paris or Los Angeles. Somehow it was not a thought that brought any sense of fear with it, nothing much stronger than curiosity, and up to this point he had never actually been proved right. But it had been that way since what happened in New York; any daily routine, now, could contain this news.

He remembered that he'd been late getting to work, the morning it had happened; he'd been standing in line at the bank, and had gradually realized that the line was moving so slowly because the tellers kept leaving their posts to cluster around a small radio. As he got closer to the desk he'd been able hear bits of the broadcast, stories of airplanes and skyscrapers. 'Ah geez,' one of the tellers had muttered, a huge man with a shiny bald head. 'I just hope they don't start a war over this, you know?'

So it was like that now, catastrophe inevitable at the most empty moments. Everyone waiting, almost wanting it, a secret, guilty desire for meaning. Their time in history made significant for once by that distant wall of black cloud.

But there was no such news this morning, Susie gone before dawn and Alex sitting by the radio with a cup of coffee, trying to pay attention; it was all about UN weapons inspectors and fluctuating currencies, an outbreak of Marburg virus in a tiny distant country, and a confusing story about an arrest in connection with incidents not precisely named. The subway, he guessed, and wondered who they'd found and what they were thinking.

The small explosion of order in his own life happened later that day, ephemeral and unexpected, when a bird somehow entered the hospital, in a way that no one was ever able, later on, to understand. When Alex arrived, unsummoned but pulled away from his lunch break by rumours of excitement, it had been contained in an empty room where it huddled in a corner, grey feathers fluffed angrily out, a disoriented disease vector, potential reservoir of avian flu, West Nile, any number of other infections.

'Just let me kill the fucker!' an orderly in a mask and industrial gloves was shouting, grabbing for the pigeon as it leapt from his hands, its wings slicing upwards.

Alex slipped unnoticed into the room, and knelt with his camera as the pigeon exploded towards the ceiling in a scatter of fluff and droppings, crashed into an iv stand, and started to make a break for the door before someone slammed it shut. The orderly ran at the bird with a canvas bag and it veered up again, greeny-white shit falling into another orderly's long hair. 'Jesus!' she screamed, her hands flying up.

The pigeon began to spiral, high out of reach, and the orderly dropped the bag and picked up a mop, began stabbing the wooden handle at the bird. 'Open a window!' someone else called. 'Open a window, let it out!'

'They don't open that way!' yelled the first orderly, and a male nurse, seeming now in a state of pure panic, picked up a chair and bashed at the window, trying to break it.

'Kill it, kill it, we have immuno-compromised patients in here!'

'How in God's name did it get in?'

'Alex, Jesus Christ!' The long-haired orderly backed into him. 'Don't take *pictures* of this.'

'Personal use only,' said Alex, as the pigeon wheeled in lunatic circles, wings beating into the walls. Then it sank downwards, bright amethyst slivers of light splintering from its chest, and dug its festering claws into Alex's hair.

'Fucking hell!' he shouted, stumbling forward, the thin talons piercing his scalp.

'It's gone on the attack!' cried an orderly.

Alex fell onto his knees, his teeth sinking into his lip, his hands beating uselessly at his head as the window gave way.

'Oh, good going, Stuart,' snapped another nurse. 'I hope you know you're paying for that.'

An orderly swung a pillow at the bird and it lifted off from Alex's head, leaving him bent on the floor, tears of pain in his eyes. The pillow still waving, a white flag, and the bird was herded towards the window and out, suddenly hesitating in the air and almost returning, before Stuart began cramming bedclothes into the gap.

'You're probably going to get head lice,' said the other nurse to Alex.

'What the hell was up with that bird?' asked the orderly with the pillow. 'I mean, have we got a big hole in the wall somewhere or what?'

'There's going to be an inquiry over this one.'

'Just don't sue us about the lice, okay, Alex?'

His scalp was throbbing when he got home, his head smelling of disinfectant and Polysporin. He felt shaky still, but unable to sit down. He didn't think he wanted to cook himself anything for dinner. Didn't want to stay home at all, really. He'd spoken to his ophthalmologist that morning and it hadn't been very encouraging.

He could have phoned Susie. He thought about phoning Susie, but he found himself instead with his camera on Bloor Street. He'd tell her about the bird sometime. She would like to hear about it. But not now, not quite so soon, not so he looked like he needed her.

He did have to eat something before he started working, so he went into the tiny falafel shop by the movie theatre. An older woman, heavy-set, was sitting in one of the plastic chairs, wearing a deep green velvet head scarf and peeling a mandarin orange, and as he came in she looked up and smiled at him, soft, familiar, as if he were a loved relative, or as if the pigeon had marked him, in some way recognizable only to a few. He smiled back, nervously, and she stretched out half the orange towards him; he shook his head, but she pressed it into his hand, the orange and gold-washed flesh of it shining under the fluorescent light. He broke off a segment and lifted it to his mouth, the juice sharp and sweet, a wordless agreement between strangers in the city.

There was one night when *Dissonance* was in production that a phone call had come in, and Chris had waved Susie into the office to take it. Alex was at one of the tables studying a page layout, and he watched her, resting her head on one hand as she talked, biting her lip anxiously, twirling her hair around one finger. Chris seemed to get impatient as the call went on and started gesturing for her to hang up, but she shook her head. He spoke again, more sharply – Alex could hear his voice through the glass, though not the words – and she put her hand over the receiver and whispered something back at him, her face pale and tight. It was too long for Alex to keep sitting there; he had to go back into the darkroom.

He had just finished shooting a stat on the process camera when she knocked tentatively on the inner door.

'It's okay,' he called, switching on the light. 'You can come in.'

She sat down on the stool, her feet pulled up, tucking her knees under her chin.

'You all right?' he asked.

'Why wouldn't I be?'

'I don't know. You tell me.'

She was wearing an oversized white shirt and torn jeans, a jagged metal necklace, army boots. She put her head to one side, her cheek against her knee.

'Do you think it would be easy to lose your mind?' she said, picking at a flake of nail polish at the corner of her index finger.

He lifted out a sheet of photographic paper and ran it into the developing machine. The room smelled of chemicals and stale marijuana smoke.

'It could be,' he said.

'Does it scare you?'

The stat came out of the developer, a little darker than he'd wanted. Maybe he should shoot it again.

He had never thought about losing his mind, not really; he had enough to think about when a small needle of insulin was the only barrier between him and rapid death. 'Not so much as some things,' he said – and then pre-empting her, because she would have asked, 'I just mean things in general.'

She nodded. 'Okay.' He had one of his mixed tapes on in the background, a song from Big Star's last album playing, ragged and needy. 'If somebody loves you,' she said, and Alex was glad that he was facing away from her because he could feel the rush of heat in his face, 'what kind of rights does that give them?'

It took him a while to gather his breath to speak. 'Probably none,' he said quietly, turning a dial on the machine.

'Yeah. Maybe that wasn't what I meant.'

'I have to turn the lights out,' he said, and he pushed the switch, and they were in red-tinged darkness. The flash from the process camera blurred across them and flared out. He reached out a hand in the crimson dark and stroked her hair, and he knew that his fingers were wet with the developing fluid, that she would carry the smell of the darkroom with her for the rest of the night. Her face in red shadow. He thought her eyes were closed, though he couldn't be sure.

He stepped backwards and turned on the light.

'Yeah,' he said. 'Yeah, well. I have to run this through the developer now.'

'Yes,' she said. 'All right,' and slid down from the stool, turning towards the door.

Laser photocoagulation is performed as an outpatient procedure. Each individual treatment should take less than one hour. Your ophthalmologist will tell you how many treatments your particular condition will require. If you have been diagnosed with proliferative retinopathy, you will probably require two or more treatments at two-week intervals.

You may experience some discomfort during and after the treatment. You will be given anaesthetic drops before treatment, which should minimize the discomfort. If your eyes are still causing you discomfort one week after the treatment, inform your ophthalmologist.

You may experience blurred vision immediately after the treatment. This should go away by itself. DO NOT attempt to drive home after the treatment. You should bring a friend to the clinic who can take you home. If your vision continues to be blurry for several days, inform your ophthalmologist.

'I have an appointment for Monday morning,' said Alex, putting the pamphlet back in his bag as they walked, after dark, towards

Pottery Road. 'That in itself is disturbing. I don't like them treating it as an urgent case.'

'Do you want me to come?'

'No, I'll be okay. I'll just take a taxi back. But I did want to ask you – if you happen to be free. I wanted to take some photos of you this weekend.' They passed by a man wearing a surgical mask, white gloves on his hands. 'I know I'm being superstitious. It's not going to make a big difference, not the first series of treatments, only if I have to, only if it comes back. So it's not really that important but – I'd like to do it, if you have the time.'

Susie nodded. 'I was going to spend tomorrow in the library. But Sunday, if you want.'

'Late morning? The light's good in the late morning.'

'Sure. Whenever.'

Under snow-covered trees, they made their way down the hill, past the concrete divider with the black word FEAR on the side. High drifts surrounded the prancing wooden ponies of Fantasy Farms, and the glowing flower man was breathing out clouds of ice crystals, clutching a bouquet of plastic roses to his chest. Into the sketchy dreams of the city's sunken veins, across the Don.

They climbed the steep hill at Bayview, scrambling and sliding up the slope where the brush cover was most scattered, sinking into the snow. By the time they reached the top, snow had clumped in Alex's gloves and the creases of his coat, his boots had filled with a cold layer of it, freezing his ankles. He ran quickly over the railway track, thinking how he hated crossing it, though it was small and narrow and there was clearly no train anywhere nearby; he felt sure, irrationally sure, that an engine would loom up from nowhere and flatten him.

'Should I wait up here?' he asked, as they reached the sharp downslope, just above Derek's underpass. Across the valley, he could see an array of lights, and above them a soft red glow in the sky, the city's permanent day.

'Come down a bit further,' said Susie. 'We'll see how it goes.' She brushed snow from her arms. 'I'd like to have you in sight, I guess,' she added, almost apologetically.

She went down the slope ahead of him, and stumbled, clinging to a branch, onto the level area; following her, he nearly fell himself, snow down his right side. As he found his footing on the bare ground, he heard the sound of a man crying. Susie stood still. Inside the tent, the sound went on, hiccuping, empty, desolate.

She walked to the tent. 'Derek,' she said softly. 'Derek. It's Susie-Paul.'

The crying sound stuttered and died away. Susie waited, squatting down, and slowly Derek crept out of the tent, his face still wet and crumpled. Under the emaciation and dirt and age he seemed somehow young, almost childlike.

'I'm feeling very sad,' he whispered.

'I can tell,' said Susie gently.

'I was thinking about when we were small, and Mom and Dad killed our white horse.'

Susie pinched her lips together. 'We never had a horse, Derek.'

'Oh yes,' said Derek, nodding. 'We did. It was a white horse, and it spoke to us. But they killed it. There was blood all over. You cried and cried. I tried to comfort you.'

'Okay. Sure. Let's just not get into this now.'

'They cut its head off. The blood got into your hair. That's why your hair keeps changing colour.'

Susie put a hand to her hair automatically, then shook her head. 'Derek. We need to talk about a place you can live.'

'I'm doing very well here.'

'I don't think so. It's getting really cold. It will get colder in January. I don't want you living in a tent.'

'You remember that horse. I know you remember. Mom held its mouth shut while Dad cut its head off with an axe. The blood went flying.' Tears began to roll down his face again. 'Oh. Oh. It used to talk to us. Baby sister. It would take us away to a place where we could be safe together.' His voice broke up into little gasping sobs. 'You cried and cried.'

Susie covered her face with her hands. Slowly, quietly, Alex moved towards them. Derek rocked back and forth and seemed not to notice him, and he knelt in the frozen mud beside Susie and put his hand on her shoulder. She looked up, and for a second bent her head to the side so that her cheek touched his fingers.

'Derek,' she said, her voice steady. 'I understand that you're sad. My concern right now is the weather. It is too cold to be living outside.'

Derek wiped tears and mucus from his face and took several deep, shaky breaths. 'Will you introduce me to your friend?' he said.

Susie glanced at Alex and shrugged. 'Derek, this is Alex Deveney. Alex, Derek Rae.'

He stretched out his hand. Alex slid off his glove and took it, and they shook briefly. Derek's hand was trembling, and it felt wet and clammy and very cold.

'I don't think you can take proper care of my sister,' he said.

'No,' said Alex. 'I don't suppose I can.'

'I'm a grown woman, Derek. I take care of myself.'

Derek frowned. 'But you're still very little. You're my baby girl.'

'Let's talk about this housing problem.'

'They won't let me come inside,' said Derek. 'You know that. They never let me come inside. They make me go out.'

'Well, I'm trying to find a place that won't make you go out.'

He shook his head. 'They always make me go out. They tell me about the behaviour. They don't understand my parameters.'

'If you'd take your medication, we wouldn't have so many problems with your parameters.'

Derek scowled and looked sideways, towards the concrete wall, twitching a bit. 'We've discussed this before. I don't need medication. I have my own self-regulatory system.'

'Oh yeah. That's why you're starving to death in the snow under a bridge.'

'Baby girl.' Derek lifted his eyes to Susie, and crept slowly towards her, his voice suddenly dreamy, his tongue moving back and forth across his lower lip. 'Remember when you were bitten by the snake? I saved your life. I sucked the poison from your blood.'

Susie made a small noise, and Alex put his hand back on her shoulder.

'You were lying dead on the ground. You were so pale. You had no heartbeat. I picked you up in my arms and sucked the poison from your blood. Don't you remember?'

'That isn't what happened,' said Susie. She reached up to her shoulder and held on to Alex's hand with her own.

'I saved your life a hundred times. It was so hard. They kept trying to kill us, but I protected you. I will always protect you if you let me.' He touched her knee with his hand. 'Mom and Dad put the snake in your bedroom.'

Alex felt Susie's nails through the back of his glove. 'You know that it didn't happen like that,' she said weakly.

'They tried to kill you so many times. Then they realized they'd have to kill me first. But I won't let them, baby girl.'

Susie shook her head, exhaling hard.

'The snake was five feet long and golden, and it sank its teeth into your little thin arm, your poor little arm, while you were sleeping in your innocent bed. The poison went straight to your heart and you died. You died in my arms.'

'Derek.' Susie pushed herself backwards decisively, and her voice was sharp and businesslike. 'Forget the damn snake. I never died of snakebite. Let's talk about your medication.'

Derek sat up, his legs going into a nearly convulsive twitch. 'Susie-Paul, I don't want to hear any more of these dangerous ideas. You know that I regulate my own fluid patterns. I had a buildup of semen this week and I dealt with it by my own measures.'

'Oh God. Not this again.'

'It was semen of a particularly thick and corrosive nature. Building up and expressing itself into my penis and interfering with the release of urine. It was quite urgent to find a means to discharge it.' His hands were twining and untwining, his voice getting higher, more anxious.

'Cut it out, Derek. Drop the subject *now*.' She looked up at Alex. *I'm sorry*, she mouthed.

It's okay, he mouthed back.

'It was building up from my penis and testicles and entering my kidneys. It could have been very very hazardous. There was a leakage of semen from my penis on a regular basis.'

'Jesus Christ, would you please shut up about this? I have a friend here.'

Derek rolled his head slowly from side to side. 'Oh. Oh dear. It's a problem. It's a serious problem.'

'Shit,' murmured Susie, and motioned Alex away; he backed off a couple of feet, still within the circle of pale light. Derek was rocking and wringing his hands, his tongue working at one side of his mouth.

'And they say, and they say, we can't tolerate this, no no, we can't tolerate this, but I never did the crime. I never did.'

'Derek. Derek. Listen to my voice. Calm down.'

'And you say, oh God, and oh God, but what kind of God is that? When they do these things? This is what kind of God. And why did they want to hurt you? I don't understand, and I say, I don't understand, but why would you hurt her, and I tried to protect you, baby, I tried and tried.'

'Oh, please,' said Susie. 'Please don't do this. Just calm down, can't you calm down?'

'Fucking hate, fucking hate, fucking hate this, but I never did the crime, did I, so why do I, why do I, why the hell, oh God, *why do I have to live like this?*'

Susie stretched out her hand and tried to touch him, but he was a dystonic scatter of movements, unpredictable. His own hands flew up and began to claw around his eyes, saliva trailing from his lips, and she seized his wrists and pulled them fiercely down. He crashed into her lap in something like a spasm and threw his arms around her, wailing, *'Why don't you stay with me? Why don't you ever stay?'*

'Derek, *please.*' Susie fell backwards under his weight, thrusting one arm into the mud to support herself, as Derek pressed his head against her chest, sobbing, his hands grasping up to her face.

'Oh God, oh Jesus, what did I ever do to deserve this? They say I did the crime and they have to kill me, but I never did it, baby, I never did.' Susie was almost flat on the ground now, dangerously close to the edge of the hill, Derek's mouth on her neck, his body covering hers, and for a moment her arms seemed to go limp, helpless. Alex started forward.

But then she was moving again, she struggled free, and Derek slid down in a heap, his hands in his hair, a high hollow wail pouring out of his throat. Susie scrambled in the mud and pulled herself up, pressing her fists against her eyes.

'I know, Derek. I know you didn't,' she said, fighting for breath. 'It's all right. Just please. Try to calm down.'

'They poison me and fuck me up the ass until I bleed.'

'I'm sorry.'

'They want control of my mind so they can make me do the evil thing.'

Her face tense with effort, Susie leaned back towards him and rested her hands on his head, pulling his fingers out of his hair. 'Oh, Derek. It's okay. It's okay.'

'I'm not the bad garbage,' he said, his voice a thin whine.

'No. No, you're not. Sit up now, please. Sit up, Derek.'

He lifted his head, pulling his shoulders up until he could look in her eyes, wiping mud from his face.

'Will you talk to me, Derek, about coming inside?'

'No. No no. It's not a good choice. I'm sorry.'

'Then I have to leave now. I'll come back another day. I could bring you, I don't know, a warm blanket or something?'

'I have my resources. I'm not in need.'

'Well, I'll see what I can do.'

'Will you give me a kiss before you go?'

Susie frowned, a deep furrow between her eyes, and bit at her thumbnail.

'Please, little sister?'

She leaned towards Derek, and briefly, softly, touched his wet lips with her own.

'I won't let them hurt you,' he whispered.

'Yes, Derek. Thanks. I appreciate that.'

She came back to Alex, and they scrambled up the short slope and crossed the railway track. Susie didn't hurry across, he noticed; she saw that there were no lights, there was no sound of an approaching train, and walked over it at a normal speed, unafraid. She put her hands in her coat pockets and stood at the top of the hill, her jeans dark with mud and melted snow, staring across the ravine.

He remembered that night in the bar, all that time ago, when he had watched her crying, and he thought now that it had never been because of Chris at all, not Chris and not him, none of the things that had seemed so important.

'I've been the lucky one, Alex,' she said softly. 'Just lucky. That's all.'

The door of the Donut Wheel's smoking room opened and then shut nearby, and the smell of cigarettes drifted around them at their table.

'I don't know what options I have. He hasn't done anything that could be grounds for involuntary hospitalization.' Susie ran her finger over a bead of moisture on her beer bottle. 'I don't think I'd want to do that even if I had grounds. There's – there's trust issues here. It's just I'm really worried … I don't think it's an accident he's living so close to the railway tracks. He's tried to hurt himself before.'

The alcohol seemed to be affecting Alex disproportionately; he felt nearly drunk already after a single beer, and so drained and tangled up in confusion and, God help him, a sick kind of jealousy, that he could hardly put words together. 'Aren't there social workers? Anybody?'

'Well, what are they going to do with a guy under a bridge who won't talk to them? I mean, in a bizarre sort of way he's quite functional right now. Except for the not eating and the freezing to death.' She picked at a maple-glazed doughnut, rolling bits of white pastry between her fingers. 'I'll call up social services, though. Maybe one of these days they'll have a useful idea.'

Alex went to the counter and bought two more bottles of beer, thinking that she would kill him yet. Watched her pretty mouth on the brown glass, the slight movement of her throat when she swallowed. His mind full of serpents and severed heads, and the things that can happen to children.

'I don't know anything about you,' he said.

She raised her eyebrows. 'You know more than most.'

He took a long drink of beer and shook his head. 'Nothing, really.'

'Oh well.' She broke a fragment of icing off the doughnut and licked it from the end of her finger. 'It's probably not worth knowing.'

Outside on Broadview, in the cold, he slid his arms clumsily beneath her unbuttoned coat and kissed the side of her mouth – he really was drunk somehow, it was ridiculous. She took one of his hands and pressed the knuckles to her lips, but he could see that this was already a movement away; he knew before she said it that she wouldn't want him to come to her house that night.

'But, you know, Sunday, if you want to do the photo thing.'

'Yeah. Yeah, I do.'

'Take me somewhere you know about,' she said. 'Some weird hidden place. Show me the city. I promise not to criticize.'

'It's okay if you do. It's your job in a way.'

He walked down to the Danforth where the street signs were all in Greek, and he might as well have been in a foreign country, he knew so little, he was so far away.

Teenagers and old men wrapped scarves over their faces, picked up canvas bags and set out on newspaper routes with the early editions. One of the papers carried an article on the front page reporting, disapprovingly, the release on bail of the suspected terrorist, the man who had been parking his bicycle, now charged with assaulting a police officer.

On the next page, an article about the girl who had died of meningitis, the number to call if you had known her, the symptoms you should fear.

And at five in the morning Alex was walking around the west end, in the rising chill before dawn, his ears numb with cold and his blood sugar off, wondering why he couldn't stop doing this, surfing these waves of self-destruction, wanting her with the sick pain of a physical lack, the skin-twitch of hunger as her hands withdrew. And his eyes went on bleeding.

Derek Rae beneath his bridge, writing on scraps of paper, trying to bring back the numbers he once knew.

Remember this.

A boy and a girl, dark-eyed and small. The grass of the lawn is cut short, a perfect chemical green.

Listen, says the boy. I will save you. I will always save you. He pokes branches into the earth, a pattern, a star or a helix. I will learn about the nature of time, he says. I will learn how to change the world.

The girl, even now, understands that he will fail. But she loves him. There is no one else. The girl knows too much, for a child this small, about having no choices.

Gusts of dirty smoke unrolled across a landscape of broken glass, in the bleached light of a winter dawn, and between the smoke, parting it like curtains, the white figures moved, flames at their feet. Raised arms to signal to the others, the masks over their faces smeared with black dust, their breathing harsh. The strange cracked sounds of fire.

The hoses stretched out, long paths of canvas, and the firefighters, masked as well, their uniforms coated with ash, directed the streams of water towards the windows of the warehouse, and the smoke turned heavy and dark, clotted clouds hanging low to the walls.

The white figures moved in the doorway, bloated and clumsy, turning in gradual motion. Within the doors of the warehouse, a livid blackness. They held up their ashen hands, their instruments, their mysterious process. Their slow-dance liturgical beauty.

The smoke divided, inside the warehouse, and revealed the signs on the walls, on the yellow barrels, the chemical hazard signals.

Bioterrorism, said someone, standing a street away. *That's what I heard.*

I don't think so, said somebody else.

I'm just telling you. That's what they say.

Coming back inside from hours of cold was more than a shock; it was an unpredictable series of pains as Alex hung up his coat and sat down on the sofa in his apartment, a swelling ache at the back of his sinuses, fingers and ears burning, lightning darts of pain through clenched muscles, even the cuts on his scalp beginning to throb again as blood flooded the extremities of his body. Jane pulled herself heavily up into his lap as the shimmery waves of hurt subsided, and he shivered and held on to her gentle mammal warmth. Reached over to turn on the radio, the mildly eccentric music of the early morning, avoiding any stations where they might break in with news.

When he had stopped shivering, he checked his blood sugar, worked out the dosage he'd need to balance it this time, and decided to make himself a bowl of porridge and a pot of tea with cream, invalid food, soft and soothing. He sat on the couch watching the golden swirls of melting butter through the oatmeal, the thick caramel lumps of brown sugar, and then slept for a little while, Queen Jane on the bed draped over his legs. When he woke up, he drank a cup of black coffee and thought that, after all, this might be a good time to visit Adrian.

He was uncertain what went on in churches on Saturday afternoons, and was afraid he might interrupt something or walk in on a service, but when he opened the side door to the hall, all he found was a small group of people sitting on the floor in sweatshirts and tights, reading from bound scripts.

'But in what other way can we exist, in this consumer society?' recited one of them.

'No!' cried someone else. 'I don't accept this solution to our crisis!'

A man with a thin red ponytail looked up at Alex. 'Excuse me? We're rehearsing here?'

'I was looking for Adrian Pereira,' said Alex. The man nodded his head towards the back of the room.

'Through that way,' he said. Alex stepped carefully past the circle of performers and down a narrow hallway. There were doors leading in several directions, but he could hear the faint sound of a guitar coming from one of them, so he opened it and found himself in the church proper. It was dark; the first thing he made out was a wooden altar at the front, with a stained-glass window, the spiky outlines of figures he couldn't recognize. A circle of empty chairs, and in a far corner, by himself, Adrian playing a guitar and singing very quietly.

His voice had lost a bit of its upper register maybe, but it was still clear and oddly weightless. A voice that it was never really possible to sell, not a successful voice. He wasn't singing one of his own songs, and he wasn't singing a hymn either, though Alex briefly thought he was, and was made nervous by that; it was just one of those old odd floating songs about cryptic love.

> *Build me a castle*
> *Forty feet high,*
> *So I can see him*
> *As he rides by.*

sang Adrian, who did sometimes sing songs meant for women's voices without bothering to change the pronouns.

> *As he rides by, love,*
> *As he rides by.*
> *So I can see him*
> *As he rides by.*

Alex sat down in a chair, trying not to make any noise, but Adrian noticed him, of course, lifted his head from the guitar and stopped singing.

'Well. Hi there.'

'Hi,' said Alex.

'Waiting for someone?'

'No. Just hanging out.'

Adrian nodded and put the guitar down into its case. 'Okay.' He snapped the case closed and seemed to be thinking for a moment.

'You want to see our miraculous lightbulb?' he said at last. 'It's been burning for more than eighty years without ever being replaced. The angry little old lady wrote to the Archbishop of Canterbury about it.'

'Did he come and see it?'

'He never wrote back. I think she was pleased, it gave her something else to be mad at. "There's *no* excuse for this! Doesn't he open his *mail*?"' Adrian stood up and led Alex over to a niche in the wall that held a baptismal font and a small light with a red glass shade. 'Now, you understand I can't personally verify that it's been burning for eighty years. All I know is that we haven't replaced it in the two years we've been here. But I'm firmly told that it's been the same lightbulb as far back as the oldest person in the parish can remember.'

'Awesome,' said Alex.

Adrian looked at his watch. 'Well. I've got a kid coming in for a guitar lesson in a little while. But I could make some coffee if you want.'

They went into the little kitchen off the church hall, the actors throwing them suspicious looks. 'It's not just you, James,' one of them was reading solemnly. 'We men have to tackle our sexism as a group! And we'll do it as a group!'

'There's an idea,' said Adrian, pushing the kitchen door closed. 'We could do that.'

'Is two men enough of a group?'

'I've never been part of a bigger one.'

'I'm not sure I'm up to heavy-duty tackling, though.'

'Oh well. Another great opportunity lost.' Adrian reached up into the cupboard. 'Is instant okay? 'Cause if not there's, well, nothing actually. Maybe a teabag.'

'Instant's fine. By the way, your cupboards are full of herbal shampoo.'

'I know. Crazy Larry's been dumping his hot goods on us again.'

'Is this a routine thing with churches? Receiving stolen goods?'

'Pretty much, yeah. I mean, the general public would be surprised.' Adrian set a kettle onto the burner. 'So, there's a fire burning at a warehouse out in Scarborough,' he added. 'They were talking on the radio about evacuating people. Chemical fumes. There's a theory it was set on purpose.'

'By who?' asked Alex.

'The Mad Poisoner, I guess. He'll be dropping acid in the reservoirs next. Do we have reservoirs? I'm not sure.'

'We have Lake Ontario.'

'Yeah. That'd kind of dilute it, I suppose. When you were a kid, did you get those scenarios about the Russians putting LSD in the water supply?'

'Not that I can remember,' said Alex.

'Okay. Maybe I just had weird parents. Anyway, the thing about the Scarborough fire, everyone in Scarborough is just sitting in their houses waiting to be told what to do. We don't have much of a gift for chaos.' A twist of steam rose up from the kettle, and he poured the water over coffee crystals in two white mugs. 'I don't think people are as scared of LSD these days,' he went on. 'So it'd have to be something else in the water. PCP, would that scare people?'

'No,' said Alex, taking one of the mugs. 'Chemical warfare stuff. Or maybe disease. Ebola. Smallpox.' The imaginary doctor, pouring a test tube of cloudy liquid into a vat at the R. C. Harris Filtration Plant. Putting a match to a pile of rags in a suburban warehouse. Thinking of love.

Adrian poured sugar into his coffee from a tall glass dispenser on the counter, and stirred it again, hiking himself up onto one of the counters. 'That's true. It's an infection-based paradigm.'

'You like the word paradigm, don't you?'

'I like that it's gone out of fashion. Slightly obsolescent terminology is my deal.' He blew on his coffee. 'I could say they're just worried about nothing, but maybe that's the thing precisely. Nothing can be extremely disturbing.'

Alex sipped the coffee, which tasted of little except a certain artificial bitterness. 'I was listening to one of your old tapes the other night,' he said.

'Huh. That's something I don't hear very often.' Adrian looked down at his mug. 'I put too much sugar in this. Anyway, infection. It's all about people touching each other, isn't it? Proximity. Half the congregation won't drink out of the common cup any more. I've been counting.'

'Susie, Suzanne, she's planning to write an academic paper about it. But she thinks she has to talk to the girls from that first incident. Which I doubt she's going to be allowed to do.'

'Proximity's a difficult issue for people,' said Adrian. He pushed his glasses up on his nose, and then spoke quickly. 'You should have kept in touch, Alex.'

Alex leaned back against the other counter. 'I thought I did,' he said softly.

'When you moved? You never told me, remember that? I tried to call you and your number was disconnected, you didn't even have a message with the new one. So you can see, you know ... yeah, I could've looked up Deveney in the phone book, but it seemed like you were sending a kind of signal there.'

'I didn't mean to. I just forgot.'

'Well. I guess that's kind of true.'

'It *is* true. I mean, I don't even remember now, honestly. But I'd know if I'd done it on purpose.'

Adrian nodded. 'Okay. That's okay.' He looked up, took another sip of coffee and grimaced. 'It's really bad with all this sugar.'

'You could pour some water into it. But I don't suppose that'd solve anything.'

'So which tape were you listening to, actually?'

'The live one. Remember? You can hear Harold Kandel yelling in the background?'

'Oh yeah. He had this plastic bag with a radio in it. And when I asked him to turn it off he went into this thing about Minnie the Moocher. How she was a low-down hoochie-koocher and so forth. But I knew he was trying to be supportive.'

'It was meant as political commentary, I think.'

Adrian stirred his spoon around the oversweetened coffee. 'I did kind of like that tape.'

'It was good. Your songs are good.'

'I guess. In their way.' Adrian checked his watch. 'I should get back. I don't want my student being forced to tackle sexism as a group. But it's nice to see you.'

He let Alex out by the church door, and as Alex left he looked back and saw him standing in the doorway with his hands tucked into his armpits, watching down the street for his student, small and quiet, perfectly alone.

At the corner of Yonge and Gerrard, four men sat on the ground in handcuffs, in a ring of police and campus security. Two of them, manic and agitated, were arguing about who had hit who first, while the other two leaned back against the wall with a strangely cheerful air, as if this were an interruption in the daily routine staged only for their entertainment.

'He's a fucker, that guy,' commented one of them.

'He's a bum,' said the other. He laughed languidly. 'But hell, so am I.'

'He's fucking screwed.'

'I didn't hit fucking nobody.'

'Me neither, man. Didn't lay a hand.'

'He's a fucker.'

In the business district, figures in coats hurried across a windy corner below a looming pixelboard display, a loop of stock prices and headlines and weather reports. Suspicious fire of unknown origin. Security Council negotiations. The cold front stationary, hovering like a hawk above the city.

A man walked through a corridor, quickly, thinking of events set in motion. On the twenty-third floor of a half-empty office tower, a woman backed away from a wrinkled envelope that had been pushed beneath the door, a piece of paper marked with the type-written words THIS IS NOT ANTHRAX. Backed away, hands shaking, from the threat understood in the denial of threat. Reached for a phone.

When the fire trucks arrived the alarm system was activated, the building emptied. The workers from the twenty-third floor hosed down, their clothes dripping, inside a white tent in the icy chill. In the surrounding apartments, people came to the windows and saw them filing into the street, evacuees. A woman in a nearby church sat in the centre of a meeting room, huddled in a chair, hearing the sound of the alarms gliding up and down in the air.

A tall man stood under the freezing spray, his feet in a plastic pool, water cascading from his dark suit, and felt suddenly emptied of everything, staring along the winter buildings outside the door of the tent and into a clear blank freedom.

Some distance away, a rock smashed through the window of a shop at Coxwell and Gerrard, scattering glass across the display counter, the bright-coloured honey-and-milk array of sweets. A television over the counter played on to no one, the news crawl picking up the rumours of anthrax, the hazmat team on the screen with their purifying hoses.

'You'll probably hate this place when it's finished,' said Alex. 'It'll all be very expensive. But I thought you'd like it right now.'

He stood with Susie in a long channel of mud, under the heavy brown-brick walls of the abandoned Victorian factories, slabs of wood laid over the wet dirt where there would someday be cobbled walkways. The sun came over the high buildings in shards of cold brightness, breaking out from a soft dense sky. It was a good day for light, slightly diffused through cloud, not too harsh.

Here and there, new businesses had already opened – a coffee shop, a microbrewery, a small art gallery. But most of the space was still inchoate, forming itself out of the memories of fallen industry, sweat and dust and darkness. Susie looked around intently, and Alex supposed she had a theory, she always had a theory, but she only nodded, apparently pleased. They walked up a temporary wooden stairway to a metal door, set in a massive brick wall, and Alex took a set of keys out of his pocket.

'Are you really supposed to be in here?' she asked.

'I know people.' He turned the key and pushed the door open. 'It's going to be artists' studios in this building. And if I say I need it for a photo shoot, they know I'm not really going to bring in twenty friends and a keg of beer.' He motioned for Susie to come inside. 'The thing is there's no heat. And no artificial light, but I know where there's a good exposure.'

The hall they entered was dark and wet, but the spiral stairway to the next level had already been built, and he led her down a corridor of drywall and metal spars, into a half-finished room where a large south-facing window filled most of one wall.

'I think there's a photographer going to rent this one,' he said. 'It'd be good. If you wanted to have a studio in a fashionable place, I mean.'

Out of the wind, it was not quite as cold, but the chill was damp and clinging. Susie put her red hat into her pocket but left her coat on, over a black sweater and jeans.

'Do you think you could take your coat off?' he asked. 'It's okay if not. It's not exactly warm in here.'

She blew out a small puff of visible breath and smiled, but shrugged the coat off and left it in a corner. 'Just don't take forever, all right?'

'I'll try not to.'

He bent down and opened his camera bag, took out the Leica and selected a lens. It had to be the Leica, but he was glad that she didn't understand how much that meant to him.

'Let's try near the window,' he said. 'You could just stand over there.'

He didn't do a lot of portraits. A hand spot and an umbrella would have been useful, but he would have needed to rent them. He hung the Leica around his neck and got out his light meter.

'Could you lean against there, by the window?' he suggested. 'Yeah. That's good.'

He loved the way this camera felt in his hands, the gentle action of it. The planes of her face, her hair loose around her neck, the sharp corners of the window frame.

Part of the trick was shooting around the eyes, those dark-chocolate eyes, not letting them dominate her face entirely. Get light on the cheekbones, the rather thin pale lips, the slight emerging grooves from her nose to the edges of her mouth.

'So what's up with the dissertation?' He was forcing conversation, he knew; if he didn't get her to talk, she'd end up with that awful rigid portait face you so often saw. He took in the rough texture of her sweater, almost feeling the thick knots of black wool, synaesthetic. 'Arms down a bit? Thanks.'

'Oh. Um, working on a chapter about homeless youth.' She looked out the window, moving her face into three-quarter profile, and licked her lips once, nervously. 'No one makes things these days, do they?'

'How's that?'

'I'm just thinking about this place. The city used to be about manual labour, didn't it? Making things, tangible things. Now it's all service industries. It's all, do you want fries with that?'

'Well, they made whiskey. It's not exactly, I don't know, like hammering stone.'

Light spreading, honey-yellow, across her body, her left breast edged with shadow, outlining the soft shape. A rectangle of sunlight on her right hip, against the broken plaster wall.

'Nevertheless,' she said. 'It's as if there's no such thing as primary production here anymore.'

'The terminal stage of capitalism?'

She smiled a bit, self-conscious but not as much so, the tension in her arms beginning to release. 'You've been talking to Vojcek, haven't you? He's a bright guy, but I think his theoretical framework's kind of outdated.'

He adjusted the focus. The strong line at the side of her cheek, a wedge of shadow between her face and the window frame. She was quite objectively beautiful. It probably hadn't made her life any easier.

'Sit down now?' he suggested, gesturing towards a wooden spool with insulated wire curled around it. He was concentrating too hard, he was making her nervous. 'Or you could just do whatever. Pretend I'm not here.'

'Oh, sure,' said Susie, and this finally got her to laugh, he took a series of shots quickly, didn't want to lose this chance. 'This is such a natural location.' She sat down on the spool, good, her movements were less constrained now, she was adjusting to the camera.

'Could you turn your head that way? Yes. Thanks.' Loose strands of fine hair along her neck, the inch of exposed skin pale with cold. He sat back on his heels, reaching into the camera bag for a second roll of film.

'You're not digital?'

'I'm digital at work. I'm kind of a luddite personally.' He checked the light meter again. His shirt was damp at the armpits. 'I don't know where that puts me in terms of, ah, types of production.' Susie shifted on the spool. Folded up her legs, her hands around one ankle, her thighs a complex swell like a pool of water. He checked his light meter and moved further to one side. The action of the Leica under his fingers.

'This is kind of weird,' she said. 'I'm not used to, I don't know, I'm not used to this.'

'Yeah, I know. Photo sessions, they're a funny thing, they're ... ' he ran out of words. She smiled, and pushed at her hair as it slid back over her ear.

'I trust you, though,' she said. Pale hand resting on her knee, the pattern of wear in the fabric of her jeans, the sun-filled hollows in the curves of her legs. He picked up the light meter and walked around the room, his eyes off her for a moment, half dizzy.

'Could you stand over here?'

She stood up from the spool and crossed the room again, stood awkwardly against the unfinished wall.

'It's okay. Relax. Just stand normally.' She bent one leg and put her hands behind her back, leaning her head against a spill of light, a good accident.

'This isn't really normal.'

'It'll do.' He went down on one knee and held the camera upwards. She tipped her head slightly to the side, suggestion of tendon along her neck, a shadow on the opposite cheekbone.

'I hope you're not thinking of exhibiting these.'

'They're yours.' He leaned back. 'They're completely yours. I'll give you the negatives if you want.'

'I was kind of kidding, actually.'

She swept her hair over her ears with both hands, letting it down in front of her shoulders. Folded her hands loosely in front of her, cupped low on her stomach, her wrists resting above the small protrusions of her hipbones. The inevitable upwards tension of her legs, the bowl of her hands.

'The police are going to come and accuse you of making nerve gas in here,' she said.

He adjusted focus, still kneeling in front of her, and moved the shot in tight to her face. The fine crinkling of the skin around her eyes, the maple-syrup fall of hair, indirect light on the golden strands within the soft brown. The small space of floor between them, the lens of the camera. The way the Leica felt, like a human response.

'Okay.' He put the camera down, staring at the floor and feeling the pulse of blood in his head. 'I think that's enough.' He looked up at her, and tried to smile casually. 'You're free to go.'

This was the strangest moment for the person being photographed, he knew, suddenly released from the control of the lens and unsure how to move. There was always that second of forced ·informality, a small nervous laugh. He took a deep breath and wiped his forehead. Susie shook out her hands, more shy now than when he was photographing her, and then walked across the room for her coat, pulled her hat down over her ears, and sat down not far from him.

At that moment he was prepared to give in completely, to let her eat him alive if that was what she wanted. He blinked at the skittering hint of a floater in one eye, and swallowed.

They sat on the floor, across from each other, in the frozen half-built room.

'I'm not really a terminal case,' he said. 'I'm not really going to end up blind tomorrow.'

'Of course not.'

'It's a thing I have to do. It's not anyone's good scenario.'

Outside the window the sun broke through cloud, a broad slab of light suddenly detailing the flawed uneven plaster of the wall, the unsanded wood floor. She stood quickly and walked from the room, and it seemed to Alex as if her image in the doorway froze in a hanging moment of time, her head in profile. Susie leaving.

She must have expected that he would follow, shivering with the bright cold and the need of her; and in the dark hallway at the bottom of the spiral stair she reached out for him, the chill of her hands like needles on his skin, the rough grain of the brick wall scraping the fabric of his coat as his body rose to hers, her heat pouring into him. But the image was as fixed in his mind as any picture, the sequel to every photograph he had ever taken of her. Susie turning away.

A woman fell down at Glencairn, the long sweep of her coat spreading over the tiles of the floor. A few hours later, the police entered the back room of a pizza restaurant on Ossington and arrested a Nigerian man who had been seen near the warehouse before the fire, taking a picture with a disposable camera.

At the Healthcare Divisional Operations Centre, men and women sat around the table in an emergency meeting. Two paramedics who had attended at the College Street restaurant were off work, collapsing suddenly, their symptoms unclear. A flipchart by the table was scribbled with handwritten notes. Under the heading *A) Unknown/ fainting*, written in blue ink, were the words *Contact CUPE asap. Working quarantine possible?*

Then a slash across the page, and a second heading, this time in red, a pointer to an urgent fax lying on the table: *B) MENINGITIS*.

In the crooks of the ravine, men and women reached out for survival, scooping water from the river, and at the shore of the lake someone walked through the small stone spirals of a garden, and saw the word FEAR on the side of a building across the road.

The girl who had fallen went back to the park bench, and the can of tuna and the money had been taken.

It could have been anyone.

She walked to the bushes at the edge of the hill, and she thought of going past the line of trees, but the thistles caught at her clothes, and she stepped back.

It was late when Alex left Susie's house on Carlaw, late enough that the subway had stopped running. Late enough that he was expected at the eye clinic in a matter of hours, and he still had to develop the film in his camera bag. He walked down to Gerrard, turning off Carlaw to pass beneath the bridge, where snow and damp litter piled up at the edge of the wall, the smell of urine lingering on the concrete. He was tired, he hadn't had enough sleep for days, maybe weeks.

He leaned his head against the glass of the window as the bus travelled along Gerrard, and almost wished that he was twenty-five again, able to live on devotion and drama. To promise her he would do anything, for nothing in return, and to believe it was true. Give up, give in, whatever the state of his blood, though she was always poised in a doorway on the verge of departure.

But he couldn't; he couldn't go on like this really, he would kick this, he would let it go.

The hopeful phantoms of the city's night passed briefly under the streetlights as the car turned onto Carlton – a large bearded man in a white tutu, a fat little Franciscan monk eating a burger from a paper bag, a woman with a shopping cart full of newspapers. He rode further, onto College, past the university and the frayed margins of Spadina, into the small shops and cafés of his own neighbourhood, and he got off the streetcar and stood at College and Grace feeling once again that the city was just about to give up its secrets, that point in the depth of the night when everything was transparent and lucid, one impossible step from a final meaning. When he saw the man held hostage leaning against the wall, he greeted him like a kind of colleague, a fellow worker in the fields of madness.

'Thank you so much, sir,' said the man, taking the two-dollar coin. 'You're very kind. They're assembling the forces to protect me, sir. There's been a great improvement.' He hid the coin away somewhere among his layers of sweaters. 'And the man you were looking for, have you had good luck in finding him?'

'Oh. We found him, yes. Thanks very much for your help.'

'It's no problem, sir, I'm happy to do what I can. It was approved by the government, you see. It's all part of a larger plan. The terrorists want me dead, sir, because of the pretty people falling from the air, so I have to keep on top of an intelligent strategy.'

'It's not easy,' said Alex. 'I don't find it easy myself.'

'But you've always been kind to me, and they're sure to give consideration to that.' He scratched at the hair around his ears. 'There are different ways that a person could come to die, I guess. Like when blood comes out of the ears. But you could also die if you happen to walk on the subway tracks and a train arrives. Do you ever think about that, sir?'

'I try not to.'

The man nodded. 'The terrorists try to put me in front of the trains. It's pretty bad, sir. But I have the support of the military now. They're getting the forces in position. So thank you for the help, and things are getting better all the time.'

'No trouble. Really. And I hope ... ' he shrugged, unsure what he could hope for this man.

'They're mobilizing the forces on the border, sir!' the man called after him as he reached for his key and opened the door of his building.

III

This is what happened. Alex Deveney sat with his head in a box – though it was not actually a box, it was in fact a medical device of some sophistication, but he experienced it as a box, a metal box. And in the darkness of this device they fired lasers at his eyes, burning the overgrown blood vessels, and burning, as well, the tissue around them. This was unavoidable, the risk could be reduced but never eliminated; there would be some spontaneous repair, but also some permanent scarring. The lasers were a specialized type known as Argon Green, used in many similar procedures. More than one eye condition is treated with Argon Green lasers, but for proliferative retinopathy the burns are harsher, the number of burns is many times greater. It is an intractable illness, difficult to treat.

Alex sat with his head in a box, repeating the words *Argon Green* in his head with each painful flash, about a thousand burns on each side, green knives of light from the dark ground. He lost, for a while, chronology and proprioception, existence distilled to the world of Argon Green and the small fluid arc of the eye.

And the rest of the world went on, planes fell out of the air and diseases were quarantined, amazing rescues were performed from burning buildings, people married and died and played air guitar.

In a biohazard lab, instruments scanned the single sheet of paper that had arrived from nowhere saying that it contained no anthrax, and again and again the machines proved the claim to be true. It made no sense, the only reason to deny such a thing was its ultimate truth, but the instruments ran the results again and returned the same answer. Nothing.

On a late-morning street in the centre of the city, Alex Deveney leaned against the wall of an office tower, his hands over his face.

He hailed a taxi and rode home trembling. He couldn't see, he couldn't properly see, everything was obscured by glare and blur, and his eyes were throbbing with pain. And he knew it wasn't really so bad. He was blowing this out of proportion, he had to be.

The blur would go away, the blur was not permanent damage. The permanent damage he couldn't be sure of right now.

The glare was probably lasting. He would have trouble with bright sunlight forever, he'd have to wear dark glasses or some stupid baseball cap. This intense lovely light of winter, the crystal drifts.

He couldn't really tell if his field of vision had narrowed. It felt constricted. He could be wrong. It was easy to imagine, hard to be sure.

He turned out the lights in his apartment and lay down on the couch. It would get better. Of course it would get better. And he would go on taking pictures. He would go on as long as he could distinguish light from darkness and maybe after that. Perhaps he could make a living as a kind of inspirational novelty. Hallmark would put his photos on their cards, beside poems about how you truly see with your heart. But he wasn't going blind right now, that was absurd, self-dramatizing.

He had a vague memory of reading somewhere that if you drank a lot of water it would wash anxiety-causing chemicals out of your system, which seemed like probably spurious science, but he went to the sink and drank two glasses of water anyway.

He remembered the tulips he had seen lying in one of the city's concrete planters the past summer. Squirrels had got at the bulbs, dug them up and eaten them, and left the stalks, with the flowers still in the bud, lying scattered across the planter's soil. But they had gone on growing, they had gone on turning red, the buds opening into distorted and burned-looking flowers, even bending upwards on the torn stems towards the sun, a futile and terrifying pantomime of vitality. He had wished that they would just give up and die, or that someone would throw them away, but he had never done anything himself, just gone on staring at them every day, at their horrible stupid post-mortem life.

In the hospital, the specialists held their vigil over the burned man. They supervised the debridement of the dead meat from his body, watched the progress of the skin grafts. The man woke and slept again, and saw always the fire as it came towards him.

He knew that he had not been a good man, not really, that he had failed in work and in love and talked to himself sometimes out loud. *Speak to the bones*, he would say to himself, thinking of her disappointed face and the carton of expired milk. Things happened badly. But no one could tell him why – how it was he had been burned like this, why he was the person that young men had chosen to hurt.

The burned man could not remember their faces, those angry young men equipped with fire. When he saw them in dreams, coming towards him, he could not picture them clearly. These things he knew, that they had lighters in their pockets, alcohol on their breath, that they had tense, implacable muscle. That they were full of lack and desire, and they hated him because he was weak. Because he was no one.

They were angry before these troubles started, these young men, and they would be angry afterwards, formlessly angry, and only rarely would they cross the path of the public world. They were not the city's only threat, and not the worst, but in the burned man's dreams they came to him, and he woke to pain and purple infection and the constant drip of liquid in his arm.

Pray for us now and at the hour of our death, he whispered.

Alex went down the winding slope of Grace Street and walked for a while in Trinity-Bellwoods Park, kicking at snow, throwing a badly formed snowball at a tree. Then the pain got to be too much for him and he went home and took a Tylenol and sat with his eyes closed, listening to the radio.

'And phone in those pledges right now, people,' the announcer on the campus radio station was saying, 'because we are $15,000 behind on our rent, and if you don't get on those phones, we're going off the air at midnight!'

He would have to remember to check the station tomorrow and find out whether they were still around.

This is what it would be like, he thought, an aimless little life of walks and radios and pointless diversions. Because he couldn't really believe that it would work out well, that they would arrest the disease with a few treatments and cause no major damage to his sight. His ophthalmologist, he suspected, didn't really believe it either. It happened that way for some people, but it wouldn't happen for him.

The girl watched the late afternoon light move across her desk, deep yellow, the sun glowing orange behind the dark mass of trees beyond the window. Her notebook was open in front of her, a purple pen with gold sparkles lying across it. The English teacher reached for a dictionary and set it down on Zoe's desk. 'Okay. Definition and derivation,' he said. 'Read that part?'

Zoe glanced at the page. 'What? The whole letter B?' she said teasingly. The teacher pointed at a line.

'Beel ... no way. You're trying to make me look dumb.'

'Oh, come on,' said the teacher.

'You read it.'

The teacher shrugged and picked up the dictionary. 'Beelzebub,' he said. 'Definition 1: the prince of demons; the devil. Now you read the derivation.' He passed the book to Lauren, who ran her finger down the page and found the line.

'Hebrew – oh, wow! Hebrew for Lord of the Flies! Awesome!'

'Oh my GOD!' exclaimed Zoe, putting her hands up to her face. 'How did you even *know* that? Were you just, like, reading through the dictionary one day and you found it?'

'Um, it's just more like – general knowledge,' said the teacher, who was a very young man, though he didn't seem so to the girls in his class. 'It's a thing people know.'

The girl drew a flower in the corner of a page, watching the rest of the class from the corner of her eye. Looked outside at the woods.

'That is so *awesome*,' said Lauren.

The girl played with her pen for a moment, and then closed her exercise book and carefully inked the word FEAR onto the cover, in tiny, precise, very dark letters.

'You know, if William Golding had kids, his kids would be *totally* upset reading this book,' said Tasha.

At the St. Patrick station, on the stairway leading to the street, a woman collapsed and fell down half a flight, breaking two bones in her hand. A dead smell, she said it had been, a dead, sweet smell that pulled her down.

How could she be expected to do proper blood tests, asked the doctor in the toxicology lab, when no one could tell her what to look for, when all they could tell her was what they supposed it was not, not sarin, not cyanide, probably not a virus? Was she meant to search down to infinite degrees of abnormality? There could never be an end to that.

In the storage rooms and passageways below the subway lines the hazmat workers moved, breathing through heavy masks, slowly searching each room, each corner, for traces of powder or chemical marks, for doors opened that should not have been, cigarette butts in forbidden areas, for any sign that someone had hidden here, waiting, contaminants in open hands.

Other things happened that were innocuous and fairly ordinary, the little troubles of winter. A common enterovirus infiltrated several playschools and caused a large number of toddlers to start vomiting. Many adults exhibited upper respiratory tract infections. Some of them, remembering the men who had lost their breath at the King station, understood their symptoms to mean that they had been poisoned. Hospital emergency departments began to overflow.

A man was admitted to one of the hospitals with a high fever, the transaction that had passed between himself and a dead girl breaking violently to the surface. This man got to a doctor in time; he was treated effectively with intravenous antibiotics. Public Health was notified, and began once again the process of tracing contacts, discovering those he had been close to, those he had lived with, those he had touched. Meningitis is fast, faster than organized plans, and the dead girl, the vector, with her weak immune system and her coded, hidden world, she was moving the authorities now in a way that her life could never have done.

Alex went out again in the early evening with his camera, and tried dismally, experimentally, to take some pictures. That everything felt wrong was surely a function of his mood as much as the state of his eyes.

Anyway, some of the photos might turn out all right. There was a quality of light and movement that he liked, outside the windows of the Diplomatico, a girl in the doorway of the Bar Italia, these might be okay after all. He had to believe that.

When he got back to his apartment, there was a message on his voice mail from Susie. Asking how he was. He didn't want anyone asking how he was. Telling him that she was going to see Derek that night, that she'd be leaving around ten, he could come to her house anytime before that.

In theory, he could simply not turn up. She had left him that choice. She might even have been suggesting it.

He could do other things. He could phone his sister, his pleasantly normal, dissatisfied sister, and listen to her stories of the folly of her co-workers. He could call in a pledge to that poor campus radio station. He sat on his couch stroking Jane and thinking about the things he could do if he didn't answer Susie's message, and then it was quarter to ten. He stood up and got his coat, put the photographs of her in a new manila envelope, and packed his insulin kit in his camera bag. He was halfway out the door when he turned back, grabbed the string of the balloon and brought it along with him.

He would come when she called. Watch when she left. Lose her, lose his eyes. Lose the winter light, and end up with nothing.

Two of the smaller restaurants along College had posted handwritten signs in the windows, announcing themselves to be Closed on Account of Illness. Whether this was the illness of the proprietors, or whether they were entrenching against the illness of the city, he wasn't sure.

He was late. She'd probably go ahead without him.

End up with nothing.

He rode the streetcar up Bathurst, noticing that the gold foil star was sagging a bit now as the helium leaked slowly away. He didn't look out the window, not wanting to know how much he was unable to see. As he got off the car at the Bathurst station, he saw the word FEAR spray-painted in big black letters on the concrete wall. He entered the station and caught the subway going east.

As he arrived at the house he checked his watch – it was past ten-thirty. But when he went inside the front door, he saw that the door to her apartment, at the foot of the stairs, wasn't actually closed. Slightly ajar, it swung open further at his knock.

'Alex?' she called down the stairs.

'Yeah, it's me.'

'Are you okay? Come on up.'

She was sitting at her desk chair, lacing her boots, but she stood up when he came in.

'How are you? I tried to phone.'

Alex moved away from her, slumping down on her futon couch, and fought back another irrational spasm of anger. He twitched his shoulders in a tight shrug. 'They cauterized the blood vessels, I guess. I can't really, you know, it's too early to say if it's affected my vision. It's just the first round anyway. I have to go back.'

'How are you feeling, though?'

'It hurts. I'd rather not talk about it.' He realized that he was still holding the balloon, and stretched his hand towards her. 'Here. This is for you.'

Susie took hold of the string and wrapped it loosely around the back of her chair. 'Wow. Mafia balloon,' she said with a faint smile. 'Thanks.' The star didn't pull the string taut anymore, but hovered softly a few feet below the ceiling.

'I was just going to see Derek.'

'Yeah. I know. I got your message.'

'I don't have to go right now necessarily.' She played absently with the string of the balloon. 'I talked to this guy, this psychiatric social worker, he's going to come with me and see him next week, if he's got my okay maybe Derek'll talk to him.'

And suddenly he couldn't bear any of it, the hunger and the damage, the constant covert search for signs of other men in her life, the moment when she would leave him this time. He shoved his hands into his pockets. 'Good. Great. You won't be needing me anymore, then.'

She pushed her hair back and looked at him, frowning. 'What does that mean?'

'Oh, nothing. Never mind. It's probably just as well.'

'Alex.' She sat down on the couch beside him, and he edged away.

'I said it's okay. Look, I was convenient. I'm aware of that, and if you've got some other guy to take over, that's fine. I can't really do this any longer anyway.'

Susie lifted one hand to her mouth and began to chew on the edge of her thumb. 'Okay, I don't get this. Where is this coming from all of a sudden?'

'Oh, come on.' He stretched out his legs and crossed one ankle over the other. 'We both know where I stand. I mean, you never bothered to call me for thirteen years, did you? You called Adrian and not me, for God's sake.'

'This is bullshit.' She twisted her thumb between her teeth. 'In case your memory doesn't extend back a full three weeks, I *did* call you, how the hell else would you even be here?'

'Yeah. Eventually. You did.' He didn't know why he didn't stop, but he couldn't, the rush of it, high and reckless. 'Your brother was missing and you wanted somebody to be your, your good luck charm or whatever. And apparently you didn't happen to have any other admirers around at that point, or, or your husband, whoever the hell he was –'

'His name's Nick McCawley,' said Susie fiercely, biting off a strip of nail. 'He works at Legal Aid. Why don't you give him a call, collect a few more stories you can throw in my face?'

'That's not my fucking point!' He didn't mean to shout, but it happened, a stab of pain in his head. 'I'm trying to tell you, I can't do it again, Susie-Paul, I can't go through this again.' He put his hands up to his eyes and rubbed them. 'For God's sake. Of course I want you. You're smart, you're beautiful, probably everybody wants you. But it costs me too much. It costs me too fucking much to hold your hand until you feel like going away. I can't give up everything else just to be a marginal player in the dramatic life of Suzanne Rae.'

She stood up then, without saying a word, picked up her coat and walked past him to the stairs and left, closing the door hard behind her, and suddenly he was alone in her apartment, half-panicked by what he had just accomplished. He couldn't stay here without her, that was ridiculous, he had to – oh Christ, he had to follow her again. He ran down the stairs and out into the street.

She was far ahead of him, a distant little figure under the street-lights. He had to keep running, his camera bag thudding awkwardly against his hip, to catch up with her, and for a minute he thought that he wouldn't, that he'd have to stop and lose sight of her. In the darkness she kept receding, a small shadow in the shadows, and by the time he reached her he felt such relief that he almost didn't expect her to be angry.

'Get lost,' she snapped. He tried to touch her shoulder, but she shook him off, still walking.

'Susie, cut it out,' said Alex, struggling for breath. 'I wasn't making fun of your life. I've seen what you go through with Derek, I know it's real, and I know the breakup with Chris must have hurt you in its own way, but Jesus, it nearly killed me, and you never even noticed.'

'That is not true.'

'Okay. You did. You noticed that I was someone who would just hang around and be in love with you forever and never ask too much of you. But I,' he tried to catch his breath; she was so much smaller than him but she was moving fast, 'I have a chronic illness, okay? I don't like to say that, but it's true. The first night we went down into the ravine, I nearly had a hypo episode, and then my sugar went up way too high, and I had something close to a hemorrhage from the stress, I had serious damage to the blood vessels in my eyes, I'm, I'm, I'm losing my sight for fuck's sake, you can't do this to me!'

She didn't stop walking, but she slowed down a bit. 'You didn't tell me.'

'Well, what was I going to say?'

'I'm sorry, then. About that, I'm sorry. But about everything else, you're just wrong.'

'I am not.'

'Do you really believe – God, Alex, do you think I could ever …' she moved her hands in the air as if she were trying to shape a sentence. 'Alex, I'm sorry about what happened back then. I fucked up. I treated you badly, I know I did. But you have no idea. You have no idea what it took to call you, what it – Alex, *you*, you are not, you have never been marginal. You can't believe that. You can't really believe that.'

'It's actually not very hard, all things considered.'

'No. No, you just want to think that.'

'Fuck that, Susie-Paul.'

'You do. You don't want to think that I was confused too. You don't want to think that you mattered. That's too hard. You just want to live in this pretend world where you aren't responsible for anything.'

'*I'm* not responsible? You left. You just *left*. You never even sent me a fucking postcard.'

'Go home, Alex,' she said quietly. They were nearing the intersection with Broadview now. 'I don't need you.'

'No kidding,' said Alex sourly.

'God, you like that idea, don't you? Poor Alex, out in the cold, all fragile and powerless. As if you … as if it never hurt, knowing you were always there – wanting things I couldn't give you or, or anyone …' She turned her head sharply, scanning the road for a break in the traffic. 'As if you never hurt me. Jesus.'

'It's not the same at all.'

'Okay, then.' She turned to him. Her face was cold and very still. 'I had an abortion in Vancouver. Will that do?'

He wasn't immediately aware of any emotion. The first thing he thought was that he needed to sit down, and his legs folded up onto someone's front lawn. He saw the outline of Susie standing in front of him in the darkness, a faint red wash from the Christmas lights of the house beside them, her arms crossed.

'Good enough, Alex? Happy now? You think maybe you did enough harm after all?'

'Oh God. Stop. I don't … I don't … '

'What I really hate,' she went on, her voice tight and controlled, 'is that I can't tell you for sure if it was yours. Because I don't know.

You have no idea how much I hate saying that, but I don't know.' He pressed his fingers against his temples. 'Not that there are a million candidates. It was either you or Chris. I just can't be sure who.'

'It's not … ' he said, and the words came out too high-pitched, ' … surely it's not very likely it was me. I mean, it was only … '

'No. But it's not very likely it was Chris either. One way or another, something unlikely happened, all right? It's true I was sleeping with Chris on and off until I actually left town, which in retrospect seems pretty sick, but on the other hand,' she took a breath, 'when I slept with Chris, we used birth control.'

He dug his hands into his hair. 'Oh Jesus.'

'Yeah, well.'

'I'm sorry. God, I'm sorry. I thought … I assumed you would have said something if … oh, hell. I guess it doesn't help to say I wouldn't do the same thing now.'

She sat down on the grass beside him, and he put his head on his knees.

'I shouldn't have told you.'

'I don't know. I don't know. Yes, you should've.'

'I don't blame you. Not really. I'm sorry I brought it up this way.'

'No. I had to know.'

'Chris doesn't know. I don't plan to tell him.'

A car drove by, lights passing over them. His eyes were throbbing. 'Suppose,' he said hesitantly, 'suppose you had known … say you knew for sure it was Chris's … would you have … '

'Please. Don't. It's not worth going that way. I was by myself in Vancouver, and honest to God, neither one of you was looking like fantastic father material.' She swallowed once, and he thought she was trying not to cry. 'I nearly did tell you. I had my hand on the phone once. But how the hell can you say to somebody, I'm pregnant and it could be yours, but then again maybe not?'

'I don't know. I guess most people just lie.'

'Anyway,' he saw dimly that she was lifting her hand and wiping her eyes, 'that wasn't the only thing. I just … Alex, my twin brother is schizophrenic.'

He bit his lip. 'Yeah. And I have diabetes.'

'Oh God, you don't get it,' she said, her voice choked. 'Do you think I meant – '

'I don't know what I think. I don't think anything.'

'It wasn't like that, I wasn't thinking about the, the child having it. I was thinking about me. I was thinking,' and now she really was crying, he heard the small gasping sounds between her words, 'I would lose my mind, I would go crazy like Derek, and I would have this baby, this poor little baby, and it would have to love me, it wouldn't have a choice because babies don't, and it would have to watch me lose my mind. Probably just when it was old enough to really – to have its life totally destroyed, and I could see it so clearly, I could see how I would fall apart, little by little, and I would, I would do awful things, I would *hurt* it, hurt it in all kinds of horrible ways, and it was so easy to picture, so easy … '

'But why … for God's sake, why would you … '

'I was sitting in, in this chair, in this house in Vancouver, and there was this picture in my mind of putting a baby's hand on the burner of the stove, and I thought, *I will believe that I'm helping it. I will do this and I will think that I'm helping it.* And I couldn't, it wouldn't go away, and I couldn't get up from the damn chair, hours, a whole day, I don't know how long. *I would believe it was kindness.*' Her voice broke up completely, and she had to breathe fast and shallow for a minute before she could speak again. 'Alex, it shouldn't have been just Derek,' she said, her voice faint and strained. 'It should have been me. You didn't grow up with us, you don't understand, you think these things are far away, but they're not far away, they're close, God they're close, there's nothing there I don't already own. It's right here inside me, all of Derek's sickness, it's in me too, and maybe it won't ever get me, maybe I'll always escape, but it's still there, it's still mine.'

Alex sat with his head on his knees, trying pointlessly, stupidly, to remember if there had been a clinic in Vancouver back then or if she would have gone to a hospital. He hoped there had been a clinic, but he couldn't remember. He hadn't kept track of those details. He'd only taken pictures.

He imagined a past where he might have said different things. Where he might have said, *I will love you, I will look after you, whoever you become and whatever you do.* Where he might have said, *Stay here. Stay with me. We are all of us mortally sick. Stay here.* But it wouldn't have been real. He wouldn't have understood what he was saying.

'I was a stupid scared kid, but I think I did love you sometimes,' said Susie. 'So fuck off out of my life, okay?' She stood up, wiping her nose, and crossed the street, without looking back at Alex as he followed her.

They walked in silence down Pottery Road, into the darkness. The night-vision problem was worse. He could see very little. He remembered the day that he caught her as she fell from the railing, and the sudden feeling that was like a revelation. *You are mine.* He thought that, after all, it was nearly true, and that it was far more painful and complicated than the person he was could ever have dreamed.

Along the narrow shoulder of the highway, the lighting was unpredictable and sporadic, and the route seemed too precarious, the cars curving directly towards him, each missed step a waiting disaster. They crossed the Don River and he felt gravel under his feet along the curve of the road towards Bayview. An ambulance raced past them in the other direction, its light pulsating.

At the foot of the hill, she could not any longer pretend to be unaware that he was behind her. 'I never invited you to come,' she said.

'I know.'

'What makes you think this is any of your business?'

He had nothing to say to that, so he simply shrugged. Susie turned away and began to climb, towards her brother, her magnetic north. He waited a few moments, leaving a distance between them, before he started up the slope himself.

But when they reached the top, above the streetlights, he was nearly blind. The ambient light that he remembered was useless to him now, his eyes unable to register it. He took an uncertain step forward, unbalanced, and reached out for something to put his hand against, but there was nothing there. He walked another unsteady pace and stopped.

'I can't see where the railway track is,' he said.

Susie didn't speak. He would not have been wholly surprised if she had left him there. He heard her moving in the darkness, the soft friction of boots in snow. Then her gloved fingers closed around his wrist.

'This way,' she murmured, and led him forward. 'Now.'

He stepped out carefully and felt the track under his feet, stumbled across and stopped sharply at the other side, remembering that the steep downslope was very close. Susie let go of his wrist, and he shuffled downwards in a crouch, clinging to dry branches, until he saw a dull light to the left. Derek's lantern. He could make out the shape of the tent by the concrete wall now, pick his way to level ground. Susie went ahead of him. 'Derek?' she called.

There was no answer from the tent.

'Derek?' She moved closer to the front flap. 'It's Susie-Paul. Are you there?' Then frowned, tipped her head as if she heard something faint. 'Hello? Derek, are you okay? Talk to me, Derek.'

Alex wasn't aware of any sound except the distant traffic, but Susie leaned closer to the flap. 'Hello? Please, Derek, answer me. Hello?'

Her hand moved out, and Alex caught his breath as she unzipped the tent flap. In the light that spilled from the opening, he could see her put a hand to her mouth, her eyes widening. 'Derek, Jesus Christ, talk to me!' She disappeared into the tent, and he was crouching and heading towards the entrance when she looked out.

'Alex, come here,' she said shakily. 'He's really sick. Physically sick.'

He got down on his hands and knees and crept into the tent, the cold nearly as bad inside, the wind crawling through small rips in the fabric. The rotting sweet smell of unwashed human, sticky acrid male smells of urine and semen and sweat, and something else, the swampy scent of illness. Derek was lying on the ground on his side, unmoving, and Alex realized now what Susie had heard, the rasp of hard breath. He had heard this before in the hospital. Not agonal, not the last breaths, not quite, but very bad.

She had moved to the side of the tent, deferring to his quasi-professional status. The lantern was inside, and he could see well enough. He didn't want to touch this man, but there was a duty here, some elusive transfer of the medical oath to Alex, the next best thing.

He put a hand on Derek's dirty forehead, and there was a trace of response, a twitch and a moan, consciousness.

'He's burning up.' He tried to think what to do about fever. Derek's mouth was open, the lips dry and puckered. 'He's extremely dehydrated.' He looked around the tent, piles of ragged clothing, old books with foxed pages, rat droppings. There was a bottle of water in one corner. 'He's kind of semi-conscious. It's possible I can get him to take some fluids.'

Susie handed him the bottle, and he took hold of Derek's shoulder, thinking of fleas and mites, and pulled him over. He would have to hold on to him. He put one arm around the other man – realizing for the first time he was a fairly small man, of course he was, he was Susie's brother – and lifted him partway up. *Bodies in space.* Derek muttered, and his legs flexed up spasmodically; then his whole body moved, and a thin stream of stringy vomit ran from his lips down the side of his face. Alex put down the water bottle, reached for a rag and wiped the vomit away, then picked the bottle up again and tried to pour the liquid into Derek's mouth.

He should have noticed it earlier, but maybe he hadn't been at the right angle. Derek's shirt was partly unbuttoned and hung open over his skinny chest, ribs like sticks, and Alex saw the rash, the dark purple explosive spots scattered across the skin. He froze where he was.

'Do you have your cellphone?' he asked, trying to control his voice. Susie nodded. 'Call an ambulance now. Right now,' said Alex. 'This is meningitis.'

She took the small phone from her pocket, but she couldn't get a good signal under the tracks, had to crawl outside the tent and stand on the hillside in the open air, leaving Alex alone counting how many days it had been since he'd shaken Derek's mucusy wet hand, trying to remember whether he had touched his own mouth or nose afterwards. How many days it had been since, oh God, Derek had kissed his sister.

Susie crept back into the tent. 'They're on their way. You should take the lantern up to the top of the hill so they can see you. I'll stay with Derek.' She was unnaturally calm, her face stiff.

Alex was still holding Derek, the heat of the fever close against him. 'Susie, honey, he's very contagious. I've had more exposure than you up to this point, maybe I should ... '

'Don't be an idiot. Leave me with him.'

She was right. Of course she was right. He lay Derek gently down on the floor of the tent and moved out, his eyes on Susie as she knelt beside her brother, and as he backed out of the entrance he saw her bend down, and put her lips once more to Derek's.

He pulled himself up the slope of the hill in the circle of light from the lantern, hearing her voice behind him, a soft continuous sound. He couldn't make out the words. He passed over the tracks and stood at the highest point of the hill, holding the lantern up, level with his head.

Outside its pale circle there was nothing but blackness, a chaotic punctuation of lights moving in meaningless patterns. Dry seed-heads broke through the snow at his feet, and the invisible city stretched out on every side. In front of him, the Don River, the slope upwards to the east side, the plane trees and small brick houses, and behind him the wetlands, and the landscaped sloping enclaves of Rosedale. To the south and west somewhere was most of his life, his apartment at College and Grace, the osprey on the wall in Kensington Market, the little brick church, the woman in the room-ing house on Bathurst and the man being held hostage by terror-ists, the new Sneaky Dee's on College that would always be the new Sneaky Dee's although it had been there for more than a decade; to the north, his office in the hospital, the operating rooms where he moved quietly among the surgical teams, the burned man in the isolation ward. The girls falling down in the subway, the Don River running past him and away into landfill, where the shore of the lake used to be. All dark. He closed his eyes and listened to the traffic on Bayview, the hum of the engines, the wires connecting in networks above his head, like the hiss and thud of his defective blood.

And here, on the edge of this valley, half-blind and tainted with disease, he felt the city inside him with a kind of completeness, all the tangled systems. Money and death, knowledge and care, moving constantly from hand to hand; our absolute dependence on the actions of bodies around us, smog and light and electric charge.

There was a sound like music at the bottom of the city's noise, far distant. And it grew louder, and closer, and he knew it now, the wail of the siren, the ambulance come to them in this strange retreat, this place at the heart of everything.

IV

At the corner of College and Spadina, a man with a torn bit of blanket around his shoulders and a bottle of Chinese cooking wine in his hand stood in the radiance of a neon sign and watched the show. A streetcar stalled in the middle of the intersection, the sound of car horns surging around it at all four corners, as the traffic lights spread smears of green and red on the wet asphalt, and a woman lay in the road, flat on her back, her arms and legs spread, her hair fanned out, eyes open and white, the pupils rolled up. A fire engine pulling out from the station a block away. The streetcar driver climbed down onto the tracks and knelt by the woman, and the lights of the vehicles seized them there, etching them in high relief, a frozen sculpture on a city street.

Further south, the hazmat teams in their white gowns descended to the PATH, to a dim corridor where a man crouched and trembled half-conscious against a wall, and the friends around him spoke of roses and incense. The white figures raised their instruments again into the air.

And the hill on Bayview was public and crowded now, filled with noise. Alex had been partly mistaken – it was not the ambulance but the fire engine that arrived first, the firemen clambering up with flashlights and a first-aid kit, as if they attended to people under railway bridges every day of their lives, and for all he knew perhaps they did. He led them down and into the tent, where Susie was sitting with Derek's head in her lap, and they moved him away from her to check his airways, do whatever other preliminary things could be done. Susie, irrelevant suddenly, crept out of the tent to stand with Alex on the hillside.

The paramedics came, and Alex was needed to help them pull the stretcher up the hill. A fireman carried Derek out from under the bridge, cradling him in his arms like a child, and lay him down on the padded surface, strapping him in for safety before they brought him, slowly, dangerously, down the steep slope to the emergency vehicles, Alex holding on to the metal side of the stretcher with his gloved hands, pushing his feet into the earth and leaning against the weight. Susie followed them, empty-handed, the tent abandoned.

They were down beside the road, standing in the blue light of the ambulance, a police car pulling up, too many things being said that he couldn't quite grasp. Derek's cracked lips were bleeding, or perhaps the blood was inside his mouth, it was hard to tell.

'When blood comes out of the ears, there's no possibility to survive,' whispered Alex.

'You *walked* here?' asked one of the paramedics, incredulous.

Somehow it ended up being agreed that Susie and Alex would ride behind the ambulance in a police car, and he was aware that this was a deeply unusual arrangement, that they must look like a pair of orphans on the roadside, grimy and confused.

The policeman talking through his radio to the ambulance ahead of them. Crackle of static. 'They can't *all* be on emergency redirect,' said the policeman. 'You're shitting me, right? All of them?' The radio chattered again. 'Oh, sure, that's great. We'll take him to Sick Kids, give 'em a laugh, eh?'

The ambulance wound up and down the streets, south and west. More static from the radio, and then they turned north again.

They pulled into the parking lot of one of the central hospitals, and Alex saw four other ambulances sitting in the bay, their lights revolving. One attendant was standing on the pavement, smoking; he threw the butt angrily to the ground and stomped on it, went to the glass door of the emergency entrance and shouted something.

The police radio crackled, and they pulled out again, heading further north.

'Fuck this,' said the policeman. 'Somebody's bound to die soon, eh? That'll open up a space.'

Susie was looking silently out the window, biting her nails. He wanted to tell her not to put her fingers in her mouth. He searched in his bag for an alcohol swab and handed it to her. 'You can wipe your hands with that,' he said softly. 'It's kind of small, but it's better than nothing.' She held it in her lap and stared at it for a while before she opened the wrapping and rubbed it across her palms.

The car stopped suddenly, pulled over to the side of the road. He saw the word FEAR again, spray-painted on the wall of an alley nearby. They were somewhere above Yonge – on Avenue Road? He wasn't quite sure. His hand was shaking a little, though he guessed that this was probably just the stress. 'Excuse me?' he said to the policemen in the front seat. 'I'm about to check my blood sugar. I just wanted you to know that's what I'm doing.'

'Sure. Knock yourself out.'

It was okay, a little bit low, not dangerous. He would need to eat something in the next little while, but not immediately.

The radio crackled, and the car pulled out and continued north. At a red light, he saw a tall man with long greasy hair, his skin like old leather, holding cramped arthritic hands in the air and screaming, 'Fuck OFF! Fuck OFF!' over and over, in an ascending scale of agony. At another corner they passed two police officers bending over a woman, down on all fours on the pavement, her blonde hair covering her face, drunk or desperate or poisoned by terrorists, it all seemed much the same.

If he were going to imagine a terrorist, Alex thought, his murderous doctor or whoever, he would have to decide who this person had failed, where they had betrayed or misjudged; something terrible and public or very small, but there had to be that failure, a loss, a crackup, a falling down. He could see how releasing poison gas on the subway might seem like a valid choice.

Not that he himself was the kind of person who released poison gas, more the kind who sat politely inhaling it, not wanting to cause a fuss.

His eyes were still sore, stinging, and after a while he closed them, and for a moment, in the darkness and the motion of the car, he thought he might sleep. The car kept travelling through the streets, then paused somewhere else, but he didn't open his eyes.

The impossible thought that in a different world he would have a nearly teenage child, a girl falling down on the subway for all he knew. Or maybe not, maybe Chris would, maybe nothing in his life was any different than it had been the day before.

And it wouldn't have been like that anyway, there was no reason to think that he would have been a father in anything except the most crude genetic sense. All that he could ever have given it was his weakness, his own sickness, nothing better.

They stopped finally, inevitably, at the emergency entrance of his own hospital, so close to where they had started that they might as well have sat in place for half an hour and avoided the whole journey, and he stepped from the car in a circling tide of light and darkness, Susie rushing past him towards the ambulance they had followed. But the stretcher was disappearing through the doors and down a dim corridor at the end of emergency admitting, and Alex and Susie pressed into the crowd – the moulded plastic chairs in the waiting area already full, a crying girl in one corner, people standing with styrofoam cups in their hands and bits of tissue clutched to their mouths and noses. A nurse with a clipboard led Susie towards a desk and began writing down information.

'He had a health card,' Alex heard Susie saying. 'He did have a health card. But I don't know the number.'

'You can't find it? We're going to need that to admit him.'

'It's very complicated,' said Susie, and put her head down on the desk.

'Oh, now, stop that,' said the nurse sharply. 'We can get this sorted out. You just have to be sensible.'

A family pushed between them at the triage desk, parents supporting a wheezing girl who clutched her chest and wept, and Alex was separated from Susie and the nurse. He threaded his way across the room and stood by the wall, reaching into his bag for a granola bar, watching them assemble Derek's story in bits and pieces, in questionnaire form. There were Christmas decorations hanging above him, cardboard Santas and holly-wreathed bells. A small boy was sitting on his mother's lap, throwing up into a plastic bowl. Two middle-aged men in different corners of the room were clutching plastic oxygen masks to their faces. The nurse went away and looked something up on a computer, and then came back.

'… risperidone last year,' he heard Susie's voice briefly, breaking out of the general clamour. 'But he's been off it … no, no allergies that I'm aware … '

Another man arrived, breathing hard, and then a girl with red welts on her face, hanging on to the arm of an ambulance attendant. A woman with a baby in her arms and pale clumps of sick-up clinging to her coat. Susie was standing with her elbows on the counter, her hands on her forehead.

'If we can't determine his health coverage, we will have to ask you for payment. You may be able to get it refunded if he's eligible.'

'Oh, for God's sake,' said Alex loudly. 'I *work* here. Take it out of my damn paycheque.' The nurse turned around and glared at him, snapped a file closed as loudly as she could. He stood by the wall, eating his granola bar, avoiding Susie's eyes.

Outside the movie theatre at College and Yonge a woman knelt on the sidewalk, her arms wrapped around herself, cradling her body like an infant.

'You shouldn't touch her,' shouted someone. 'We don't know what it is.'

'She's just sick to her stomach, it's nothing,' said someone else, as they stood in a circle around her, not quite near her, and she swayed back and forth and vomited onto the sidewalk.

It's nothing.

Don't touch her.

A man leaned against the glass window of a coffee shop with one hand in the air, holding a fluttering magazine, trying to summon a taxi before he fell, and an ambulance rounded the corner, the sound of its siren slowly flowing through the night.

They stood in emergency for a couple of hours, or it might have been longer, he hadn't checked the time. One of the nurses had set up a preliminary triage station at the door, collecting the breathing problems in one area, the children with intestinal viruses in another. Alex could see the ambulances lined up in the parking lot, paramedics and orderlies waving their hands at each other in the pools of light on the asphalt. An intern dragged two more portable oxygen canisters into the waiting room, fastened the plastic masks on two more patients slumped in the chairs.

A man with a press card and a camera came in the door, and an orderly grabbed his shoulder and pushed him outside again. Someone turned up with his hand wrapped in a blood-soaked strip of canvas and was sent to the corner of the room, one of the lowest priorities, a trail of blood running slowly down his arm, a smear drying on his face; then the paramedics ran in with another stretcher, a body strapped down in restraints, foam curdling at the edges of the mouth. Solvents probably. Glue, or plastic bags of gas. The nurse at the door was handing around a bottle of antibacterial alcohol gel now, demanding that everyone wipe their hands as they entered. The man with the camera got inside again and was again expelled.

Alex wondered what was happening in the city outside the doors, as chaos arrived at the lobby in tiny pieces. He was very tired, and drained of almost every possible emotion, and his mind was wandering in half-connected ways, probably about as valuable as the insights you had when you were stoned. Wondering if it was possible to distinguish, really, between illness and fear, immune systems equally mobilized now against germs and dreams. Susie blew on her coffee, the fluorescent lights reflecting on its surface. Her eyes were red-rimmed and damp.

'Are you okay?' whispered Alex.

'Don't talk to me,' she said.

He stared at the TV hanging from a corner of the ceiling and tried to take an interest in a replay of a hockey game. Conscious in a crystalline way of how much knowledge they shared, and how far it estranged them. A hundred dead things stood between them, and not one of them a clear death that could be mourned.

'Alex?'

His eyes snapped open and he jerked in a quick startle reflex when a hand touched his arm; he thought at first it must be Susie, then saw an intern he recognized standing beside him.

'Are you on call tonight?'

Susie was sitting on the floor, her head lowered, her hair veiling her face.

'No, I'm … Look, I'm in my winter coat, do I look on call? I'm here with a friend. Is there … '

'Oh geez.' The intern, Sam, that was his name, frowned nervously. 'Could you do us a favour, man? We've got an assault over there, and … '

Assault. He rubbed his eyes. Sam was still talking.

' … some kind of glass bottle, and they said he was talking about an anthrax letter, but the thing is he's all cut up … '

'No. No.' Alex pulled his coat around himself, though he was sweating from the heat, his shirt wet under the arms and along his back. Thinking of flesh and broken glass, the metal tang of blood, shards in the muscle. 'No, I can't do it. You'll have to page Laura.'

'Please, man? The police want this on record as quickly as – and we've got this reporter hanging around who … '

'Go,' said Susie from the floor. 'Just go, Alex.'

His chest was half collapsing on itself, his eyes filmy. 'Sam, call somebody else,' he said, as if he hadn't heard her. 'I can't do it. I'm sorry, but I can't.'

'I told you to go,' said Susie. But then a nurse was kneeling down beside her, touching her shoulder and telling her she could come up to intensive care now. Susie rose, and began to walk, and then the nurse turned around again.

'Wait. Are you the person who arrived with her?'

Alex nodded, Sam still gesturing to him.

'You'll need to come with us as well. The doctor needs to talk to you about infection.'

They rose up in the elevator to a different world, insulated from the crowds below them, and walked down a long low corridor, the sound of their boots hollow in the sudden quiet, into the waiting room. Armchairs and couches upholstered in dark blue fabric, pink and white prints of flowers on the walls. Someone was lying on a couch wrapped in a grey blanket, other people eating takeout sandwiches from plastic plates. The nurse left them standing in the centre of the room, assuring them the doctor would be there soon.

Alex went to a vending machine in the hallway and bought two more cups of coffee, and when he came back he saw that a resident, a tired young woman with unwashed hair, was sitting in one of the soft chairs beside Susie. He started to walk to another corner of the room, but the doctor beckoned him over, and spoke to them about vectors of transmission, how the bacteria rode on the fluids of the mouth and the nose. How, where, people touched each other.

Alex told her about the damp handshake, about wiping Derek's mouth when he found him in the tent, and the doctor nodded.

'I don't think you're high risk at all, but I'm going to prescribe you a course of Rifampin as a precaution. And … ' she glanced at her file '… and Ms Rae? Would you have had any very close type of contact?'

Alex looked at Susie, who was biting down again on her index finger.

'You shared a bottle of water,' he said.

'Yes,' said Susie. 'Yes, that's right.'

'Last week.'

'Yes.'

'Okay, that'll be Rifampin for you as well. We won't have a definite diagnosis until we get the bacterial cultures, but it's presenting pretty clearly, and we're aware of other recent cases, so it's best to start the prophylaxis right away. Can you tell me – I understand his lifestyle was a bit unusual – but do you know if there's anyone else who could be at risk?'

Susie shrugged. 'The street nurses visited him. I doubt he would have let them get very close, but I can give you the number for the group.'

'I'd appreciate that. Public Health will need this kind of information.' She looked at her file again. 'Now, again, this is really something that Public Health will take up, but the particular outbreak we're experiencing right now seems to have started with a young sex worker. Would your brother,' she glanced down again, 'would Derek, to your knowledge, have any reason to be in contact with … that type of activity?'

Susie put her head down on her knees. 'Low end of the street trade?' she said, her voice muffled. 'Probably an addict?'

The doctor cleared her throat.

'Okay, doesn't matter. But yeah. I mean, it may not have been sex as we know it. Do you really need to hear the details? Because I can probably tell you, but I'd honestly rather not.'

'That won't be necessary.' She took out two small slips of paper, scribbled a few words on each. 'There's a pharmacy downstairs where you can get these filled.' She rubbed her eyes and sighed, a momentary vulnerability she should not have shown them. She'd recognized Alex, maybe, let down her guard in the presence of a co-worker. Then she caught herself, straightened her shoulders and left the room.

'It's not open, actually,' said Alex, when she was gone. 'The pharmacy. I expect she's forgotten what time it is.' He looked at his watch. 'It opens again at seven.'

'Okay. Whatever,' said Susie, her head still on her knees. Alex pushed a cup of coffee towards her, and she unfolded herself enough to reach for it.

'The doctor says he'll probably live,' she said, her voice low. 'He's still breathing on his own. Not too much cerebral edema.'

'That's good, then. You found him in time.'

Susie picked a bit of styrofoam from the edge of the coffee cup. 'There could be brain damage, of course. Epilepsy. Hearing loss. It'll be a while before they know.' She lifted the cup halfway to her mouth and lowered it again. 'I wanted ... '

'It's okay.'

'Alex, I wanted him to die. I did.'

'I said it's okay.'

'I'm the only one who loves him. And even I wanted him to die.'

He tried to touch her shoulder, but she pulled away, and he was left feeling as if his hand had hit the edge of something broken.

A boy and a girl, once upon a time, among the green lawns of the suburbs. The boy makes a DNA spiral from drinking straws and hangs it over his bed. This is what we are, he says. This is what we have to be.

He draws a picture on his wall and labels it *the inevitable heat death of the universe*. The girl raises one hand to it and thinks that this, if nothing else, would be a means of escape; but she will find another one, she will do what she has to, she will make herself a way.

I will save you, says the boy, I will always save you, and she knows again that he is wrong. That neither one of them can really be saved.

V

In the centre of the city, several men, unknown to each other, are receiving Rifampin from their doctors; a powerful antibiotic, not commonly prescribed. Each of these men has taken care not to mention it to anyone else, to obscure their thin line of connection, the single young body shared between them all.

They cannot imagine, most of these men, that they could have had anything at all in common with Derek Rae, as he lay under his bridge, or stood on the corner of Parliament and Jarvis, trembling with the impending traffic and the bad chemicals in his body, looking for a girl who would accept money to perform a temporary rescue. But these men are linked to Derek now, all of them equally marked.

This is not Derek's only tie to the city. Among the bleeding ghosts of his mind there are recent memories. He remembers, yes he does, the girl with fishnet stockings, who touched him and gave him her sickness. He remembers his sweet small sister, his one love, her face streaked with black as if she were part of some archaic drama, spotlit in darkness.

And there is another memory, one that Derek himself does not recognize as part of this pattern.

There are many transient pains in Derek's life. He is weak and withdrawn and passive, most of the time, and he has been beaten on the streets for saying strange things, he has been robbed of his disability cheques on several occasions, his nose has been broken. He does not expect much better from the world, and he doesn't think much, or for long, about all the small terrors and abuses. But he has not forgotten, not really; it's only that he has no idea of the role that he played, and there is only one person who could tell him, and she is someone he certainly will never speak to again.

Falling

'No, but I think monkeys are more morally superior than people,' Zoe was saying. 'Because monkeys don't use like landmines and stuff, do they?'

'Unless they were really horrible monkeys,' said Tasha, and then they were at the park.

But there was no one playing soccer, no one their age at all, only a few old people walking their dogs along the grass, and a man on a bench, a skinny dirty man, talking to himself.

'Well,' said Lauren. 'This is pretty random.'

'Was that guy here before?'

'Yeah, he could seriously creep you out.'

'We should just go to the mall. It's getting too cold.'

A woman with an apricot poodle walked by, glancing with disapproval at the girls' shortened skirts. The man on the bench moved one hand in the air, frowning and muttering.

'Maybe I should go home and write my assignment anyhow.'

'Oh!' cried the man on the bench, suddenly, loudly. The girl turned, startled. He lifted his head and stared around the park. 'Once upon a time there was a little girl,' he said, his eyes fixing on them suddenly. 'Yes. Once upon a time there was a little girl.'

Zoe's hands flew up over her mouth and she moved backwards. 'Oh my God!'

The man dropped his head again, and his voice slid down, a low constant murmur, a rhythm rising and falling.

'Oh my God,' Zoe repeated, her eyes wide. 'That was so scary.' The girl opened her mouth, but only a small noise came from the back of her throat. She folded her arms around herself, sickness pitching up in her stomach. Lauren touched her arm.

'That was really bad,' said Tasha.

'They shouldn't allow it,' said Lauren, with a little nervous frown. 'They shouldn't let people like that even *be* in the park. He could be seriously dangerous.'

'This is not fair. This is like, this is like he's stealing the park nearly.'

The man's face was full of hunger, lost and empty. Adults and their needs. What they wanted. The geography teacher's damp hand on her thigh.

'Pervert,' she muttered, feeling the sting of tears at the edge of her eyes.

He said something again. He said something about a girl.

She hated him.

'Hey!' called Lauren, raising her voice, putting an arm around the girl's shoulder. 'Get out of the park! We want to walk here without being harassed!'

It wasn't clear if the man heard her. He lowered his head and shook it from side to side, slowly, and kept on talking.

'I said get outta here!' said Lauren, pulling away from the others, walking closer to him. He looked up at her and scowled, as if he were confused, and pulled his shoulders in.

'But about the sodium hypnothol, it's not that simple,' he muttered. He was chewing his lower lip, it was soft and bloody. 'Because I said to her, you have to look at the system as a whole. It's a problem of chemicals.'

'Weirdo,' said Tasha. She hesitated, then took several fast steps forward, and he shrank away. The girl stepped forward as well. There was another feeling stirring now. That he pulled back from them. That he was afraid. The other girls around her.

'Excuse me. But you have to look at the system as a whole,' he repeated softly. He put his hands up to his mouth, his hands were shaking.

'This is not your park,' said the girl, her voice abrupt and half excited. 'Leave us alone!'

'Yeah. Yeah.' Megan giggled in terror and excitement. ' Why don't you go home?'

Zoe was hanging back. 'Maybe we shouldn't get so near him,' she said softly. 'He, he might grab us.' But somehow that made it even more sick and wrong and thrilling, yes, perhaps he wanted to grab them, probably he did. But he was a little broken weak man, anybody could see that. The girl felt gooseflesh on her arms but her heart was pushing heat through her body, her limbs warm with it.

Lauren moved in even closer suddenly, almost touching him, then darted back. '*God*, he *smells!*' she cried. 'God, mister, you're so disgusting.' She grabbed the girl's arm. 'He smells like *puke*.'

The girls were in an arc around him now, just out of reach, quick, feral, power moving between them. The man dropped his head in submission, surrender, and his hands moved into his lap in an instinctive gesture of self-protection.

'*Jesus!*' screamed the girl. 'Look at him! What a pervert!'

'God, it's so disgusting that he's allowed in the park.'

'He's jerking off, he *is*, he's getting off on it, the pervert!'

Their bodies lit up like electricity, scared thrilled burning little girls, and without really being conscious of it the girl arched her back and lifted her arms, her smooth white stomach exposed, her long thighs angled.

'Please,' said the man. 'I'm not a bad person. I just need a minute to think. Please.'

'Sicko bastard,' said Lauren.

'Get out, you pervert,' said Tasha, though of course the man could go nowhere, he was surrounded by their tense wild bodies, could only shrink further back into the bench.

'Please don't hurt me,' he said. 'Please. I never did the crime. I never did it.'

Megan bent down and picked up a rock. It wasn't clear if she meant to throw it. Maybe she didn't, maybe she had no intention, only a thing in her hand. She tossed it from one hand to the other and might have been thinking of throwing it.

'You have no right,' said the girl desperately, clenching and unclenching her hands. 'Being like this. *God*.'

Megan lifted her hand. It wasn't exactly a throwing gesture, it was a soft compromise lob, deniable, scared. But the rock struck the man in the shoulder, and he ducked away and whimpered. The girl put a hand across her mouth, the hot flare of excitement in her throat.

Megan bent and picked up another rock. This time she threw harder, and it struck the man's head, and he lunged away, and when he fell back against the bench there was a gout of blood on his forehead. His arm flew up, and the girl could smell him as he moved, that close to her, and he could have wanted to hit her, or to grab her, or to push her away.

'Stop it!' he shouted. 'I never did! Ask her!'

The girl moved her own arm. She did not know what she meant to do.

'I never did!'

He was so near her, that smell, dirty and thick and animal. She had nothing in her hands to defend her. There was a rock in the air. The man ducked.

'You have no right,' she said, and her nails were nearly against his skin. Her nails were long. The skin would tear. She felt saliva in her mouth, and the clean burn of anger, and she didn't think, she pursed her lips and spat at his face, and then the sickness hit her again, instant, the sticky wad of saliva shining on his dirty skin. She thought of blood on her nails, and it was as if she had been standing there forever, her spit on his face, her hand

Someone pushed in beside her. Zoe. She stumbled, and her arm fell.

'This is stupid,' Zoe was saying, her voice harsh. 'This is fucking ridiculous.'

Megan turned. 'What's your *problem*, Zoe? You in love with this guy or what?'

The girl looked at her hand.

'I just think it's stupid, it's … what's the fucking point, Lauren? I'd rather go to the mall.'

'You like him, don't you? You wanna marry him? The sick pervert?'

'Oh, fuck you,' said Zoe.

'I think,' the girl started to say, her hand held awkwardly in the air, and her legs began to shake; but Lauren glanced at Zoe and said, 'Go ahead, then. Go to the mall yourself. We're *busy*.' And Zoe yelled, 'Fuck you, Lauren, fuck you!' and ran weeping out of the park.

The man had his head between his knees now, his hands folded above them, but the circle of girls had been broken, the shivery current was dissipating. The girl wiped her mouth, tasting sweat from her palm. She had a pain in her stomach.

She stepped backwards. The man glanced up, and she didn't want to look at him but she did, the trapped grimace of his mouth, grotesque. Broken man. The dark hurt eyes.

'Zoe's a moron,' said the girl. But she was moving, suddenly, drawing the others with her, away from the man, laughing and pushing each other.

They were moving away. She was taking them away.

'God,' said Lauren. 'That is so random, letting him be in that park.'

'He was so *weird*,' said Tasha.

'Yeah,' said the girl. 'Yeah.' And she laughed, a strange high forced laugh, and walked fast towards the sidewalk, and they followed her. She was doing this. She was taking them away.

'Stupid pervert.'

'Sick bastard.'

And when they got on the subway she was thinking *wrong*, she was thinking that certain things were wrong, were very wrong, and she thought *somebody could hurt me*.

They could, they could do that, though she didn't know who they were or what they might do, but there was hurt in the world and she was just too close.

She was thinking *wrong*, she was thinking *I don't feel well*.

'He was such a pervert,' said Lauren.

'I bet he goes home and jerks off all night long,' said Tasha, and the girl laughed her high stretched laugh again. *Wrong*. And her own half-distorted memories of being pulled from the subway car in the darkness, and trying to understand what she had done to make this happen. Bodies falling around her. As if it were a war.

You could get hurt. People could hurt you. People could hurt you for no reason, to make you scared, to make you go away.

It wasn't right.

Because she *had* done something wrong. Or something was wrong, near or around her. But she had. And you couldn't get away with it. You couldn't. The man's eyes, black, his twisted mouth.

'I don't feel very good,' she said.

'What?' said Megan. 'You feeling all upset for him? You wanna marry him too?' But Lauren looked at her coldly, this was too much. Megan never knew when to stop.

'Shut up, Megan,' Lauren said.

'I just don't feel good,' said the girl. 'I feel … I feel really weird.'

'Jesus,' said Lauren. 'You look sick. You're scaring me.'

'Oh my God,' said Tasha, her eyes expanding. 'Did you smell anything? Is there anything wrong?'

'I don't know,' said the girl. 'I don't know.' And then she did, there was a smell all over the car, it was like roses, it was everywhere. *Somebody could hurt me.* And her throat started heaving, and then vomit was pouring out of her mouth, burning, violent.

'Oh my God!' cried Lauren. 'Oh God, oh Jesus!' The girl was dizzy, she bent down, nearly collapsing, her skin starting to itch and redden, and the others gathered around her but she couldn't make out their individual words, and then the train pulled into the station, jerking her back against the wall, and a grey-haired man walked over to them and asked, 'Does she have an EpiPen?'

Girls fall down because they have come to know too much, and have no words for that knowledge. Sometimes girls fall down and bring chaos to the city, not just because of the bad things around and outside them. Sometimes girls fall down because of a tiny emergent good.

Every Safe Thing

'You should go home,' said Susie, curled up in a waiting-room chair, an old copy of the *New Yorker* lying unread in her lap. There was no expression on her face that he could read.

'I guess.'

'Or are you supposed to go to work today?'

'I'm not sure. I think I took today off. I can't really remember.'

And he should have gone home, he meant to go home. There was no reason to think she wanted him there. He left her his beeper number, but he didn't expect her ever to use it.

It wasn't much of a way to leave, but he wasn't sure that mattered.

He went down into the dim lobby, and even here there were traces of the night, shadowy worried figures drifting back and forth in the darkness, lost relatives maybe, wandering patients, doctors who had been working for thirty-six hours. Outside, he saw another ambulance pulling around to the emergency bay.

There was a cab parked near the entrance, a warm orange light on the silent street, and he sank gratefully into the soft fake leather of the back seat. He did mean to go home. It was just that he could see the sky starting to fade from black to a dull lead blue, the suggestion of bare tree branches emerging, and he thought of something that needed to be done.

The driver looked at Alex skeptically as he stood on the shoulder at Bayview and Pottery Road, counting out the fare. Nearly morning now, the streetlights glowing pale and redundant under the wet clouds. 'What you planning to do here, man?' he asked. 'Nothing here at all. You sure you got the right address?'

'It's okay,' said Alex. 'Really. I know what I'm doing.'

A police car came speeding around the curve in the opposite lane, siren wailing. 'I take you where you want to go, you know,' shouted the cab driver over the noise. 'You tell me where you need to go, I be happy to take you.'

'This is where I want to go. Honestly.'

'You got something to do, I wait for you and drive you on.'

'I'll be okay. Thanks, but I'm fine.'

'I'm a good driver.'

'I'm sure you are. I just, this is where I need to be, that's all.'

'Things pretty crazy on the subway, you know. Better not rely on that.'

'I'll keep it mind. Thanks.'

'Your business, man. But you know, this very strange behaviour, I must tell you.'

He waited until the cab pulled away – slowly, and with obvious reluctance – before he began to climb the hill, fearing that otherwise the driver might come after him, furious with an insistent mixture of concern and the desire not to lose a fare.

Something, a raccoon or a skunk, had been in Derek's tent already. The sleeping bag was torn, half the stuffing pulled out; the opened tins of Ensure had been scattered. He pushed through the mess, leaving his gloves on, kicking aside a small pile of dirt-stiffened clothes. There were some bottles of water, some Ensure tins that were still sealed, but nothing worth saving. By the side of the bed he found a few ragged books, university textbooks. Physics, chemistry. An edition of Chaucer. He opened one and looked at the copyright page. Yes. About twenty years old. They were the talismans of Derek's life before madness, maybe the last things he had owned in the daylight world. Alex searched among the contents of the tent for a plastic bag – there had to be a plastic bag, there was always a plastic bag, all human activity seemed to generate plastic bags – and put the textbooks in it.

Maybe there was a health card somewhere. It seemed vastly improbable, but there could be something, maybe medical records, something with Derek's health number on it. He came out of the tent and looked into the first milk crate.

It was lined with more plastic bags, then a pile of crumbling bricks. From the old brickworks, he supposed. For a minute he thought there was nothing there but bricks; then he realized that there were two layers, and in between them a thick sheaf of papers, lined three-hole pages torn from notebooks.

> Dear Mr. Kofi Annan, I am writing to inform you. FUCK FUCK FUCK SHIT CRAP FUCK. the laws against the evil thing 1) avoiding

the touching 2) periodic table equated with hyposodium = GHB
tranks. But he had the knife but it didn't go like that snick snick.
     once upon a time there was a little girl

Derek would want these, he thought, and put them as neatly as he could into the plastic bag, beside the textbooks.

The other milk crate was filled with more books, water-bloated and smelling of decay. These seemed to be a selection of whatever Derek had been able to scavenge – a Gideon Bible, a novel by Leon Uris, two copies of *Jonathan Livingston Seagull*. He didn't think many of them were going to be worth saving, but he began to sort through them, checking to see if there was anything beyond the standard leavings of rummage sales. As he took them out and piled them up beside him, he noticed that there was something else at the bottom of the crate. He shifted another stack of books and saw a photo, an old snapshot, sealed in a clear plastic folder.

It wasn't a posed shot exactly, but a bit of a coerced family group, some aunt or uncle behind the camera marshalling the four of them together momentarily in front of a Christmas tree, two adults and two children, maybe thirteen or fourteen years old, sitting on the carpet. It was the worst picture of Susie-Paul he could imagine (was she Susie-Paul then? He had never known where that odd nickname came from, though he'd always assumed she had come up with it herself – it wasn't her parents, he was sure of that. But Derek called her Susie-Paul, so it must go back some way. It occurred to him for the first time that it might have been Derek who gave her the name). Her eyes were half-closed from the flash, her skin blotchy and her face sullen; her brown hair was pulled back tight in an unflattering ponytail. She could not have communicated more clearly that she wanted to be somewhere, almost anywhere, other than this. The spectacled boy beside her was smiling, embarrassed; he looked scholarly and gentle, held a book in his lap. They were very like each other, the same hair, the same features, both wearing jeans and plaid wool shirts, Derek's in blue, Susie's red. Derek's shirt was tucked in neatly; Susie's was far too large for her, the sleeves hanging down over her hands. Derek had scribbled over his parents' faces with a ballpoint pen, so Alex couldn't make out much about them, except that they were old to be the parents of teenagers.

It told him nothing, really. That she had been an unlovely girl who didn't like having her picture taken. There was nothing here that could explain it to him, what had happened to these children to make them so alone in the world together, to leave them so terribly bound to each other. Nothing that predicted Derek's long ordeal, or Susie on the hillside, his heart in her hands.

He touched the girl's face through the plastic, and put the folder carefully into his camera bag.

He sat under the bridge for a while, watching the edges of objects grow slowly definite as the light crept down the hill. There was some shelter from the wind here; at moments it seemed almost warm. But every safe thing is taken from us in the end, and maybe he was not so different from Derek sometimes, their lives a long training in how things went away. He came out from under the bridge into the open plain of snow at the top of the hill, and walked over to the edge of the slope.

It was a white cold morning now, the sky a scrambled mixture of dark cloud banks and sun. And someone had parked a bike at the foot of the hill and begun to climb. This seemed like such an insane development that he could not immediately think how to react, and by the time he had decided that he should go down towards this person, she was already nearly at the top, and he could see that it was Evelyn, in a black toque and duffel coat.

'Alex, how are you?' she said, as she pulled herself up and stood. 'You look tired.'

'I'm sorry,' said Alex. 'But this is too much. I think I'm finding this too much to deal with.'

'I came to get Derek's stuff.' She looked at the plastic bag. 'I guess you thought of that already.'

'Did Susie call you?'

'No,' said Evelyn. She dusted snow from her arms and took a breath. 'Derek – Derek's awake. He asked the nurse to phone the church. He's, well, I know him, is all. I've known him for years, actually.'

'Oh. Susie didn't tell me.'

'No. She wouldn't. She doesn't know. I, well, I've spent a lot of time working in the shelters. For a while I didn't even know he was her brother. But, yeah. After a while I knew.'

Alex felt his shoulder muscles lock. 'Fuck,' he said softly.

'I'm sorry. But he asked me not to tell her. I have to respect that.'

He looked at Evelyn's serious kind face, and thought that she was in some ways a very disturbing person. 'You should have said.'

'I couldn't. I really couldn't. I am sorry.'

'I mean, what, does he have a whole social circle that she doesn't know about?'

'No. Just me. As far as I know.'

'Why would he ... oh, never mind. There's no point getting into his motivation, is there?'

'It might not make much sense to the general public, if that's what you mean,' said Evelyn with a small shrug. 'I keep saying I'm sorry. I really am.'

Alex lifted a hand and rubbed his eyes. 'You shouldn't be telling me this, should you?'

'No. I certainly shouldn't.'

'You must know that I'll tell her.'

'Just don't say that, all right? Just – pretend you didn't say that.' She tugged at one finger of her woollen glove. 'He's in five-point restraints already, you know,' she said sharply. 'I mean, he hardly woke up and they put him in restraints. But he was pulling the IV lines out, so I suppose they had limited choices.'

Alex was concentrating on staying upright in the dizzy flowing air, his body numb and fragile. 'I guess you should take these, then,' he said, handing over the plastic bag, feeling it as as a loss.

'Thank you.' Evelyn looked into the bag, sorting through the contents. 'That looks like the main things he'd want. This was good of you.'

'I don't know.' He wasn't sure if this made Susie less alone or more so, that she had shared Derek's pain all along with someone else, with a friend who had never told her. Whether he himself would tell her after all. Or even have the chance. 'I just, it was just an idea.' He rubbed his eyes again. 'I had some free time, I guess.'

She reached out and put a gloved hand on his arm, and his nerves startled at the muffled contact.

'This is where we live, Alex,' she said.

'I … what?'

Evelyn shrugged, her hand still on his sleeve. 'This is where we are. Right here. It's a fallen world, or whatever you want to call it. Derek's not exactly wrong. There's dangerous chemicals all over the place. We just … follow it down. Make it what we can. That's all we do.'

She turned away, the plastic bag hooked over one wrist, and slid down the hillside.

In the snow by Holy Trinity Church a man fell to his knees, the Eaton Centre like a cliff of glass behind him, a red flush spreading across his hands. He cried out, an inarticulate noise, stretching his arms towards the men who lived in the square, blankets wrapped over their heads, and one of them stood, staggering towards him. A woman by the icebound fountain saw the falling man, saw him jackknife now and retch on the pavement, and she picked up her briefcase and ran.

A man sat on the steps at Summerhill subway station and wept, not even sure what he was crying about. Because there could be no end to this, not a proper end with catharsis and resolution. Because there would be neither a single evildoer to cast out of the community nor a moment of realization to draw us together, because there would be no shape or sense but only the ongoing confusion of our lives.

Because our bodies are permeable to the world, and ash and poison are moving in the air, and we have to persist like this, in anxiety and longing, on high alert.

Alex hadn't considered how he was going to get home. He felt too awkward to follow Evelyn on the Bayview slope, so he went back to Derek's tent, then skidded down the long valley wall that he and Susie had climbed the first night they came here, towards the brickworks, his camera bag over his shoulder, his trousers covered with snow up to the knees. Pulling himself out of a tangle of dried thistles, he made his way along the path to the side of the abandoned building, where a network of footbridges spanned the frozen wetlands.

He was more tired than he could have imagined possible, his head floating, unable to form coherent plans. His eyes were starting to hurt again. Morning sunlight splitting through heavy cloud to shatter on the snow, drowning him in a milky blur. He thought longingly about the restfulness of the taxi's back seat, the smell of fake leather, and it seemed to him now like the softest, the most comforting place he had ever been.

He'd never find another taxi here. The road was thick with rush-hour traffic, but any taxis passing this way would have fares on board already, no one would cruise around the highway turnoffs looking to pick up stray photographers and flower sellers. He'd have to walk to Castle Frank station.

He went into the old factory hall and sat down for a minute, holding the bag against his chest. He was still feeling somehow deprived of Derek's remnants. Lonely without them, though he had been their custodian for only a few minutes. But he still had the photograph with him, he remembered. That was reassuring but not proper, he would need to return it somehow, and this gave him a small residual duty, a thing to hang on to. There were the pictures he had taken of Susie as well, the ones he had promised were hers. He was accumulating quite an archive in his bag, and none of it should stay with him. He was terribly tired. But he could do this, he could get to the top of the hill, and it would be easier after that.

He wasn't sure what he would do with the photographs. Maybe he would give them to Adrian; one more small thread of knowledge and silence, but Adrian could handle it, he could take them back to Susie and it would be a straightforward thing, not the random complicated mess that it was bound to be if Alex tried.

He stood and came out of the hall, wet and chilled, blinking hard, onto the shoulder, and began to trudge alongside the road, dishevelled and unshaven, clutching his camera bag. West on the first turnoff, and then up the long slope of highway ramp, under the bare trees, orienting himself towards the great viaduct that spanned the Don Valley, its massive black arches, the delicate suicide veil bending harp-like above, shining silver in the breaks of sunlight.

He couldn't shake the feeling that when he reached the top of the hill there would be someone there waiting for him – Adrian or the imaginary doctor, or possibly the police, he didn't know which of these it might be but he felt crazily sure that he was awaited. A wave of vertigo hit him, and he stopped, an acid burn in his throat as if he might need to throw up on the gravel, but it wasn't that bad, the moment passed.

He heard the sound of a motor behind him and moved further over on the shoulder. Somewhere behind the trees a car alarm was going off, a mechanized voice barking commands at no one. *Please step away from the car. Please step away from the car.* He was out of breath, but close to the top of the hill now, and there had to be something conclusive in this. Some expected moment.

He let himself think that it would be Susie who was waiting for him, though he could not imagine a circumstance which would cause that to happen; and it was not a particularly good thought, a fragmentary swirl of shining brown hair and anger and failure, but it pulled him forward with a quick deceptive longing. He came around the last bend, where the ramp curved through the last edge of the woods and opened up to Castle Frank subway station.

Of course there was no one there. *Please step away from the car,* the alarm repeated. It was parked near the subway station, he could see now; someone must have brushed against it on the way in. A woman with a sky-blue helmet rode a bicycle onto the viaduct and spun quickly out of sight. Beyond the traffic island, someone pulled open the door of the station and entered.

He had never really thought there would be anyone there. He had never really supposed there was anyone waiting, but he stood at the edge of the sidewalk for a while, looking across at the subway entrance, and no one came.

He wouldn't see her again, he thought. That was what it meant, that he had looked for her at the top of the hill and she wasn't there. He needed sleep so badly. He would have a bowl of soup, he would lie down and rest, his cat curled up against his legs, and Evelyn would guard the secrets of the world, and that would be enough.

He walked across the traffic island, kicking at the snow, crossed the street and entered the station. Inside, a skinny old man stood in the corner leaning on a cane, wearing a bright red coat and a base-ball cap with a large Molson Canadian sticker on the front. At his feet, a mechanical clown doll was jerking and gesticulating frantically, reaching out from a paper bag. Someone had scribbled the word FEAR on the glass wall in black marker.

Maybe she was right that he had chosen to live his life so much alone, though it wasn't a choice he remembered making. But it hadn't saved him anyway from the network of debts and payments. It hadn't saved him at all.

The doll stretched out its palsied arms to Alex as he passed, as if it were begging him for rescue.

He was waiting on the platform at Castle Frank, leaning against the wall, when he saw a young man, mid-twenties maybe, with wire-rimmed glasses and a small goatee, sliding an oversized black marker into the pocket of his army jacket and exchanging a covert glance with the woman beside him. She was tall and athletic-looking, dressed in a short black skirt and rainbow tights, her long hair a bright lime green. She was carrying a canvas backpack, and as she turned to look into the tunnel for the lights of the train, Alex could see the top of a can of spray paint. He smiled to himself. So these were the city's editorialists, then. He was relieved to discover that they were not people he knew, that the FEAR graffiti was in no way connected with him, that there were still a few people around with whom he did not have complicated emotional ties.

He would have liked to signal to them somehow that he was on their side, a supporter of graffiti in general and largely in agreement with their message. But they would never believe that – he was too old, and despite his current slept-in state too respectably dressed, outside of their world, a stranger. It didn't stop him from privately wishing them luck.

The train pulled into the station, and he and the young people got into different cars. He had managed to walk into the morning rush hour, so there was no chance of a seat, but he was pressed so tightly against the people around him that it seemed almost relaxing, as if he were not wholly responsible for supporting himself, and he closed his eyes, one hand on the metal bar, a dark velvet blanket of exhaustion surrounding him. The train swayed through the tunnel, hot and close and filled with intimate bodily smells; and though he had not really decided if he was going to change at Yonge or stay on until Bathurst, he found himself conveyed almost automatically out with the wave of other passengers at the Yonge/Bloor station, onto the narrow platform of the east-west line. He blinked, his eyes watery, and looked up and down for the sign pointing him towards the southbound train, got onto the escalator, wanting to sit down on the metal steps and see if he could sleep for the few seconds it would take to travel upwards.

The boy with the goatee and the green-haired girl got off at Yonge as well, and moved quickly through the crush onto the north-south level, then up another flight of stairs and through the turnstile into the mall. Near the drugstore, in front of a large poster advertising a new perfume, the girl turned and raised her eyebrows interrogatively. The boy frowned, doubtful, but she nodded her head, and he slid the marker carefully out of his pocket and into her hand, taking up a position in front of her as she slipped the backpack off and he hooked the straps over his own shoulders. Holding the marker below chest level, she began to slash it across the glass case that housed the poster, moving it in quick rapid strokes, but then the boy's hand shot out and grabbed her arm, and she stopped, the marker uncapped in front of her, the letters FE scrawled on the glass, and a security officer a few feet away, his mouth opening in a sharp command.

They both knew what you did in this case. You dropped your eyes, you handed over the marker, the spray can, you apologized, possibly cried a bit if you were a girl. You went with the officer, you said you'd never do it again. They both knew this. So there was no explaining what the girl did next, why she suddenly grabbed her marker and ran, the boy coming after her, encumbered by the backpack, the security man chasing both of them. She dashed down the stairs to the subway level, and then reached the turnstile, launched over it with her hands and landed in a neat crouch on the other side, a transit guard appearing out of a booth as the security officer fumbled with the gate and shouted, 'Stop her!' The girl bounced up and ran for the escalator, and the transit guard followed.

'Sasha, come back!' called the boy, as the girl leapt from the bottom of the escalator into the mass of commuters on the platform, colliding with a man in a duffel coat and then springing away, dodging into the crowd, head down. The man's briefcase crashed to the tiled floor and he made a grab for the girl's arm but she was long gone, her swift feet skating over the fake marble, people pulling away from her on either side. As the boy reached the bottom of the escalator the transit guard overtook him.

She was weaving now, through the mass of bodies, putting them between herself and the guard, her rainbow legs and flying hair darting in and out of sight. The guard moved fast and heavy in a long-legged run, reaching for her as she sped along the edge of the platform. 'Leave her alone!' shouted someone, while someone else tried to take hold of her arm, and she jumped sideways, away from his hands.

The lights of a train swept through the tunnel in the distance as it swung in towards the station. And the girl was going the wrong way, one long leaping step threw her onto the yellow line, and her own momentum was moving her forward.

'Jesus, stop, stop!' yelled the transit guard, throwing his hands out towards her. Her lead foot crossed the edge of the platform.

'Shit, oh shit, oh shit!' cried the guard. She tried to turn but the turn itself threw her off balance, and she was rocking on the edge, her arms spiralling, her green hair fanning out in the wind of the approaching train, and the lights of the train were washing her out in a haze of white, her mouth wide open and soundless. And now people were running towards her, a dozen people had realized what was happening and broken into action, converging on the girl from every side. A man in a knitted Rasta cap reached her first, jumped out of the crowd, grabbed her wrist, and pulled.

A man in a dark coat pushed past Alex, holding a package wrapped in brown paper. *He looks like the doctor,* Alex noted, a quick twitch of fear, but the doctor was imaginary, of course. Like most of his problems. His own imagination and his own damn fault.

That man's going to drop the package and poison us all, he thought. He was thinking this on purpose, wasn't he? A weird variant on punishing himself, and he reached the top of the escalator and walked onto the platform.

The PA system was explaining that delays on the Yonge line had now been cleared but that normal service might take some time to resume. Passengers might experience longer than usual waits between trains. All right. He put his head back against the wall, retreating again into something near a dream, only his commuter reflexes still awake, attending for the sound of a train arriving.

Then everything fell apart.

He heard a shout, somebody screaming, and his head jerked up. The mass of people on the platform had fragmented, beginning to run in different directions, and an alarm going off. Emergency.

The man with the package. For one terrible moment, only half awake, Alex believed that he had done this, somehow he had done this, he had thought it and it had come to be.

A wave of people parting at the edge of the platform. Uniforms at the edge, on the stairway. He held the camera bag against his chest, and as he tried to step forward the glare hit his eyes and obscured the space ahead of him. He blinked again, dizzy, shook his head, and he saw a series of frozen pictures, like screen captures flashing in front of him. The man with the package opening his hands and letting it fall. An old man with a baseball cap, his eyes wide with terror. And then he saw her, the green-haired girl flying forward towards the edge of the platform, and this much he understood, that whatever else was happening this girl was in danger, and someone at his shoulder began to run an instant before he moved forward himself.

At the edge of the crowd, a woman sprinted to the wall. She was a woman who worried, her brain wired for anxiety, a woman who watched for pay phones and emergency buzzers wherever she went, and she knew the location of the subway's red button, she knew how to cut the power. This was the moment she had waited for all her life. She slammed her fist into the button, once, twice, finally useful, finally justified.

The girl's hair a wild swathe of brilliant lime as she pitched forward, lifted off her feet by the force of the man's arm, her muscular body colliding with his at the edge of the platform, both of them hitting the ground.

The situation at the edge was a blur of colour and light, and Alex was still running and someone beside him running, when he lost his footing, and staggered for a moment, and a heavy man pushed past him and knocked him backwards and he felt the impact of metal on his skull, reached out for a wall, there was suddenly a wall in front of him, but it banked at an angle and then sped towards him, and the tiles struck him in the face as he fell.

Bodies in Time

I

Somewhere, people are talking.

An alarm goes off for an indefinite period of time.

Somewhere there is the gentle continuous action of gravity, and the hard push of tile on the body's weight.

'He's got a medic-alert bracelet,' said a man's voice.

After what seemed like some time, Alex realized that the man must be talking about him, that there was a hand on his wrist and another on his forehead. He should really open his eyes.

'It says he's diabetic. Do you think it could be insulin shock?'

Alex cleared his throat and looked up, an unfamiliar face leaning in towards him anxiously. 'It's not,' he said. 'Not insulin shock.' He lifted a hand and wiped his eyes, and he could see that the girl was sitting on the platform, quite near him. If he had blacked out at all, it could only have been a matter of seconds. 'I think I just, ah, just sort of lost it. I'm all right.'

'He hit his head,' said a woman's voice. 'On the pillar there. He could have a concussion.'

'Should we call an ambulance?'

The girl was holding her forehead, dazed, and the boy with the goatee had pushed his way towards her now. Another group had formed around the man in the Rasta cap, who was waving them away, laughing, his hands trembling. The train was sitting still, frozen halfway into the station, the conductor leaning out the window.

The transit guard took a step towards the girl, his face stern, but a shiver of energy suddenly went through the people around her. Alex heard someone shouting, *Ain't you scared her enough for one day, man?* The guard tried to speak, but he was cut off by someone else. *Leave her alone. Jesus Christ.*

And Alex saw what was happening now. It could have gone in any direction, she could have been their enemy, their terrorist threat. But the crowd, that strange volatile creature, had decided on protection, a soft animal embrace. For no reason, for this moment only, it had adopted the girl, the two fallen men; they were its wounded young.

He felt a man's arm behind him, supporting him as he sat up. A curly-haired woman was at his shoulder. 'I do think we should get you an ambulance.'

'No, honestly. I'm fine now.'

'At least a cup of tea.'

'I have a glucometer in my bag. I need to check my blood sugar. But I really think I'm okay.'

Someone pulled the bag over to him and began lifting items out, a light meter and several lenses, before finally locating the insulin kit.

'Can I help?' asked the woman.

'Thank you. But not really.' They had found a thermos of tea, somehow, somewhere, and were carrying the plastic cup to each of the casualties in turn, the girl, the man in the cap, and then Alex. He sipped the tea, a man holding the cup to his lips; it was hot and sweet, and he was aware of an extraordinary feeling of comfort, which confused him, because he hated being looked after, he had hated it all his life.

The man with the Rasta cap was the first to stand, exchanging handshakes with some of the people around him and heading towards the stairway for the east-west line. The train had pulled fully into the station now, and people were coming off, a bit bewildered, moving in a slow arc around Alex and the girl and those who were still surrounding them, checking them for injuries, offering them mobile phones to call home, one elderly woman pulling a thick brown herbal remedy out of her purse. Eucalyptus, thought Alex, eucalyptus and something else, the smell dark and weedy and medicinal, weirdly pleasant. It was not clear if he was supposed to drink it or rub it on his skin; he settled for inhaling deeply above the bottle, and this seemed to be satisfactory.

The boy had found the felt marker – the girl must have dropped it at some point in her dash down the platform – and he handed it over to the security guard, eyes lowered, then sat by the girl and muttered, *Fucking fascist's mad at the world because he couldn't even be a proper cop.*

Somehow Alex, on his feet now, was being led past a line of transit staff and up to the street, still accompanied, wrapped in the foolish kind concern of the crowd, and he hated this sort of thing, he really did, but this was so purely impersonal, so nearly abstract, as they hailed a taxi for him and helped him into the back, that he could almost accept it as a kind of joy.

You could stand on the upper level of the subway and look at the letters FE scrawled on the tile poster glass, and not have any idea what had gone on below. You would assume that it was someone's initials, probably.

Above, in the shopping mall, exchanges of goods and currency continued unbroken, the inhabitants of the city purchasing candied pineapple and disposable razors and stocks and bonds and geranium-scented shower gels. A woman at a corner of the street hummed under her breath, sipping from a small paper cup of espresso. A driver climbed down from his streetcar to switch the tracks. White birds fell from the cold air towards the rooftops, and men and women crossed at the flashing lights, their selves a silent accidental balance, norepinephrine and serotonin, infinite tiny adjustments. These are the actions of the world, the small repetitions by which it runs.

And there is always this respite in the morning, misplaced and temporary, but a breathing space at least. Alex sat back in the taxi's soft seat, conveyed without effort towards his destination.

The cloud cover had thickened while he was underground; the streets had gone shadowed and dim, as if the sun had barely risen, and the sky was a low churn of black and dark slate grey, the undersides of the cloud drifts edged with brilliance. The taxi pulled into the parking lot of the hospital.

People were crossing the tiles of the lobby, the lights fully on now, a wide fluorescent space. Near the information desk, a woman with thick hair like yarn was sitting on a bench, turning her hands in her lap. She stared at Alex as he passed.

'There's going to be a wind,' she said loudly. 'There's going to be a great wind tomorrow.'

'Yes,' said Alex. 'You're probably right.'

She turned away from him then, and he walked on into the hallway.

He went to the pharmacy on the ground floor, handed over his prescription slip and got back a plastic bottle of antibiotics, then took the elevator up to his office.

The Rifampin was chalky and foul-tasting, and Alex drank some fruit juice and ate a stale muffin that had been sitting in his desk drawer, then called Fiona to find out if he was working or not. No, she said, he had taken two sick days for the laser surgery, and what was he doing in his office at all?

'I've been having trouble keeping track,' he said.

Susie wasn't in the ICU waiting room, but her gloves were sitting on the table, beside an unopened bottle of Rifampin. He waited in the doorway until he saw her coming, walking slowly down the corridor from the ward, each footstep deliberate as if she were balanced on a string. She was still wearing her coat, though the rooms were warm; her hair matted on one side, her face blotchy and raw. She pushed through the double glass doors, but she didn't notice him right away – she went to the vending machine outside the waiting room and pushed the buttons with delicate disoriented precision, knelt down to remove a chocolate bar.

'Hi,' said Alex.

'Yeah. Okay.' She walked into the waiting room and sat down.

There were any number of ways this could have ended that might have seemed simple and sad and final, satisfying in an elegiac way. But our lives are great shambling stupid things, the flawed nerve paths of memory and randomly built excuses for the body, and we are mostly still trying to make them come out right when we die. He followed her into the room.

'How are you?'

'I don't know,' she said. 'I need to find his psychiatrist, I think. They aren't sure about meds and stuff.'

'Can I help?'

'I can't see how.' She crumpled the candy's foil wrapping. 'I told you to go home.'

'Yes. I decided not to.'

She shrugged. 'Not my problem.'

'All right.'

'I fell asleep for a bit,' she said. 'I had this dream where I had a sort of a baby, this little wet white rag doll thing, but it just sort of fell out of me and I forgot about it, and it fell in a corner with its face against the wall and it couldn't breathe and it died before I found it. It was like, how do you do CPR on a rag doll? I hate it when my dreams are so fucking obvious.' She broke off a corner of the chocolate and put it in her mouth.

'How is Derek?'

'I don't know. How is he ever?' She set down the chocolate bar and wrapped her arms around herself. 'I never meant to lose him,' she said softly. 'I tried, you know, I really did.'

'You saved his life.'

'No. Not in the way that counts. I let him go. I let him go away.'

'Susie, there was nothing you could have done.'

'But there should have been, don't you see? There should have been.'

He heard a soft shimmer sound at the window, and looked up to see that it had started to rain, a filmy veil spread over the glass.

'You haven't taken your antibiotic,' he said.

'I will. In a bit.'

'Well, when?'

'I don't know. Soon. When I feel like it.'

Alex watched her as she pulled her fingers through a tangled bit of hair, and he remembered something else about that day at the clinic, Susie hanging in the air and refusing to speak, knowing the policeman had his nightstick out, knowing he would hit her. The strength of her refusal. Derek's tremendous negative power, under his bridge renouncing the world, the extreme and appalling force of doing nothing.

'Take it now.'

'Drop it, okay? I told you I'll do it soon.'

'No,' said Alex. 'Not soon. Now. I want to see you take it.'

'Is there something wrong with you?'

'I swear to God, Suzanne, if I have to pour it down your throat myself, I will do it.' He felt like a fool, he was probably making himself ridiculous. Susie stared at him for a long time, and he looked back at her, and he didn't know which one of them would break first.

'You don't own me,' she said at last.

What he was going to say next terrified him, but he said it anyway.

'Yes, I do,' he said.

She stood up abruptly, the plastic bottle in her hands. 'Jesus, Alex. You've got some fucking nerve.'

'It's probably not even a good thing, but there it is.'

He knew that he was saying something outrageous, that you were never, ever allowed to say this, but suddenly he couldn't understand why, when no one could go on for a single day without this, all the passionate and harmful and endless ways that people owned each other. He had no right to this, none at all, it was just there, like Canadian weather; because sometime long ago she had been falling, and he had been the one nearby.

The edges of her hair were dark with sweat, but her skin was pale, and she had that look on her face again, like someone very young who wanted something badly, and believed that asking for it would doom her.

'You make it so bloody hard,' she said.

'I'm sorry,' he said. 'I'm sorry. You scare me to death.'

He stood up and put his arms around her, and she leaned into his chest and hung on to his shirt with her hands, the medicine bottle pressed between them. He was a contingent person, his time artificially purchased, but this was his life, the rest of his life was contained in this, and it didn't make him happy exactly any more than breath or insulin made him happy; it was simply necessary.

'Take the antibiotic, okay?' he murmured.

Susie pulled slowly away from him and sat down at the table. 'I was always going to,' she said, breaking the security seal on the bottle and pouring the thick suspension into the cup. 'Honest to God, I was. You just make up stories about me. You've got to stop that.'

'That's a problem,' said Alex. 'I'm not sure I can.'

Susie sighed, swallowed the dose and grimaced. 'Yeah. You and my brother. And the rest of the world, it seems like.'

'It's what people do, I think. But I really am sorry.' He reached out and combed a strand of her hair between his fingers, and she sighed, inclining her head in his direction.

There would be a time, some years later, when he would be sitting in a dim room drinking coffee and talking to Evelyn, of all people, trying to explain what this moment meant, and the only thing he would be able to say was that it was not by then a choice but more like a gravitational process, and all you could do about gravity was to love its force.

II

On the surface of the city, above the tunnels and sunken gardens, the temperature has risen just enough for a cold rain to begin falling. Inside a little brick church, the rain is a muffled sound through an opened door, as a woman in a violet robe raises her arms in consecration, the elements transformed. She turns to place a wafer in her daughter's hands. In the basement, someone is painting NO WAR on an old bedsheet, aware that the war will happen regardless. Out on the street, a man covers his mouth, and watches for signs of poison gas.

A teenage girl sits in front of the laptop in her bedroom. She is no longer pointed out as the first girl who fell. Now she is waiting to see who she will become.

She looks out the window at the letters on the wooden fence, at the ravine beyond, and imagines walking out there, what she might find. She believes there will be a change, someday, not now, but someday soon.

This girl wears pink glitter lipstick and silver bangles, and rolls up her skirt when she leaves her school. She sits in class folding the corners of pages, aware of an absence.

This girl knows a few things. This girl knows more than she thinks she knows.

Fear will find its own directions. Girls will keep falling, at least for a time; the subway will stutter and stop, and the hazmat teams will come. Men will stare at blisters on their hands and think about anthrax and death. But no particular contagion lasts forever. Troops will move at borders, and other shapes will form.

It is raining outside Derek's window, winter rain, sudden and thick, that will melt down the drifts and fill the gutters with dark streams, leaving mounds of impacted snow on the city's lawns and the slopes of the ravines. Small ribbons of ice crack from windowsills, and reach the ground as water.

Later, the water will freeze back into ice, treacherous slicks on the pavement and shimmering film on the branches of trees. These are only the early days of winter, still. It will last a long time.

The men with the masks across their faces arrive, and tighten the bands that restrain him. They hold him down and inject him with chemicals. He tries to think clearly but his mind is clogged, polluted. They move their hands around his body. He cannot stop them from touching him. He does not know what they intend to do to him. He thinks he may die here.

Derek Rae understands that he is travelling through hell.

He knows that this is his duty, to be a prisoner in this long and shadowed war.

He has heard rumours, outside the door of his cell, about troubles in the city, but he can tell that these are transient disruptions. The struggle in which Derek is engaged is longer, and deeper, and impenetrably secret.

They touch his body, preparing him for rape. They have infected him already, but they just can't stop. They just can't get enough. They will lead him back and forth like a creature and rape him in the night, their poisonous sperm contaminating his blood.

But he will bear it. He will endure.

In the muddy ebb tide of drugs, Derek's mind wallows in waking dreams. He dreams of the chemists in their secret laboratories, burning sperm and tumours on their blue flames, slitting the necks of thick writhing snakes so the corroding blood runs out, oozing over their instruments.

He dreams of lying in the earth, finally alone.

Of twin children in a pale suburban yard, playing games of escape with branches and bits of cloth, the hungry birds waiting above them.

And he dreams of the white horse that came one day, long ago, to him and his sister, as she knelt in a corner weeping. Of how it bent down, its muzzle sweet and smooth, and opened its mouth and gently spoke. A voice like cream, the girl's tears drying. The white horse spoke to them of safety. It told them no time is eternal, and all things die. It told them that there was a coming day when they would be loved.

He knows that the horse was slaughtered in a bloody feast, its head torn away. But on certain days he thinks that if only he can wait forever, perhaps it will come back to him then.

The train moves slowly through the black tunnel. Water runs in cold rivulets down the walls. Like a bird in the night, the train flies through darkness, alone. As it passes, men in safety vests stand to either side, poised on ledges, motionless, holding up implements.

In front of the train, a space of light opens up. Then the light expands, surrounds it, draws it in. The platform is bright and open. A man is playing music on a steel guitar. Beyond him, the bright colours of magazines, of candies and juices. Fruit gels, Life Savers, Aero bars and cinnamon-flavoured gum, cough drops with lemon and mint. The deep tawny apple juice, the ruby translucence of cranberry. There are muffins and cookies. There is warmth, the warmth of artificial heat and the warmth of bodies, moving near each other, the silky hair of young women. People speak, sometimes they touch. Some of them are tired, some are smiling, some are at peace. The doors of the train open, widely, softly.

And then this moment passes.

There is a three-note chime, and the doors close. The train moves back into darkness.

Acknowledgements

The lyrics on pages 115 and 116 are from the Leslie Spit Treeo songs 'UFO' and 'Heat,' by Laura Hubert, Pat Langner and Jack Nicholsen, © 1990, Spittoons. Used by permission.

For information on my characters' professions, thanks to Rob Teteruck, Senior Photographer, Hospital for Sick Children, and Dr. Metta Spencer, Professor Emerita of Sociology, University of Toronto.

Alex's imaginary terrorist actually closely resembles Ikuo Hayashi of the Aum Shinrikyo cult. My information on Hayashi and Aum is derived from Robert Jay Lifton, *Destroying the World to Save It*, Henry Holt & Co, 1999, and Haruki Murakami, *Underground*, Random House/ Harvill Press, 2000. Murakami's extraordinary book is also responsible for making me think about subways in the first place.

Alex's hospital is a fictional institution; to the best of my knowledge, no Toronto hospital has experienced a pigeon attack. Evelyn's church on College Street is also fictional, but it shares the physical location, and some of the characteristics, of St. Stephen's in the Fields Anglican Church. Thanks to St. Stephen's, and to St. Thomas's Anglican Church, Huron Street; also to Sneaky Dee's, The Cameron House, Lee's Palace, and The Nerve.

Thanks for many and varied reasons to Andrea Budgey, Maria Erskine, David Helwig, Kate Helwig, Nancy Helwig, Bill Kennedy, Jude MacDonald, Katherine Parrish, Claude Royer and Ken Simons; and also to Alan, Frank (Sasquatch), George, Joanne, Manny, Miroslav, Paul and the other Friday-afternoon folks at St. Thomas's. Special thanks to Erika Peterson, without whom this book would never have been finished.

Special thanks as well to Alana Wilcox, my editor, for taking on this strange book, reading it deeply and well, and making it possibly even stranger; and to everyone else at Coach House, especially Christina Palassio, Evan Munday and Stan Bevington.

Thanks also to my agent Lesley Thorne, to the Leighton Studios at the Banff Centre for the Arts, and to the Ontario Arts Council for financial support.

Apologies to Columbanus for the unflattering reference to hedgehogs, and thanks for the advice on vestments and other matters. And acknowledgements to the Venerable Bede, source of the book's final image.

About the Author

Maggie Helwig has published six books of poetry (most recently, *One Building in the Earth*), two books of essays, a collection of short stories and two previous novels, *Where She Was Standing* and *Between Mountains*. She is the associate director of the Scream Literary Festival. She also works for the Social Justice and Advocacy Board of the Anglican Diocese of Toronto.

Typeset in Dante and Luna
Printed and bound at the Coach House on bpNichol Lane, 2008

Edited and designed by Alana Wilcox
Cover photo by David Barker Maltby, courtesy of his estate
Author photo by Ken Simons

Coach House Books
401 Huron Street on bpNichol Lane
Toronto ON M5S 2G5
Canada

416 979 2217
800 367 6360

mail@chbooks.com
www.chbooks.com